D. J. Hedges was born in Colorado, raised and educated by a great family. His experiences and choices have not always been the right choices to make and yet, he wouldn't change a thing; for it's because of these challenges he has learned to be thankful for what he has become today.

Thank you, Mother, for bringing me a book on how to draw dragons. It was the beginning of what has become and my imagination did the rest.

D.J. Hedges

Dragons of Lanila

Austin Macauley Publishers™
LONDON · CAMBRIDGE · NEW YORK · SHARJAH

Copyright © D.J. Hedges 2022

All rights reserved. No part of this publication may be reproduced, distributed, or transmitted in any form or by any means, including photocopying, recording, or other electronic or mechanical methods, without the prior written permission of the publisher, except in the case of brief quotations embodied in critical reviews and certain other non-commercial uses permitted by copyright law. For permission requests, write to the publisher.

Any person who commits any unauthorized act in relation to this publication may be liable to criminal prosecution and civil claims for damages.

This is a work of fiction. Names, characters, businesses, places, events, locales, and incidents are either the products of the author's imagination or used in a fictitious manner. Any resemblance to actual persons, living or dead, or actual events is purely coincidental.

Ordering Information
Quantity sales: Special discounts are available on quantity purchases by corporations, associations, and others. For details, contact the publisher at the address below.

Publisher's Cataloging-in-Publication data
Hedges, D.J.
Dragons of Lanila

ISBN 9781638290322 (Paperback)
ISBN 9781638290339 (Hardback)
ISBN 9781638290346 (ePub e-book)

Library of Congress Control Number: 2022915082

www.austinmacauley.com/us

First Published 2022
Austin Macauley Publishers LLC
40 Wall Street, 33rd Floor, Suite 3302
New York, NY 10005
USA

mailto:mail-usa@austinmacauley.com
+1 (646) 5125767

To, my mom, who never stopped believing in me; this is for you. Also to, my dad, who was taking way too soon, that I see every day when I close my eyes. To, the most important myself, for never giving up and always pushing through.

The world of Lanila was so beautiful; it had two suns of red and yellow. The way they shined, it had so much life in everything you saw around it from the color, to the people that called it home. You see, what helped this land to thrive and stay so breathtaking was the protection of both men and dragons who worked together. Everyone in Lanila felt safe, they had no idea what was coming and it was like nothing they had seen. It was a darkness they could not have imagined or dreamed of, and the force that it brought left them lost. This was an evil that took all the dragons and men that protected Lanila into a fight they couldn't win, until they were all destroyed. It was at that moment those that could escaped, not looking back, hoping and praying to the Elders they would be protected and spared from whatever this was and it would not take them too. What they had encountered was a dragon of darkness that had silver scales highlighted in black and its eyes were an eerie silver color just the sight would send chills down anyone's spine. This evil was brought to life by a darkness in the world of Lanila that has not yet been discovered, his loyal sideman Saball, a dragon-like creature who stood upright, took no survivors, and obeyed his leader, taking everyone's life he encountered. Before they had a chance to react to what was happening around them, it was too late; those who could survive did so by escaping into the woods and hiding. Over time, many cycles have gone by since this terrible loss had happened. Those that had survived called themselves the Farlands of Lanila, the survivors of the great battle who were spread throughout the land, waiting. Then a day came when the suns shined so brightly, a word began to spread among Lanila to all of them; patience – they were coming to a new age. The joining of the two; one's mind being so powerful and the other with unlimited strength, this was something they heard would save them from all they had lost. You see, they believed it would bring the land and people back together stronger than before, with a protection like they had never seen. These saviors that would come were a boy named Rell and a dragon named HaVon. They would give Lanila what it's been waiting for, a chance to stand up and destroy this darkness and give them hope for a new beginning.

Chapter One

This story began in a part of Lanila where a tree could be seen in the distance, the way it seemed to cover the entire top of the hill resembled a large willow tree and it had a gold tint to it. Its size was large, showing it had been here for many cycles. At the bottom of this tree, leaning against the base of it, there sat a young boy. His name was Rell and he was barely seventeen cycles with blond hair and sky-blue eyes. Like many young boys growing up, he was a daydreamer with a big heart and a strong mind, but little did he know how important that would be for him. As time would pass, he would see it become more than his imagination; the visions of this new beginning, he would learn how he was a part of it too.

On this day, the suns shined brightly in the sky, you could feel the warmth as it covered all the land around him and it had so many different colors of blue with very few clouds that could be seen. With Rell sitting at the base of the tree, leaning against it, the smile on his face showed he had not a worry in the word, almost laughing at times. He was raised to smile and enjoy everything around him, making the best of everyday that came before him. Being only seventeen cycles he was considered a teenager and a cycle was in comparison to a year. He was tall and had a strong build showing that he had no limits to work being brought up well. Showing so much character and charm, you could see how he enjoyed being at this tree as it made him feel safe and secure. At times, he would talk out loud to his surroundings, smiling and laughing the entire time. Some might see this and think something might be wrong with him, but not Rell. At times, the way he would react, it was as if he got a reaction from what he had said from his surroundings as he would look up to the tree.

"You know, I've heard the stories that Mom has shared with me over the cycles." He began to snicker slightly, knowing he had not been around for that long. "The one that sticks with me the most and that I can't get out of my mind and stop thinking about…" He seemed to hesitate a bit with a smile.

"It's the one she tells me almost every night before I go to bed; it is a land that is filled with dragons, monsters, and darkness that at times would scare me, but also the beauty and treasures that had not yet been discovered that she would speak of." You could feel with each word he spoke the excitement of how much these stories he heard had made a place in his heart and his life.

He hesitated slightly before continuing, looking up into the branches; you could see he felt comfortable talking aloud.

"But it is what she speaks of most, how much was lost before and those that had survived started talking of a new beginning." It was then that he seemed to glow from the inside, speaking out as if someone was there with him. "You know, this excites me, thinking that there is a word of hope that is beginning to spread out there, for all those that Mom said have lost so much."

Looking up into the branches of this wonderful and beautiful tree, he was silent for a moment, with a smile on his face. You could tell his mind was working, almost daydreaming at times, by the look in his eyes of this new beginning he had been hearing about. He rose to his feet with his hand on the tree, shrugged, and smiled, almost patting it as if it were a friend. He began to walk around the inside of this massive tree, the branches were amazing as it seemed to shield him from the sun and anything that might want to bring him harm, as he was lost in what he had been saying while looking up with a great big smile on his face.

"You know, she tells me of this new beginning, that starts with the joining of two powers that have been waiting over the cycles. It would bring this change to Lanila that everyone has been waiting for." You could hear in his voice the excitement. He might have not been around for that long, but he believed and knew it was true as a tear began to roll down his face. He wiped it. "I mean, could you imagine the sight if Mom is right, looking up into the skies and seeing dragons again that we thought were lost…" He paused then with excitement yelled, "Wow! Protecting us again, how amazing would that be!" You could see how he hoped that this was true, but little did our young adventurer realize how much it would have to do with him.

Most would think and feel something was wrong, seeing how he behaved this way by himself, by his reaction that he was getting an answer to what he had said from the tree and the surroundings.

"You know, I've heard a lot of stories from my mother," he continued, looking into the golden branches of the tree, "but that's the one that I can't stop thinking of, it keeps coming back to me." He seemed to hesitate a bit with a smile.

This was an everyday occurrence; coming to this tree, talking aloud to himself and all around him, it just made him feel safe and secure. He had no friends other than his mother since this great split that Lanila had went through. His heart was pure and he was thankful for all he did have around him. He leaned up against the tree, closer to it, almost hugging it; thanks to his mother, he was taught to appreciate all that was around him and not to let things bring him down, but to think of the positive that he saw all around him. That was one of the reasons that he stood so tall, he carried himself in a positive way, seeing as the energy that kept him so strong was in his mind and heart as well.

"Well, my old friend, I need to start heading back home, it's getting late and you know it's just me and Mom, she might need help with something." He rose to his feet and paused. "Thanks for being here and listening to me, it means a lot." You could hear in voice the kindness speaking out loud to the tree.

Brushing himself off, he headed toward the edge of the branches, when suddenly they seemed to separate and show an opening. Looking around and having no idea what was going on, he shrugged it off and smiled, thinking to himself it had to be a breeze or the wind as he walked through it. Starting down the hill toward his home, he stopped and looked back, thinking to himself, *I'll see you tomorrow, old friend.* Then, he had to look twice for he thought for sure it had a golden glow to it. He began to rub his eyes and think the light of the day was playing tricks, for when he looked back, it was gone. Shaking his head, smiling, and not sure if what he had just seen was real, he continued on his way down the hill.

Approaching each hill and getting closer with each one he passed, that smile on his face could tell you he had not a worry in the world. When he came upon the top of the last hill before his house, you could see his mind was churning as he slashed about the tall grass. You could tell indeed the land was coming back to life; the colors in everything around were truly a beautiful sight. As he stopped and looked down at his home, you could see he was very proud of where he lived.

His father had taken a good amount of time to find this spot to build his home. Sitting at the bottom of the fifth hill from the Great Willow, it was surrounded by bushes and tall grass on both sides, giving it the right protection from the weather and providing enough shade from the suns during the warm cycles. The house itself was a log and stone cabin, the beauty of it showed the time and craftsmanship that his father had put into it. Rell had not been born yet when it had been built by his father; taking a lot of pride in it, making sure it would bring the security and safety that his family would need. It had a porch and an opening in the front for access, you could see two handmade chairs to the left of the front door and the roof had a golden color that he was told was to help protect it from the heat. On the side of the house on the right toward the back, you could see a large stream, that seemed to have a nice flow; the way the suns would hit it gave it a sparkle like diamonds at times. To the far right of the house stood five large rocks that almost resembled mountains that stood tall, they seemed to give it even more protection from any harm. To the left of the house fairly close was a garden, it seemed to have something built from the stream to bring the water to it. You could see the craftsmanship and it helped, you could see it in the growth and color, it had been well maintained. Rell did enjoy standing at the top of the hill and looking at what his father had done for them; sure, he did enjoy the willow but always wanted to come back home at the end of the day as well for he loved his mother dearly.

I wonder how long it will take me today? Every day, he would run from the top hill to the porch, believing it would make him faster and stronger each day he did it.

But little did our young adventurer know that this day would open his eyes to the beginning of the changes that were about to happen in his life and future. As he prepared himself to start down the hill, with a big smile he took off, but this was different than any time before as he began to notice the ground was rushing by with great speed. He noticed even the grass was bending over when he passed. Just as he looked up, he was at the foot of his porch, you could see the look in his eyes; he had no idea what had just happened.

"I'm starting to worry now," speaking out loud, as he looked back up the hill from where he started. "What did I just do?" You could hear the excitement and panic in his voice. He looked around hoping his mother had not seen.

Standing there for a moment before heading up the stairs onto the porch, you could see his mind working hard trying to understand what happened. But once again, he smiled and shrugged it off. Knowing that in time he would figure out how he did that, but he knew he needed to get in and see if his mother needed any help. Opening the door to the house, you can't help but notice how much time his father put into all the detail work inside. It was open with four stone columns spread evenly through the center, and to the front left was a handcrafted table and chairs. On the wall of the left side of the house was a fireplace that had the same stone as the columns, truly beautiful; it was so wide and went all the way to the ceiling. On each side they had hung large pans and kettles, most likely for preparing their meals. Looking up, they had cathedral-type ceilings with detailed wood work as well. The back of the house had two large windows to the back left side and an oblong window toward the right. Under this window was the a very large sink and prepping area.

There was a staircase to the right that led upstairs to where they slept, you could see rock type stones sitting on metal bracket arms spread throughout the house on the walls and columns. Upstairs, they had two beds on each side with a hand-crafted table in the middle. To the far side it seemed to have what looked like an area to store their clothes and footing wear. It had as well two windows that were above each bed; his father did indeed put a lot into all you saw around.

He began to look around and noticed how quite it was. He called out for his mother but got no response. You could see he looked a bit worried but knew more than likely she was outside. He went back out the door and walked toward the back of the house, he noticed someone coming in the distance from the stream. The smile on his face when he realized it was her – Ruthanna, his mother; she was a beautiful woman, she had brown hair unlike Rell and her eyes were hazel green.

"Mom!" he waved his arms in the air to get her attention. He noticed she was caring something to her side as he approached her.

"My son!" She opened her arm to hug him, you could see how much taller he was. "Look, are you growing more each day?" The smile on his face – she always had the right thing to say to him to get that extra glow.

"Mom, you say that to me every day," he said, letting her know how much he appreciated it. "Let me get those." It was fish she was carrying on her side. "You had me a little worried when I didn't see you in the house." You could see how important she was to him.

"My sweet son, you worry too much sometimes, but it just makes me realize I will always be protected with you around." She smiled. "While you were out being my young adventurer, I thought I would catch dinner for us."

"I wish you would have let me know before I left this morning, I would have stayed home to go with you." You could see he seemed almost disappointed; he really liked to fish.

"I'll tell you what, you come back a little earlier tomorrow and we both can go down to the stream together." She knew how much he enjoyed it; this was something she had done with him since he was a small boy.

"That I promise, Mom."

She could hear the excitement in his response. As they got closer to the porch, she said, "I hope we get some like these." They admired the ones she had caught.

"Son," she began as she reached out and stopped him. She looked up at him, "I am so proud of the young man you are becoming; your father would be proud." You could see a tear forming in her eye.

"It's because of you and how you've brought me up that makes me who I am today and will be in the future." He smiles back at her. "I'm going to take these in and get them ready for you." He headed up onto the porch and she headed around the side to the garden.

Ruthanna had done well raising her son; the smile said it all as she watched him carry the fish in to prepare them. Her little boy was growing up right before her eyes, even she knew he would become so much more. As she walked to the far side of the house to the garden, wanting to grab some greens for dinner as well, she suddenly stopped and smiled while looking at the garden, admiring all the color and the growth it had provided. There was what looked to be some kind of squash. She admired it; these were special to her for they made the pies that Rell enjoyed so much. She decided to surprise him so she grabbed one, she would prepare it when he was gone tomorrow, especially since they had decided to go fishing together; it would be a nice treat.

At the same time, Rell was doing as he promised, preparing the fish inside. It was important to him to do all he could to help. He knew at times it was hard for her after losing his father, but he never let her know he saw it in her at times and could remember the times she broke down with emotions.

"I promise to never stop watching over her and being that son you know I can be, Father," he whispered as he looked up, believing that somewhere his father could hear him.

"Who are you talking to, son?" His mother had come in and he had not heard her.

"You scared me," he said as he took a deep breath with a smile on his face. "No one, just myself." He did not want to upset her, so he it kept to himself, or so he thought.

"Don't worry, son, he knows." She smiled, having heard what he had said.

"You're amazing, Mom." He shook his head. "Wow, those greens and squash look great. You've done such a great job with this cycle's harvest." He as well knew what to say, knowing how much time she had spent on it.

"We, son – everything around here is because of us and what we have done." This was one thing about her, she wanted him to always remember he was a part of everything that they saw around them. "Let me get these greens cleaned, I see the fish and fire are ready." She felt very proud that not only the fish were ready but the fire as well.

"I just want help however I can," he paused then continued, "plus, I want to make sure I get that sweet squash pie." His smile said it all as he looked back at her. "If there's nothing else you need help with, I'm going to run down to the stream and clean up for dinner and fetch some water."

"You go ahead, son. I think I can take care of the rest and get things ready for our meal." She went on cleaning and preparing.

"I'll be right back, Mom," he called as he headed out the front door and toward the stream.

He continued on his way. You could tell it made him feel good, the way he helped his mother out with things around the house. This gave him a chance to think of what had happened to him earlier, for he had not forgotten; he was not one to let things go.

I wonder how did that happen to me, he thought as he came to the stream. You could hear the amazement in his voice as he leaned down to clean up and fill the bucket. "Mom has always told me how powerful one's mind can be." He paused to think for a moment. "That can't be it!" He shook his head with a grin and started heading back.

"Rell, meal's ready," she yelled out to let him know.

"Coming," he let her know he had heard her. "I've always got tomorrow to figure out what happened to me, plus I don't want Mom to know right now, not till I can explain it myself." It's not that he didn't want to tell her, but at the same time, he didn't know if something was wrong with him and until he knew for sure, he thought it would be best for now to say nothing.

Approaching the porch, his nose smelled the aroma of a great meal ahead. As he opened the door, he said, "Mom, you can smell that all the way outside. I can't wait to eat." He walked over to the sink and placed the bucket of fresh water in it.

"Is everything OK, son? You were down there for a while." She placed the plates of food on the table.

"I'm sorry about that, Mom, I just started thinking how lucky I was." As he came up next to her, he placed a kiss on her cheek with a smile.

"Why don't you go ahead and sit down, lucky son, and let me clean my hands." She walked over to the water he had brought in. When she heard something, she looked back at him. "Wow, you must be really hungry if that was your stomach growling."

"It's just letting you know how great things smell." He smiled. Noticing the house could use some light, he said, "I'm going to light the fire rocks, OK?"

"That sounds like a great idea." She dried her hands and walked over to the table as he got up and grabbed a stick from the fireplace.

You see, what he was talking about were those rock in the arm brackets throughout the house; his father had found them by one of the large boulders that stood behind their house. They were black with silver spread through them. The day he had found them by accident, he hit two together and it sparked, causing a small flame and it was then he gave them the name 'fire rocks.' So in time, he learned that they would stay lit in a group till forced out and got very bright as well, so he made the arms that would hold them and brought a natural light to the house as Rell lite them and set back down at the table.

"Would you like to say thanks tonight before we eat, son?" she asked as she lowered her head.

"I'm thankful for this great meal before us, to the day we had, and to the one ahead." He paused a moment, then continued, "To you, Father, for what I am and what I'll become." He slowly looked up, not sure if what he had said was too much.

"I couldn't have said it any better." She smiled as she grabbed his hand and looked into his eyes. "He knows and is very proud of you. Trust me, my son, he knows what you will become." She smiled again at him.

"Thanks, Mom. Now, let us enjoy this great meal." You could tell he enjoyed her cooking with each bite.

"So what type of day did my adventurer have?" She asked in-between bites. This was something that happened every night; being sure he realized her interest in all he did.

"Nothing more interesting than the rest." You could see how he wasn't trying to bring any attention to what really happened to him.

"You know, son," she took a bite and looked at him, "I have that power to know there's more to your story than you're telling me." She took another bite.

"What do you mean?" He tried to get past the topic as he took another bite as well.

"You know, even your father would say things to me and in time would realize that there was no reason to even try it." She paused, looking at him with a smile. "We're connected by our hearts, son. We will always know if there is something that has our loved ones bothered."

"You are wise, Mom." He shook his head with a grin. "Something did happen today, that I can't even explain." You could see the sigh of relief as he told her.

"What happened?" He had her attention.

"I don't know how to explain it." He paused. "First time ever this has happened to me." He looked at her then.

"The first time for what?" By this point, she was becoming a little bit worried. "Did this harm you in anyway, son?" You could hear the concern in her voice.

"No, Mom." He paused, not sure how she might react. "When I approached the last hill today, you know how I like to run every day and see how fast I am?"

"That's what it is?" She was confused why he was so worried.

"Well, not exactly. Today, when I took off, Mom, the ground passed me by so fast I didn't know what was happening." He looked at her thinking she probably thought he imagined it. "I know what you might be thinking, but it was real, Mom, and I stopped right at the porch."

"Son, I've told you since you were able to speak, the mind is a powerful weapon." You could see from by his reaction that he didn't expect that. "If you continue to try and believe in something, anything is possible."

He loved the way she always made things seem right.

"I was worried at first, but you're right, Mom." You could see he seemed more relaxed. "You have always taught me that my mind and heart are a very important part of how we live, knowing anything is possible."

"I'm glad to hear that, son, and hope that shined some light on it." She could see he seemed more relaxed. "Why don't you go on upstairs and I'll clean this up and be up soon," she said as she stood up and gathered the plates.

"Sure you don't need help cleaning up?" He didn't want to leave without helping.

"I have it," she said as she smiled at him, "but thank you for asking." She had raised him well.

"OK, I'll see you upstairs." He smiled and headed up.

With Rell upstairs, she continued to clean up from the meal. When everything was done, she walked throughout the house putting out most of the fire rocks and leaving a couple going for some dim light; this was something she did every night. She walked to the bottom of the stairs and stopped, turning and looking around the house with a smile on her face,

"I miss you, my love, and think of you every day." She wiped a tear from her eye. "You would be so proud of our son. Help keep us safe." She blew a kiss into the air and walked up the stairs.

"Hey, Mom, what is it?" He noticed she was standing in the doorway looking at him. "Everything OK?"

"I'm fine, son. I realize standing here how much you're growing up." She smiled. "But don't you forget, no matter how much you grow, you'll always be my little boy."

"I know that, Mom." He chuckled. "You're not going to let your little boy wait any longer to hear more of an adventure, are you?" A smile came over both of their faces.

"Now that wouldn't be right." She made her way over to his bed and sat down on the edge.

These adventures that he spoke of were stories that his mother had told him of since he could remember; it was one of the most important things he looked forward to at the end of the day. From trees so big they would compare them to mountains and would reach into the skies, to part of the land that had no life with so many walls you could see your reflection. Lands that could swallow you if you were not careful, there were so many that he had heard of passed down over the cycles. Through the fathers before and their fathers, he enjoyed them and by the way she told them, he knew how important they were to her.

"OK, where did I leave off?" You could see by the way she asked, it was a way to see if he had been listening.

"They have all been great." You could see him thinking. "How about the story of the two that would take back all that Lanila had lost?" Even though he had not yet been born, he knew the land had lost so much through all the stories.

"Your mind amazes me all the time, son," she said as she smiled. "You're right, this is something that we all have been raised on. I was your age when it all went dark and changed for everyone."

"Dark? What do you mean?" You could see she had his full attention.

"It was like nothing that we had seen." You could tell this brought back memories she had tried to forget. "I myself had no idea what it was; it was my parents that shielded and protected me as we all fled for our lives." She paused, taking a breath.

"You OK, Mom?" he asked as he looked at her, noticing she had never reacted like this before.

"I'm sorry, it just reminds me of terrible things that had happened." She turned to look at him. "Life continued as they all waited and hoped for, what we all had spoken of, even your father knew of this." She hesitated. "It was one of the reasons he was so protective of you." She touched his hand with a smile.

"This is a new part of the story you have never completely told me." He seemed to be sitting on the edge, waiting to hear more. "What was he protecting me from?"

"From everything waiting, son." She saw he seemed a bit worried. "Don't worry though, my young one," she tried to reassure him.

"Waiting?" he was puzzled. "For what, Mom?" Eager to hear her response, he was silent.

"Remember the joining of two, my son, where two powers would be brought together?" She could see she had his full attention. "These powers would make an unbelievable force to bring back what we all have missed." She smiled, placing her hand on his cheek. "Hope, my son – what most of this land has forgotten."

"Wow! You're telling me this is something that could happen?" You could hear the excitement in his voice. "Can you imagine how great it would be to see that, Mom, to even be around when it happens?" He laid back in his bed with a smile.

"I can see you are enjoying the new parts to this story, but never forget, son, for everything that rises as good, there will always be an opposite that will try to stop all from happening." She noticed his smile slowly fading. "Now, don't lose that smile, that's the hope we need." She then paused. "I'm just reminding you for all the good, there will always be something that will try to oppose it." She leaned over and hugged him. "I'll tell you more tomorrow night." She had noticed his eyes were getting heavy.

"If there's one thing I'll never forget you have told me," he said as he yawned, "it is to believe in yourself and to never give up." The glow in eyes said it all as he pulled the covers up.

"Rest well, my young savior," she said and placed a kiss on his forehead. "You are becoming very wise." She proceeded over to her bed and lay down.

Thinking to herself, indeed, he was becoming what they had been told and hoped for. She kept it to herself for now, wondering indeed how much longer it would be. Looking over at him lying there so peacefully, she put out the fire rocks. She lay herself back in bed, knowing that the new day would bring them closer in so many new ways.

Chapter Two

Now with them both falling asleep from the long day as the moon rose higher into the sky, the suns were only beginning to rise on the other side of Lanila. This side was slightly different; it had not seen as many changes since the great battle. It had so much color in everything around it and was truly beautiful. From the mountains to plants and trees spread throughout, it did seem almost magical the way the first rays of the suns shone upon the entire area. The lakes were spread throughout and some of the mountains even had pockets of water that rested at the bottom of them. In the distance, a large peak reached beyond the clouds into the sky – truly an amazing sight. There was one set of mountains in particular that stood out the way the trees and grass grew around the water; it had three peaks – the one in the middle was massive in comparison to the others and at the bottom of this one, you could see what looked to be a large opening in it.

Suddenly, the ground began to have tremors and they were getting closer together and louder, something was coming from inside the opening. Suddenly, appearing from the shadows of the cave was the most magnificent and beautiful creature, it was what everyone thought had been lost. It was what Rell's mother had told and hoped for; a dragon – he was large for his age and his colors were amazing. They changed as the rays of sunlight hit him. With a sudden lunge, he took to the sky diving in and out the clouds with such grace, his name was HaVon; he was a young dragon. Flying through the air so effortlessly, his wings seemed to blanket the sky with each stroke, continuing these marvelous dives in and out the clouds. Noticing an opening just ahead, he began to dive down toward it. As he approached it, his wings spread out wide. Doing so caused him to land gracefully and silently, totally the opposite of what you might expect considering his size.

HaVon stood there looking over the land, you could see the expression in his face as he seemed to enjoy all he was gazing upon. He had landed on a clearing that sat fairly high where he could see far. When suddenly in the distance, something got his attention. It was coming from the peaks that reached into the clouds. As he focused in on it, his eyesight was something we all wish we had. You see, no matter the distance it would seem as if it was right in front of him, every young person – or in this case, young dragon – needed guidance and knowledge of life as they grew and matured. It was no different for HaVon. What it was he saw coming from the distance was his elder Ravin. She was smaller and longer than him and her scales had a purple tint to them with fur that surrounded her face and legs. Her beauty was mesmerizing as well. She was one of the last survivors of the great battle; no one knew she had survived and all this time she had watched over her young dragon.

This battle was the same one Rell's mother had told him of slightly, it had happened before either one of them were born. It caused all the land and life in them to separate into what they were today. Before this happened, the dragons and people used to work side by side and throughout the entire land. It was then when there seemed to be no problems and everything was great, the discord came from within, taking control and destroying all that stood in its way and nothing could stop it. Anyone that was lucky enough to get away never looked back, fleeing from the land, hoping it would never be seen again. Ravin was one of the survivors and before she fled, the Elders approached her with an egg, telling her at no cost was anything to ever happen to it. They went on to explain she would be the one to take care and raise this dragon, letting her know what he would become one day and they would always keep a watchful eye on them both. Knowing this, she fled to the skies with the egg in her possession, not looking back and staying low, not to be seen flying for days. She knew what she had to do.

It was then she came upon where they lived today; taking care and raising HaVon as one of her own, knowing what he would become and the Elders of the great peak helping along the way. On a daily basis, she would leave before he would wake and fly to the peak and let them know of his progress. This was where she was coming from when he noticed her. HaVon knew of the Elders and had even been told of this new beginning; it was the joining of two different powers that would bring peace and control back to Lanila, like Rell's mother had told him.

"How is my young one doing today?" Landing next to him as she looked up at him, you could see the difference in size and by his expression you could see how happy he was to see her.

"Great. I started early today on my lessons, when I stopped here to look around and noticed you." She had raised him to always better himself as each new day came.

"You seem to be growing more and more each day I see you." She raises her neck to look at him. "Your colors, body, and wings." She always had the right thing to say to him.

"Thank you." He looked at her with a grin. "I'm not the only thing growing. As I look about the area, Ravin, I can't believe how much everything has changed." He was growing and so was the life around him.

"That's a good sign though, young one. With all you have learned that has happened, even after something so terrible we all find a way, even life itself, to grow stronger," she said as she admired the land.

"I am very thankful and lucky to have someone that cares for me so much," he said as he looked over at her.

"OK, lessons. What have you had been doing since I was gone?" He knew she appreciated what he had said. "Was any of those of your speed, knowing like I told you there is no limit?" She had taught him to never have a limit, even though she knew of what he would become, only time would let him know.

"I have flown with no limit." He paused a moment with a grin. "Would you like to see if you can catch me?" There was eagerness in his voice as he waited for an answer.

"I indeed would like to see." She could see how much he wanted to do this and agreed. "When you're ready." Not sooner than she finished, he had taken off to the sky with a great force.

"Was that a go?" He snickered to himself as he looked back, noticing she had not moved, thinking this was the jump he needed.

"I guess it was." She grinned, shaking her head and admiring as he took flight to the sky. She was quite proud he was turning into this amazing dragon the Elders had spoken of.

As he climbed higher and higher into the sky, it was time for her to follow, so she spread her wings and took to the sky as well. Watching them both, you could see the similarity in the way they flew, she had taught him well. As he looked back, he noticed she was catching up. With each stroke of his wings, he flew even quicker, he wanted to stay ahead of her so bad. Then suddenly, it was like a burst; he took off with such force. Ravin stopped in mid-flight, hovering, admiring what she had just seen as he began to fade into the distance. He noticed it as well as he looked back and let out a thunderous roar that filled the air, bringing a grin to her face as she still hovered in one spot knowing, indeed, he was getting stronger and faster. But she still had some secrets she had not told him yet. As he got out of sight, you would think there was no way she could catch up to him still hovering. She closed her eyes as if she was concentrating on something, when suddenly, her body was overtaken by a gold glow, then a blinding flash followed and she was gone.

By this time, HaVon was so far ahead he had no idea what just happened, as he would look back every once in a while to see if he saw her, you could see a grin on his face knowing she was not getting closer, and he took off even faster. He knew there was no way she could catch up to him now unless he stopped and waited for her. Then he thought, *Wait, this will be a great time to try and hide and scare her.* Thinking he was far ahead enough; he was going to do it; this was something our young dragon had tried many a time but never succeeded. She was always one step ahead. He knew for sure this time he had not seen a sign of her. As he noticed a clearing up ahead, it had tall grass with a bunch of large trees by a mass of water. This was it, the perfect spot, he just knew it would work. He took to the ground, landing with grace. He looked back and still no sign of her, you could see how excited he was as he started to conceal himself. Staying still and hidden, he began to chuckle to himself. He knew it would finally work. It was like he had played it out already in his head and seen her reaction.

So as he lay there being sure not to move, thinking he had the upper advantage, or so he thought, but remember that bright golden flash that overtook Ravin's body? It was the power of teleportation from one place to another she had learned from the Elders. He had no idea about it and as he waited, she was already there using invisibility to hide herself, another power she had as well. She stood behind him being quiet, to see if he would notice her presence; another lesson in her teaching. Much time had passed since he had seen her and you could see the concern as he looked to see if he could see anything. Looking to the sky, he saw no sign of her. He became unsettled, worried now, when suddenly he heard from behind him a familiar voice.

"What are you trying to do, young one, scare someone?" Suddenly, she appeared before him, shaking her head. "I had hoped I trained you better to always be aware of your surroundings."

"So did I!" The look on his face said it all. "How is this possible? I left you so far behind me, I thought for sure I had the element of surprise." He was eager to hear her response.

"Even when you might think there is nothing that can surprise you, it is then that you learn of something new." This was her way of letting him know every day was a new day of lessons.

"You're right, Ravin, I should always be aware." You could see he almost looked as if he had disappointed her when he lowered his head.

"My young one, don't look so disappointed. I'm very proud of you; what you do every day and how well you listen shows me you are learning." She raised his head up, and you could see she always knew what to say.

"So does this mean you will show me how you were able to do that?" He waited for an answer hoping it was a yes.

"In time not only will you be able to do that but so much more as you learn and grow with each lesson." You could hear in her voice how much she believed in him and what he was becoming.

"So much more, what do you mean by that?" Still learning, he didn't quite have all the answers as he seemed confused by what she had said.

"In time, you will excel and surpass a lot, my young one, you are becoming a very powerful dragon." You could see him stand tall, he loved to hear praise from her, it made him feel special. "But never forget, the Elders even knew no matter how powerful you become, the real journey is to never feel you're alone."

"Feel alone?" Looking back at her, he shook his head. "We're a heck of a team, I would never be alone or leave you behind. We're here for each other." You could tell how much he cared for her.

"Yes, we are, but you never know what lies ahead." You could see she felt the same. "That's why it is so important you must always be ready for the worst, so you're prepared for anything that might come before you," she said, giving comfort to him.

"Well, if I have any control or say about it," he stood taller and erect, "no one will ever get close enough to bring harm to you or me while I'm here." You could hear a slight rumble in his voice as he spoke.

"I understand what you mean and I know you would do anything to keep me safe, I thank you for that." She didn't want to think of life without him as well. "This is just something that our Elders have always taught; even if you're alone, there is limit or stopping what can be learned." She was trying to make it simpler for him to understand.

"I think I get what you're trying to tell me." He paused and looked down at her. "Even when things seem to be at their worst and there looks to be no hope in sight, never stop believing and learning to make the best out of every situation." He waited for her response.

"You truly amaze me, HaVon. How far you have come with all I have taught you, the wise knowledge you show me!" She was so very proud of what he was becoming and had come so far in his learning. "The Elders were right about you," she spoke softly under her breath, or so she thought.

"The Elders know of me?" You could see the look of surprise on his face as he looked at her.

"What?" she realized she had not spoken softly enough.

"I heard you say me and the Elders in the same sentence, what's going on?" He waited thinking was it possible they did know of him.

"Sometimes I forget how well you can listen," she laughed slightly as she said it. "There is a lot the Elders know of you; this is what they do to keep an eye on all of us." You could see she was trying to get him to lose interest, saying it like everyone knew of this.

"OK." He noticed she seemed to be trying to avoid a direct answer. "Sorry, it just kind of got me excited." He knew she had her reasons and didn't mind.

"I promise you if there is anything you need to know, I will tell you." She had her reasons and knew when the time would be right. "We have been here a while and the day is growing longer, the blue moon of the night will be upon us." She could see he was wiser and curious, not wanting to let it go. "We need to begin our way back to the lair."

"I owe everything to you, Ravin, so no matter who knows of me it is all because of you and what you have taught me." He looked at her with a grin. "I see you in me every day." He had a lot of respect for all she was doing for him.

"That means a lot to me, HaVon." Of all the things he could have said, this was most unexpected but appreciated. "You have always been a great pupil, eager each day to learn more and get stronger," she pauses, then continued, "so thank you for what you do for me. Let us head back. You want to race?" There was playful sarcasm in her voice.

"No, I think we'll fly this one side by side, unless you want to show me that trick you did earlier?" he followed by a big grin, knowing the answer.

"Nice try, young one. We should go before it gets any later."

They both took to the air side by side.

With them both taking off and heading back, it was truly an amazing sight to see as they extended their wings to pick up speed, at the same time staying next to one another. They had such grace; it was like they had the entire sky to themselves. She did notice every once in a while he would look around and behind him, as if he might be bothered by something but at the same time, he knew surely he would say something. They continued and said nothing about what she had seen him doing. They were getting closer to where he began his day, the mountains could be seen in the distance.

"That is a sight for sore eyes. What a long day it has been!" the relief in his voice could be heard that they were finally here.

"Yes, it is." She was just as relieved to finally get back.

As they both approached the opening of the mountain, you could see how much larger it was than the both of them, as they both landed one behind the other and entered the cave. The further they got into it, you could see a blue glow coming from the distance, getting brighter the further they went in, giving light to all the walls. There was no doubt that Ravin had put a lot into finding a safe place to raise him. As they approached the end it opened up, seeming as if the mountain was hollow, giving more than enough room to them both. Looking around, you could see what was giving off that blue glow was a large spring, which looked to be warm from the steam that came off the water. It was truly beautiful to look at and without any hesitation, he walked into the spring with her following close behind. You could it was more than deep enough as they both were submerged at times – from the look they both showed, you could see how relaxed they felt. When they began to get out, they appeared to have a blue glow to them. It had some magical effect to them as any abrasions or cuts would begin to heal that they might have had received from the day.

"I'm truly starting to look forward to the days ending more and more, when I get into the spring." You could see he enjoyed it.

"You're right about that, my young one; it makes me feel even younger each time," she said and smiled.

He made his way from the springs to an area of the cave where they had made what looked to be a bedding that covered a large area. He proceeded to lay down and rest from the day. As she watched him, you could see she was admiring how he had grown. As she passed in front of him, he noticed.

"What is it, Ravin?" there was curiosity in his voice.

"I see someone that has grown so much and has never forgotten a thing, you make me very proud of what you're becoming." She could make him feel so good, always saying something that made him feel so special like no other.

"I thank you as well for what you do for me in my teachings and life, and for always being there for me." You could feel the love and respect they had for one another.

"For the cycles to enjoy together, my young one, now rest and be at peace with yourself, for the new day ahead brings all new adventures for the both of us."

Hearing the security in the way she spoke to him brought a smile to his face.

"You as well, Ravin, may your dreams be as blessed by the Elders."

She smiled walking past him. Ravin then proceeded to an area and lay down as well. You could see her thinking of the new day ahead and her having another meeting with the Elders at the great peaks. She wished so badly at times that she could tell him of what was to come of his future, at the same time knowing the Elders had their reasons for not wanting him to know right now. With both of their eyes getting heavy, the events had come to an end; they lay securely in the lair, resting themselves for the new day ahead. The day was ending for them and just beginning on the other side of Lanila as the suns begin to shine upon the willow and the land around it.

Chapter Three

As the suns began to cover more and more area, the first rays began to climb into the window where Rell and his mother were sleeping. Not being too bright but a gentle waking light, it worked as he began to rub his eyes and stretch his arms out from the night's rest. When he looked over to see his mom, he noticed she was already up and her bed was made. Sitting up turning to put his feet on the floor, he looked out the window that was above their beds. Realizing the new day was upon them, but unlike most, he didn't rush up and get ready, but instead he gazed out the window. You could see what had happened to him the day before had him already thinking, then the dreams he had last night seemed so life-like, it had him at a loss. Even he knew that was the point of dreams, to take us to places only our imagination could give us, but this was different and unlike the other one's he could remember the entire thing, all the details as if he was a part of it and there. He snapped himself out of his thoughts and began to get ready for the day, not giving it another thought. For now, he needed see if Mom needed any help getting the day started.

Like most mothers in the morning, she was always the first one up, having a meal ready for her son. You could tell this was important to her something, she needed to do, the meal usually being fruits she would have picked and juice as well. She could hear him making his way down the stairs as she had things ready on the table. The look on his face as he turned the corner showed he felt so lucky to have such a great mother.

"Good start to the day, my son. How did you sleep?" You could hear in her voice the upbeat spirit.

"Great, thank you." He hesitated sitting down. "Other than some wild dream I had. Why didn't you wake me? I would have helped you get this ready." He was very helpful when it came to his mom.

"I know that but I figured you might need the rest," she smiled sitting down at the table.

"You're amazing, Mom. Always on top of everything. This looks great." He was always sure to acknowledge everything she did for him, knowing deep down it made her feel good.

"So, you said wild dreams and after what happened to you yesterday, I don't know how you could get a good rest."

You could see him light up as she smiled, taking a bite.

"I knew you would remember, Mom," he said as he also took a bite.

"Now have I ever forgotten anything that has had you so troubled that you shared with me?" She knew more of what was going on than she was willing to tell at this time, feeling it was better this way for now.

"No, everything I ever brought to you, you always remember and that's why I am so thankful for you." You could hear in his voice the love and respect he had for her.

"You must always remember, my son, the way I have raised and told you about your mind, that is very powerful, especially when you know how to use it and believe in what you're trying to do." He had been raised to believe anything was possible and to never stop believing in himself.

"That's one thing that I will never forget, Mom." He sat there for a moment with a slight hesitation. "So are you telling me that my mind did that to me?" A sound of confusion could be heard in his voice as he looked at her.

"You are truly something special, my son. Your mind amazes me with what you ask and how you ask it at times." She reached for his hand. "Don't you worry, I promise you, in time you will learn to understand everything." You could see she was proud and believed the time was not right to say more.

"You have always known what's best for me," he said as he held her hand tightly. "But you know me, Mom, I can't stop thinking of everything that is happening, I'm excited." She could see a golden glow in his eye as he said it.

"Promise me you will never lose that imagination; it's a special thing. I was thinking, why don't I go to the willow tree with you and when we get back, we go fishing, like I promised?" She squeezed his hand with a smile.

"Really, Mom, you want to go with me?" It had been a while since she had gone there with him. "What about things around here?" You could hear the excitement in his voice.

"I think everything will be fine, we could get a few things done before we go," she said as she could see he was excited.

"I'll go take care some of the chores outside, Mom." He got up from his seat taking what fruit he had left in his hand and placing his plate in the sink. Hugging his mom he was out the door.

"This should be a fun day," she said as she cleaned up things, smiling as she could see he had a pep in his step doing chores.

"This is great having Mom go with me," he talked to himself as he fetched water, "a perfect day too," looking up at both suns with not a cloud in the sky.

"I think when we get back, before we go fishing I might start a pie." She knew how much he loved her pies and thought it might be a nice treat, as he came in from fetching water.

"Here, Mom," he said as he placed the water near the sink and turned to hug her, you could see the smile that said it all. "Thanks, Mom, I don't know what I would do without you."

"I feel the same, my son." Even though her head hit his chest, she hugged him tightly. "So, are you ready to head out?"

"I think so but if there is anything I have forgotten to do, I promise to help when we get back." You could tell he was anxious to go.

"Let's go then." She followed him out the door, shutting it behind them.

With all the excitement in the air with his mom going, little did either one of them realize how much it would change. By the end of the day, something that one thought that they would never see again, and the other being too young to remember the holocaust it brought with it before, happened before their very eyes. The smile on both of their faces as they walked on, you could see this was something they both needed. Walking side by side, she noticed something had her son side-tracked at times.

"You look as if you have something on your mind?" Always being aware of her son, she was curious.

"It was just a dream I had last night, Mom. I keep thinking about it." He stopped at the top of the hill and looked at her.

"A dream – usually those are things you enjoy. Why does this one seem to have you so bothered?" She seemed surprised to hear that.

"It just felt so real, Mom, like I was there," he paused for a moment, then said, "I felt as if I was flying. I know how silly that sounds, but this was so different than any dream I've had before."

"It's never silly, son, I truly believe it felt real but you were in your bed the whole night." She smiled up at him. "Come on, it's been so long since I've been to the willow." She was trying to bring light to what he had said, even though she knew there was more to it than she was saying.

"You said it has been a while?" he asked as they continued toward the tree, he was not aware that she used to come out here.

"Your father and I used to take walks out here and rest at the tree as you do." This was something she had never shared with him before now.

"You never told me that, Mom," he said, thinking this was great, knowing they also enjoyed the same things as he did.

"This has been in our family for a while, my son." They come to the bottom of the hill where the willow sat atop. "I forgot how beautiful of a sight it is!" She took a moment staring up at it.

"It is a sight, Mom!" Noticing her, it seemed as if she had missed it in a way, so he asked, "Are you OK, Mom?" He noticed a tear roll down her cheek and he reached over and placed his hand on her shoulder.

"I'm fine, son, it just brings back a lot of good memories," she said as she wiped the tear from her face. "Come on, it has been a while since I've been inside." They both began to run to the top.

"Is it as you remember?" He pulled back the branches for her to enter.

"Wow! How much she has grown! I forgot how much of an area is inside here and the trunk seems so much larger than I remember." Standing there, she seemed mesmerized like a child looking around.

"It's great to see you like this, Mom," he said and put his hand on her shoulder. "It has been a while since I've seen you smile like this. Now you know why I spend a lot of my time here." He could tell she had missed this place, but worried as well that the memories she had might be difficult at the same time.

"I shouldn't have stayed away for so long, I'm sorry." She looks over at him sitting down by the base of the tree.

"It's OK, Mom, you're here know. Someone once told me when you dwell on what has happened, we miss all that is in front of us right now," he said and smiled at her.

"You make me very proud of how much you're growing and the man you are becoming." She placed her hand on his cheek. "Your father would be so very proud."

"Thanks, Mom, but I had a wise teacher," he said as he leaned his head into her hand and smiled.

"Now earlier you spoke of this dream you had." She wanted to make sure he was not worried by it. She got more comfortable against the tree.

"It's hard to explain," he said, leaning back and looking into the branches. "It was large a place where the land was like nothing I have seen, Mom, it had mountains with lakes of water at the base of them." You could hear the excitement as he told her.

"Wow, sounds like a beautiful place," she said, giving him her full attention.

"You know, Mom," pausing for a moment, "I swear I even saw a dragon; it was purple with fur on it." This was what had him confused for he had never seen pictures, only been described how they looked and it was nothing like he had been told.

"You make it sound just as wonderful as the land you saw around it," she said, being supportive, "then that should tell you it was nothing to worry about."

"I don't understand. What do you mean?" He looked at her waiting for a response.

"You know I told you dragons have been gone since the great battle, son, where everyone lost everything and left the land what it is today." Even though she knew that there was more to this, she continued to listen.

"I guess you're right, Mom, but how cool it would be to look to the skies and see them again." The kid in him was coming out as he spoke of it, she could see the sparkle in his eyes.

With them both continuing to enjoy the day they were having together at the willow, talking so much, it made them realize what they had been missing. There was something about to change their entire lives together and it was coming from a land we have not yet described. This was a lifeless place with no sound and was colorless, the valley walls were of a glass like quartz, casting reflections throughout the entire area. Further into this lifeless land, at almost the top of one of these valley walls was a very large opening, the top seemed to be some large structure made from the same material as around it.

Suddenly, the ground began to tremble, followed by slow rumbles almost like a growl or a breathing every once in a while. It began to pick up and it was getting louder and closer together. The ground began to shake more violently; there was something coming from the opening. The opening had grown larger and was being consumed by a large black mass, it almost resembled clouds that seemed to be fighting to come out of the opening. It was Shaydon the Shadow Dragon of Darkness, that no one had seen in so long. Its silver eyes were piercing and his size was massive, the way it seemed to cover everything in its path. Many cycles had passed since anyone had seen this menace and something had brought him back. Taking to the sky, the valley walls reflected off of him, he seemed to cover the entire area and by the looks of it, he was heading in the direction of the willow where Rell and his mom were enjoying the day.

"This has been a lot of fun having you here with me today, Mom." The tone of his voice said it all.

"It sure has," she reached out, "but there is one thing I have not talked to you about."

"I don't know how that's possible? We have talked about so much today." He could tell it seemed important by the way she said it.

"You know you are a very special boy." As she placed her hand out, he placed his on hers.

"Of course, I do, and you tell me that every day, it's starting to stick." He smiled, holding her hand tightly, but he noticed something was different. "Mom, what are you not telling me?"

"I think I know why you've been having all these changes; from your dreams to what happened to you the day before." You could see she had his full attention as he sat there and listened.

She proceeded to tell him about a time before he was born, the day his father Darr had when he had met Dawla the Lady of Lanila. Explaining to him how she was responsible for all the life in the land that they saw around them, the day he saw her was on this hill and she told his father he would have a son. He would be one of the two parts that would bring Lanila back stronger than before. She continued to tell him the doubt that even his father had with what he was hearing, until she leaned down and touched the ground and before his eyes this magnificent willow tree they sat under sprouted from the ground.

"Dawla told your father how this would protect you, even went on to tell him where to build the house we live in today."

By this time, Rell was speechless yet captivated by every word as she continued about Dawla informing his father that there would be more than just her watching over their son and to always be aware of everything around.

"OK, wait a minute, Mom!" He stood up abruptly, you could see how he was trying to process all he was being told. "You're telling me I'm part of what you've been telling me will save this land?" he asked, looking down at her.

"Yes, son, and I'm sorry I didn't say anything until now." She felt slightly in the wrong for not mentioning him before. "We were told that we would know when the time was right to tell you."

"Don't be sorry, Mom. You've always had my best interest and always looked out for me." You could see he didn't want her to feel bad. "But why, Mom?" He placed his hand on his chest, pausing a moment. "That explains my burst of speed then."

"I believe so, son, that's one of the reasons we're having this talk." She knew this was a lot for anyone to hear. She rose to her feet.

"So the dream, was that real then?" He turned and looked at her.

"I don't know, son, but your mind is powerful and I've raised you to know you have no limit on what you can do." She reached out and grabbed him. "But no matter what, you are my son, you're not alone and we'll figure this out together."

"I know that, Mom," he said and hugged her. "It is kind of scary to think what's next for me." You could see the child in him come out as he hugged her tightly.

With all they discussed it could not have been at a better time for a danger was approaching and its name was Shaydon. He had covered a lot of ground since leaving the land of reflections, the black darkness that kept him hidden was getting closer, yet his silver eyes were very visible.

"It's going to be OK, Rell, I promise," she said as she looked at him. "You still feel like going fishing?" she asked trying to lighten the mood on what he had just heard.

"That sounds like a great idea." He could see she was trying to get things going in a different direction. "Mom, I know what you're doing, but it's OK. Today is no different than any other day." He paused then continued, "Sure, I just found out I'm supposed to be one of the two that will save everyone." His smile said it all.

"Come on, let us head home." She smiled, grabbing him as they headed toward the branches and pulled them back.

"What in the world is that, Mom?" he asked as he pointed to the sky in the distance. He noticed it getting darker and moving toward them.

"No, it can't be!"

He noticed how terrified his mother was as she began to shake slightly as he held her hand.

"Can't be what, Mom? What is it and why are you shaking?" He was getting concerned now by her actions.

"Get back to the base of the tree, quick!" They ran back to the trunk and huddled next to one another. "Maybe it didn't see us."

"Mom, maybe what didn't see us?" He could see how scared she was as she held on to him tighter than ever.

"Be quiet, my son. Don't say a word, I'm not going to let it take you too," she spoke softly.

They noticed the light through the branches disappear as it became dark as night.

Suddenly, a rumble like he had never felt before came upon them, followed by a deep voice saying he was there to end all hope of this. They both looked at one another, not knowing what would happen next as they held each other tight. It was just as they thought; they were in trouble. Suddenly, from the bottom of the tree, a golden light began to glow. It started to climb up the trunk and into the branches and leaves. It was all around them and so bright, it had a warm feeling to them as they watched, giving them the feel of security and then what happened next was unexplainable. With Shaydon hovering above, he noticed what was happening and it was like nothing he had seen in all his time. Suddenly, after the willow was entirely covered in this golden light, it let out a pulse of energy so bright and powerful, Shaydon was gone and nowhere in sight.

"What just happened, Mom? Are you OK?" He uncovered his eyes from the bright light.

"I'm fine, son, are you OK?" She looked around but could see nothing but daylight through the branches. "It's gone!" She paused, looking around. "That golden light we saw, where did it go?" Even she wasn't sure what the light they saw was.

"I'm ok, Mom, I've never seen that light before, I have no idea where it went." Standing to his feet, he said, "Only one way to find out where it's gone," as he walked toward the branches.

"Rell, please be careful." You could see she was still trying to get over what had just happened.

"I'll be careful." He very slowly pulled back the branches and looked through them. "I don't see anything. Whatever that was, Mom, it's gone." He pulls them apart even wider so she could see.

"I can't believe it's back," she said as she stood to her feet, shaking her head, you could see how worried she seemed.

"What was that, Mom? It seemed as if you had seen it before?" Seeing how it made her feel, he was convinced she had.

"Son, listen, I'll tell you everything when we get home, I promise." She smiled at him as she walked past him through the branches.

"OK, Mom." Shaking his head trying to understand what they just encountered, he felt his mother was keeping something about this from him. He walked through the branches and stopped. Turning back, he said, "Thank you!" knowing he could not explain what had happened but felt deep down the willow had something to do with it.

The day was growing longer and after what just happened to them, he could tell his mother was still thinking about it. She stayed very quiet on the way back to the house, saying nothing because he could see this had her really worried. He reached out as they continued and placed his hand on her shoulder, smiling just to let her know he was there for her, seeing how troubled she was.

"I'm here, Mom," he said, looking over at her with a smile.

"Thanks, son." She finally had said something smiling back; you could see the relief on his face hearing her.

You could see how anxious he was having so many questions for her, knowing she had promised to talk to him about whatever that was. Finding out what she knew about what they had encountered. As the day grew darker with each hill, you could see the relief on both of their faces; they were getting closer to their home.

Chapter Four

With the day passing, the suns were getting closer to the ground. That blinding light had caused Shaydon to disappear, leaving Rell and his mother free of harm for now; meanwhile back in land of reflections, we see where he vanished to. It seemed that the golden blast of energy that came from the willow teleported him back to where he began his journey. He was completely visible now as he began striking the sides of the valley walls. His legs and body were black with silver throughout his scales and head. You could see how angry and frustrated he was with what had just happened. With no answer to how he got back here, he let out a menacing roar, causing the valley walls to shake, calling out the name Saball. Suddenly from the distance, something was approaching and it was traveling with great speed, it was headed toward him as it left a black vapor trail behind him. This was who Shaydon had called for as he began to slow down entering the valley walls. His size was larger than two men that stood upright, muscular throughout his entire body. His head and body had the features of both a man and dragon; truly something to be feared. His arms were long with four fingers on his paws and very long claws on each of them. On one of his fingers he was wearing a solid black ring with a silver and black stone in the middle. His body was protected with some sort of black armor highlighted in silver, in a way resembling Shaydon's scales.

He approached him at a much slower pace, hearing the tone of his call. By his actions, he knew he was unable to complete his task. Knowing why he went to the willow but he had nothing with him, even Saball was confused; there had never been a time before that he never succeeded.

"You called upon me?" He kneeled before him with both hands on the ground, his voice had a very deep dead tone to it.

"Something stopped me from getting to him." He let out another roar, his voice had such a low tone to it, hitting the valley wall again.

"If he is what we have heard Lanila has been waiting for, we know now that he has something or someone watching over him."

Saball rose to his paws. "But what was it that stopped you?" Nothing had ever opposed them.

"I reached the willow and was right above it when this blast of a golden energy came from the tree itself." It seemed that they had been watching him, keeping their distance, waiting for the right time. "Then when the light was gone and I could see, I was back here."

"I've seen nothing to make us think the tree was special." You could tell Saball was trying to make sense of what happened, when suddenly he said a name that put it all together – "Dawla!"

"Of course, Saball, I should have known she was behind this." They knew of her when he caused havoc before, but they could never find her. "It's the tree; it must keep him protected when he is there."

"What do you ask of me?" Saball was large but still looked up to him. Shaydon was extremely muscular with a solid black underbelly, his scales had silver tips on each of them, you could see how havoc and chaos followed him.

"We must find a way to watch him, to see where he is not protected, then strike where this doesn't happen to us again." He walked along the valley walls with a devilish grin, the reflection making him seem even larger. "But you must be careful, Saball. After what happened today, Dawla might have more surprises for whoever tries to bring harm the boy's way."

"Understood. I will go and watch him, look for any way then report back to you with what I discover." He kneeled before him. "Is there anything more you ask of me?"

"We must not let this word travel along the land of this new beginning to those that have survived." From the tone in his voice, you could see this was one thing he didn't want. "There will be no new beginning for Lanila." He looked down at Saball. "We fought and destroyed all that stood before us, we're not stopping now, do you understand what I am saying?"

"I understand. I care not about the protection he has, this will not happen," he said as he rose to his feet. "With our powers, we can't be stopped," he said, looking down at the ring.

"Now go and keep me informed." He looked at the large mass of crystals at the top. "We'll be ready if it comes to it." An evil smirk appeared on his face.

So Saball had his orders and was off, leaving a black vapor behind him. As this black darkness started surrounding Shaydon, he seemed to be concentrating on whatever was on the top. So they knew of this word of how the land was supposed to restore itself, but not exactly how. They did know somehow the boy was tied in to it and had been watching him.

Time had passed since the last time we saw Rell and his mother. Instead of going in, they sat down in some chairs on the front porch. You could see the relief on both of their faces as they finally looked to be relaxing, but he knew what happened had trouble his mom in a way he had never seen before.

"You sure you're OK, Mom?" He was still worried about her.

"I'm fine now, just glad to be back home," she said, letting out a sigh of relief. It was finally time to tell him all she knew. "It's time, my son. I knew this day would come, just not so soon. You've grown so much."

"OK, Mom, what are you talking about? We've been through so much today." He tried showing compassion for her, seeing how upset she was. "It would help me to understand exactly what is happening."

"It has to do with this new beginning Lanila is waiting for, I know in my heart this all has to be linked to it." Looking over, she could see she had his full attention.

"So that black mass of darkness that we saw, it was because of me, Mom? You could have been hurt." He rose from the chair and approached the rail. "That golden flash of energy, it did come from the tree. You mentioned this Dawla had told Dad the tree would protect me," he said as he began to remember what he was told.

"Believe so, my son." You could see in her eyes how much he was growing. "You asked me earlier if I had seen that before," she paused, looking down as a tear falls from her eyes.

"What is it, Mom?" He sat back down next to her and grabbed a hold of her hand, seeing the tear fall from her eye.

"Whatever that was, I believe it did something to your father." She looked, up trying to be strong for her son, knowing how much this could upset him.

She went on to tell him of the day she had encountered it before. He listened carefully to every word that she spoke.

"It came a few days after your father had spoken with Dawla." She went on to explain it happened when he was on his way home one day, coming from the willow. It came with such great speed and force, there was nothing he could do; his eyes were glued to every word. "I was standing in the doorway watching all this take place. I started to run out toward your father, but suddenly, this dark mass let out this force so strong it threw me back into the house. I couldn't do a thing; I was powerless, hearing your father screaming for it to stop." As she wiped her eyes, you could see how much this hurt her. "Then as I looked up in its eyes, Rell, that silver was piercing. Then it let out another force, almost like a roar. It knocked me out and the door slammed shut. When I finally was able to wake up, your father was gone."

"It's OK, Mom," he said wiping her eyes and hugged her.

"Thanks, son." As she looked at him, "You know, I see your father every day when I see you." A smile appeared, followed by a tear. "I just don't want to lose you as well," she said, hugging him tight.

"Promise you, Mom, no one is going to take me. I'm always going to be here for you." She could hear in his voice the security she needed. "But Dad, why?" He didn't understand.

"I don't know but when I finally was able to wake up and opened the door, it was gone along with your father." She stood up; her puffy eyes looked down at him. "I'll be right back, there's something I need to get."

"Mom, sit down, I can get whatever you need, you've been through a lot." He began to get up and she reached over and stopped him.

"I'm fine. Wait here and I'll be right back."

As he sat there, you could see how he was taking in all he had just heard. Rell's mother made her way into the house, walking toward the fireplace. On the far side, she reached out for one of the stones; it looked to have some sort of symbol on it. Getting a hold of it, she turned it slightly, removing it from the rest. Holding it over her hand, she turns it upside down. It must have been hollow as a bright golden medallion fell from it. Smiling, she placed the stone back from where it came from and made her way back outside. He was still deep in his thoughts; she startled him stepping out of the door.

"You sacred me, Mom," he said, taking a deep breath. He noticed she had something in her hand. "What's that?" he asked, seeing the golden color it had.

"This is the only thing I found that day. I've been keeping it safe knowing this day would come." She held it out to him.

"Wow, it's amazing!" His eyes were mesmerized. "But what does that have to do with me?" he asked taking it to from her hands.

"Through the years of watching you grow; I've kept my dreams of this to myself and for that I'm sorry." You could tell how bad she felt.

"It's OK, Mom," he looked over at her, "through all the cycles I have grown, you've always looked out and wanted the best for me." That picked her spirits up.

"You make me so proud of how much you have grown, I'm so very proud." Her smile said it all. "This was what I found and through my dreams, I learned it was a gift from Dawla to help protect you."

"What does it do?" He held it up. Even though the suns were close to setting, it looked as if the light was on it.

"Let's head in and you light the fire stones throughout the house while I prepare something for us to eat before it gets to dark." The dreams she had been having were starting to make sense, she knew it would take some time to try and explain it.

"Sure, Mom, that sounds like a great idea," he said, smiling and holding the medallion tight. "This is so beautiful." The child in him seemed to be coming out with all that was happening.

With the day's end approaching and with all the changes, they headed into the house. Rell did as she asked and lit the fire stones. Holding on to the medallion tightly, he admired it the entire time. His mother put together a simple meal for them to enjoy. When he came down the stairs without asking, he began to set the table, asking if there was anything else she needed. She let him know there wasn't.

"Why don't you go ahead and wash up? I have everything." She looked at him and noticed his smile. "Be careful you don't lose that," she said, seeing how tightly he held it.

"You don't have to worry about that," he said as he smiled. Grabbing the bucket, he proceeded to the stream to fetch water and wash up.

As he walked toward the stream, his mind was busy thinking of everything that was happening. Still holding the medallion, he approached the stream, and realized that he needed to secure it. He thought to himself what better way to keep it safe than to put it on. When he placed it around his neck, it began to glow in a gold color, and as it consumed his entire body his eyes grew large. Then it was gone. The look on his face showed he had no idea what had just happened to him. He looked all over his body for any sign of what he just seen and there was nothing. You could tell he was confused; he did not have an answer and if what he saw was real, his mother had no idea for he was out of sight of her. At that moment, the ground began to tremble.

On the side of Lanila, we could see HaVon sleeping when suddenly, he woke up. Looking around, he felt as if he wasn't alone. You could see the confusion on his face. At the same time this was happening to HaVon, in the land of reflections where Shaydon rested, a sudden rumble began; it was so loud the grounds around began to shake, causing tremors throughout the entire land. It was obvious as soon as Rell had placed the medallion around his neck, it had started this new beginning, it seemed to effect more than just himself. He took off toward the house, feeling the tremors, completely forgetting to wash up and the bucket. Meanwhile, we could see HaVon moving around had woken up Ravin.

"What is it, are you all right?" She noticed something had him distracted.

"I'm sorry, I didn't mean to wake you up, I guess it was just a dream." She could hear the confusion along with the apology in his voice.

"You're fine, my young one, it just startled me; you're not one to wake up at night." She smiled. "You know I'm here for you if you need. Get some rest, for tomorrow brings us a new day," she said and lay back down.

"Rest well, Ravin, and once again forgive me," he spoke, laying himself down, knowing the new day would soon be upon them and so much was changing.

At the same time Rell was running toward the house, his mother had come out feeling the tremor. She hurried him inside, not sure what had happened. She locked the door behind him.

"Is it back?" You could see she still had not recovered from earlier as she looked out the windows.

"No, Mom!" He reached out and hugged her tightly.

She could feel he had a slight shake to him.

"What's wrong, son? Why are you trembling and why were you running?" She stepped back and noticed the medallion around his neck. "This looks great on you."

"This is why, Mom!" They proceeded to the table and he had her full attention. "It let out a golden glow that covered my body, then shortly after that the tremors began."

"What do you mean?" she asked, thinking to herself it was really happening.

"My body absorbed it, I believe, and I don't know why." You could see the boy in him coming out, looking to his mom for the answers.

"This happened when you decided to place it around your neck?" as she said this, a smile and a tear appeared.

"You knew that would happen?" he asked, looking at her. "Are you OK, Mom? Why do you have a tear in your eye?" He wasn't sure at this point if it was a good tear or bad.

"To hear you say that," she said as she wiped the tear from her eye, "I can't begin to tell you how proud this makes me, not to worry," she explained herself.

She continued from where she had left off on the porch, where her dreams had let her know of the coming events. At the same time, she let him know she had no idea it was so close to happening. But she kept reassuring him there was no reason to be worried.

"Wow, Mom! To think all these stories you have told me were of what I would become!" he said, nibbling on his food she had placed on the table while looking down at the medallion. "So this glow it had, what was that?"

"Now understand, my son," she said holding her hand out and he grabbed it, "even though I have told you what I have, there are still things I'm not sure about." She squeezes his hand firmly. "But I do believe and know that in time, all your questions will be answered."

"Thanks, Mom! You always know how to say things for me to understand," he said and held her hand firmly.

"Now after you finish up with your food, you need to get yourself ready for bed," she said, knowing it would take a lot for him to relax. "We can talk all about this when the new day is upon us."

"OK, Mom." Indeed, you could see his mind seemed busy thinking about all he had been told. Finishing up, he rose from the table and grabbed his plate.

"I'll get that, son," she said as she took the plate. "You get ready for bed and I'll be up shortly." She smiled.

"I'll see you upstairs," he said, still admiring the medallion.

Shaking her head with a smile, he went upstairs. While cleaning up everything from their meal, you could see her thinking as well; it was really happening, all those dreams she had been having were beginning to make more sense. Looking up, she spoke out loud, "Please, help show him the way, never let him feel alone in this new beginning of his life." As she closed her eyes, it was then that a warm feeling came over her body like she had never felt before, followed by goosebumps all over her body. At that moment, she knew they were watching over him. "Thank you!" she whispered. Putting out the fire rocks, she proceeded upstairs where her son was waiting.

As he lay in bed, you could tell he was still fascinated with the medallion, looking at all the detail as he held it up. It had four jewel type stones on it, one on the top, bottom, and each side of it, and each one of them inside a triangle. One on top was of white color, green one on the bottom, blueish and reddish colors on each side, and in the middle was a gold one but unlike the rest, it was in the center of a dragon head. It was made out of some sort of gold surrounded in purple highlighting and was truly beautiful. Such craftsmanship like this had never been seen before. Even with these stones he was amazed it had no weight to it. He continued to admire it when he saw his mom standing in the doorway looking at him.

"What is it, Mom?"

She could tell he was excited.

"Nothing," she answered, making her way over to his bed and sat down at the foot of it.

"You know, Mom, I've been looking at this, thinking, after hearing about your dreams and Dawla, what if there's a connection with this and the willow, it might fill in the blanks," he said as he sat up in bed.

"Son, promise me you will not to go back to the willow without me." You could hear the concern in her voice.

"But, Mom –" he started, trying to bargain and make a point.

"Rell, we have to be careful now." A tear appeared; you could see she didn't agree.

"I'm sorry," he apologized, seeing how much that bothered her. "I understand," he said, looking down at the medallion, "I just feel in my heart that there is more we could find out," being sure to include her in what he thought.

He understood what she was talking about. Not wanting him to return to the willow, she was only looking out for his safety. After all that had happened, deep in his heart he felt that there was more to it.

"Son, you're a lot like your father when you speak like that," she said, wiping her eyes and smiling, "he would say the same things, agreeing, but deep down I knew he would never give up following his heart." She placed her hand on his cheek gently like a mother would.

"That means a lot to me, Mom." Releasing the medallion, he gave her a hug. "I'll never take this off and will always listen to what you say."

He indeed was handling this very well, considering all that he had heard and encountered today. As he lay back in bed, little did he know this was only the beginning. In time, the questions he had now would only seem more complicated, but they would not be answered only by him but someone else as well.

"Now get some rest, my young adventurer, for the new day brings us all new questions," she said, pulling his sheets up around his shoulders, "so rest your mind and may the Elders watch over you in your dreams." She kissed him softly on the forehead.

She tucks him for bed then made her way to hers. Lying down, you could hear a sigh of relief for all that had happened to her family. She looked over and saw he had already begun to fall asleep. She closed her own eyes, tired from the day. Both of them finally bringing themselves to sleep from the day's events; they had been through so much for anyone to have to encounter, yet they seemed so peaceful and relaxed as they slept. The blue moon shone brightly into the sky here; meanwhile, on the other side of Lanila, the day had already begun.

Chapter Five

The suns rose into the sky in the land of the mountains, shining brightly over all in sight. There was so much color in the land, it was truly breathtaking. Suddenly, something could be seen in the air diving in between the clouds at a great speed; it was HaVon, using such precision. He was out early, doing his lessons and working on his strength. You could see by the way he was moving his lessons were coming along well; indeed, this dragon would have a lot to give Lanila and he wouldn't be doing it alone. He knew there was a reason for all he was learning, knowing he would be called upon one day. As each day passed and the more he learned, it brought him closer to the day when the Elders would be ready for him. Ever since he was young, he was raised with the knowledge of knowing he had to serve a great purpose to Lanila, and he also heard that he would have help from another. Ravin never told him who she was speaking of, only that they would be an ally who would help him.

As he flew through the clouds, the two suns shining off his scales, his colors changed like a chameleon all over his body. As he continued with his lessons, you could tell that something seemed to have him distracted. Every once in a while, he seemed to look around and behind him. Diving closer to the ground, he noticed a clearing in the distance that was next to a body of water. Bringing himself in as he landed, the ground made a low rumble. Bringing his wings to his side, he stood there just looking around, then something caught his attention from the distance. It was Ravin who was coming from the way of the great peaks, home of the Elders. This was one place he had not seen yet but that would soon change.

"How nice it is to see you. Enjoying this beautiful day?" she asked, bringing herself down and landing next to him. "How are your lessons today, any questions?" she asked as she looked up at him.

"It's been a great start. I think I'm even getting faster." He looked at her with a grin. "You would have been proud of me."

"There is not a day that passes, my young one, that I'm not proud of you," she said and smiled, "it makes me very happy to hear that. Plus, it shows me how much you're growing."

Standing there in the clearing, you could see every once in a while something seemed to get his attention, and made him suddenly look in a different direction. She noticed his strange behavior.

"I've noticed you seem distracted at times," she said.

He stood there still, looking as if he had not heard her.

"HaVon, what is it?" This time, she nudged him as she said it.

"I'm sorry." he shook his head as he focused on her.

"What is it, are you OK?" You could hear the concern in her voice.

"Well, ever since last night when I woke up, something just seems different." You could tell he seemed confused in a way by his silence. "It was my dream that woke me," he said looking down at her.

"Your dream was what woke you?" She got very quiet, waiting for an answer.

"It was so real at times; I can't seem to stop thinking about it." This made sense now why he kept looking around. "Since then, I feel something or someone is watching me."

"Tell me more, was there anything else you can remember?" She stood next to him in a comforting way.

He went on to explain the dream to her; by the way he was describing it, it seemed it had to do with what happened to Rell. What he experienced in his dream was exactly what Rell was going through at the time he put the medallion around his neck; it must have been the medallion that sparked the connection between the two.

"You know," she was searching for the right words to comfort him, "I believe like I have always taught you," pausing a moment, "they say dreams are a gateway at times to a connection for what lies ahead."

"There might be a connection with me and this dream?" He was eager to hear her response.

"Only you will be able to answer that, my young one," she said with a smile.

"What kind of answer is that?" You could hear the disappointment and the look of confusion on his face.

"Now don't be upset by my answer, it just means time will show you if there's a connection to anything," she tried to ease his mind.

"I'm sorry," he said softly, looking at her. "I just can't seem to stop thinking about it, like it's a part of me." You could tell he desperately wished there was an answer for what he was going through.

"Don't worry, there's no need to get so worked up, young one. Remember what our Elders say, never be impatient and believe all will come to you when the time is right." Her words to him were calming and secure.

"You're right," he said, shaking his head as if to clear his mind. "You're right, Ravin, time will answer everything. Thank you for all the wisdom and guidance you show me." He felt very lucky.

"Thank you. By the look of the skies, the day is passing. We should start thinking about heading back." Having talked for so long, the suns were beginning to get closer to the ground.

With a spread of both of their wings, they took to the skies. Even though he was a juvenile dragon, his size was amazing, shadowing her.

As they had started their way back, there seemed to be some activity in the land of reflections. Shaydon stood before a large mass of crystals. They seemed to be getting more spread out and somewhat larger. Standing there, before this, he appeared massive in size.

"It has begun!" The tone of his voice nearly caused rumbling in the walls. "I will take from them all this hope, reminding them why they should have stayed hidden. They must be taught a lesson, thinking a boy protected by Dawla will stop me." An evil smirk appeared. "In time, they will find out we're not alone." He looked at the formation as the ground rumbled when he laughed.

He turned and headed to the edge above the cave in the wall. Spreading his wings, he glided down to it. You could see how large of an opening it was and there was a red glow coming from deep within. He made his way into the red glow of the cave. Things were indeed beginning to change since Rell placed the medallion around his neck; it had made Shaydon aware and he was getting ready while Saball researched for his leader. It seemed things were about to go in an entirely different direction soon.

Meanwhile, HaVon and Ravin had made it back to the lair. He had decided to stay outside while she had gone on in.

He made his way toward the water. A large area in between some trees seemed to be flat, and HaVon lay down there in an upright position. He faced the water and you could see he was still thinking of the dream, wondering what he would find out and the purpose he would serve. Sitting there, looking into the water at his reflection, he wondered to himself if he would have this dream again when he would go to sleep.

"I know you watch over me," he said, looking up, "I love Ravin so much. I couldn't have asked for anyone better to raise or teach me." He looked back at his reflection in the water. "I miss you both. I see you every day in my reflection."

He was very thankful for Ravin but this was something special he tried to do every night, where he would come and reflect on the parents he never met or knew. Knowing Ravin was chosen to protect and guide him in the way of the Elders, to him this was a way to honor his parents for all they had given up for him to survive.

"I know in my heart you will help me find the answers I seek." Rising up, he headed toward the opening of the cave, looking up one last time as the blue moon showed its dominance in the sky. He smiled and headed in where Ravin was waiting.

"Did you find what you were searching for, young one?"

"It's like you reminded me," he answered, looking over at her and smiling, "time will have all the answers I seek." He went over to her and he looked down to where she was laying. "But there is one thing," he said as he lay next to her.

"What might that be?" She looked back at him, curious to hear what it was.

"Well, I'm curious," he paused, "what will I see in my dreams tonight?" Now he knew that what he saw might be a connection to what lay ahead.

"You are getting wiser and coming along so well with all you have been taught. I promise I will tell the Elders when I see them about all this new information you have told me." She also tried to assure him they would find the answers.

"Thank you," he said, looking at her. "Do think I could go with you?" This was something he had always wanted to do.

"In time, my young one, there is still more to learn." She knew in her heart how much he had waited for that day. "I must I remind you they will let me know when they're ready to see you," she reminded him it was not up to her but the Elders.

"I already knew what the answer would be." He smiles. "Doesn't hurt to ask. I hope they have all the answers."

You could see the day was catching up to him as his eyes looked heavy, as he fought to keep them open.

"Get some rest, young one, for the new day ahead brings all new adventures," she spoke softly, seeing he was finally falling asleep.

With the day finding its way to an end as the blue moon conquered the area, it had brought our young dragon so much more than he realized. Little did he know, the new day ahead would bring the answers, and even more questions he would need to answer for all that was about to happen. Finally having fallen asleep, Ravin slowly opened her eyes and being sure not to wake him up, she rose up and went past him, looking down as she did. Making her way toward the opening, she looked back,

"Your time is coming and there is still so much more you need to learn." She stood there for a moment, admiring him. "Rest, my young one, I will return."

She made her way out of the cave with the light of the moon casting a blue shadow across the area. Looking back one last time, she took to the air. This was unlike her to leave, but she felt in her heart this was what seemed to be the start to this new beginning. Taking off to go to the Elders, she knew they would want to know and have the answers they were searching for.

Chapter Six

With all these changes going on around the land of Lanila, the suns had just begun to climb and shine down over Rell's home. His mother was already out collecting melons, while upstairs still in bed, Rell was just beginning to move about from his night's rest. Sitting up in bed, stretching his arms out, you could see he was well-rested. He was rubbing his eyes when he noticed his bed seemed damp from his sweating. He began to look around; it took a moment for him to remember, then a smile appeared on his face and he grabbed hold of the medallion. He could see his mother had laid clothes at the foot of his bed when he heard her come in the front door.

"Be right down, Mom," he yelled out thinking he might have slept in too long. Putting his clothes on, he rushed down the stairs.

"Slow down. What's the rush, my son?" she said as he turned the corner.

"I thought I might have slept in too long," He walked up to her with the melons in her hand giving her a morning hug.

"No, you're fine." She hugged him back. "Just thought I would let you sleep in a bit with all that has happened." She walked to the sink with a smile, seeing the medallion around his neck.

"Thanks, Mom." He began to help her. "What is it, Mom?" he asked, noticing the smile on her face.

"It just looks so good around your neck." She was so proud of him.

"I think so too." He grabbed some plates and set the table. "I told you I would never take it off," he said, sitting down. "Do we need anything else?"

"I think that's all." She placed the cut-up melon in the middle of the table and sat down. "So how did you sleep?" she asked, placing a melon on both of their plates.

"I think pretty good," he answered, taking a bite as he looked at her. "It was weird though, looks to be as if I was sweating pretty bad, my sheets were damp," he continued taking another bite.

"Damp from sweating?" She thought that was odd, for when she left him, he seemed fine and dreaming, but not sweating. "Maybe it had to do with your dream, do you remember anything about it?"

"A little bit," he paused for a moment, "the weird thing is all I can remember is the sky." You could see even he didn't know what that meant.

"What about the sky?" You could see she was curious.

"I remember seeing the sky and clouds," he said as he took his last bite and swallowed it. "It seemed as if I was flying through them, weaving in and out of them. Seems crazy, I can't fly, but it was so real, Mom," he said, thinking that had to be the reason hearing it himself.

"It's all right, my son." Her comforting voice let him know he was not alone. "We will get through this and learn together." You could hear the confidence in her voice. She grabbed his hand and said, "I promise." In her mind, she was sure it was the medallion, but did not want to say anything till she was sure.

"I know that, Mom," he smiled at her, gripping her hand tight.

"I was thinking maybe we could do something together today." With all that was happening, she felt it might be better if they stayed together, not going too far from the house today.

"Well, we could go fishing." Even though in the back of his mind he couldn't stop thinking about the willow, he could see she wanted to spend the day together.

"I think that is a wonderful idea," she smiled, getting up from the table.

"I'm so lucky, Mom," he said, looking at her smile. "I don't know what I would do if anything ever happened to you."

"I would never see myself leaving you either, my son." She turned to look at him. "But to think the worse, my son, and if something were to happen," she smiled, "I will always be here." She pointed to his heart.

"That's not the same, Mom, but I understand what you mean." He smiled back at her.

It was as if the smiles they had on both of their faces had made them forget about all that was troubling them, he informed her that he would go and get the fishing stuff together then be on the porch. She agreed then began to clean up while preparing a basket with snacks for them.

As they prepared for the day ahead, Saball made his way close to the willow. He left behind him that black vapor trail as he seemed cloaked, everything he passed was a blur as he traveled with great speed and was very agile for something so large. He began to slow down, becoming more visible. He came to a stop at a clearing. Standing there, he could see in the distance the great willow. Just as he was about to continue toward the willow, something got his attention in the opposite direction. He saw the house looking and noticed someone on the front porch. He was not worried about being seen as he was too far away for whoever it was to spot him. It was then as he watched, realizing it was the boy. Knowing that this would please Shaydon if he indeed could find out if he was protected, he then cloaked himself and made his way toward the house. when he got closer, he noticed a woman had joined him; they were making their way around toward the back of the house.

"This was a great idea, son, on such a pretty day," she said, looking over at him and smiling.

"It sure is."

They were making their way along the trail behind the house, toward the stream where they both had their favorite places to fish.

"Look at the glimmer on the stream, Rell," she said as they got closer.

"Are you going to your usual spot, Mom?" he asked, knowing the answer already.

She smiled at him as he followed her down the path that opened up to the creek.

"I see why you like this spot, Mom." Seeing a few stumps, he could remember the stories of this place where both of his parents would come; it was kind of her way of keeping in touch.

"I know you do," she said, placing the basket on the larger stump in the middle.

"Here, Mom." He placed her pole next to the stump and a tub of some sort of grub-like creatures. "I'm going to continue down a little further if that's OK?" He waited for her to approve and without hesitation, she did, having nothing to worry about out here, but she still cautioned him to be careful.

"I will, Mom." He continued down along the trail.

Now with his mom at her spot and agreeing it was OK for him to go down further, but not too far from her, he found a spot. He called out her name, this was a way of him letting her know he wasn't too far away. She smiled calling back to him. Hearing her, he felt good with setting up where he was, but unfortunately, he wasn't the only one to hear her call out. Saball had made his way down the path as he heard them call out to each other he was getting close. Instead of continuing in the same direction, he decided maybe it would be wiser to cross the stream. He did so while making sure to stay quiet as he made his way through the woods. Moving along the stream on the opposite side, he kept looking out for either one of them and realized he might be getting closer. He cloaked himself, being sure not to be spotted if he wanted to learn more.

You could see being out here was a great idea for them, seeing how relaxed Rell seemed. With the changes that he was going through at this time, he needed this. He looked down at the medallion, unaware of the connection with the changes in Lanila, and what it had to do with him. But by the end of this day, something would happen to him that would bring a realization – the trouble that was coming for him was very real. You could see how much he was enjoying himself sitting there, hoping his mom was feeling as relaxed as he was. But instead, she seemed troubled as a tear fell down her cheek. It looked to be finally getting to her, all that was happening to her son, but she didn't understand why was this happening now.

Just then, the medallion began to emit a pulse of light that got his attention. Not quite sure what was going on, he decided to grab a hold of it. Just as he did, he saw a vision of his mother as if he was right in front of her, noticing she had tears coming from her eyes. He let go of it immediately and rose to his feet, thinking how was it possible as he just saw her. He went back to where he had left her, not knowing what was wrong. When he came around the bend, she didn't hear him and it was just as he had seen in his vision.

"Mom, are you OK?" could hear the concern in his voice.

"I'm sorry I didn't realize you could hear me." She felt a little embarrassed and did not want him to know why she had been crying.

"What is it?" He leaned down next to her.

"I just can't believe the time has already come."

He then realized what had her upset.

"A lot is going on, Mom, it's OK to cry." He hugged her then looked at her. "We'll figure everything out together." He smiled to reassure her.

"You have grown so much; I can see your father in your eyes." Reaching out, she placed her hand on his face. "I see how brave and strong your soul and heart are." A smile appeared on her face.

"That may be true, Mom, but don't think you're not as much a part of my heart and soul as he is." Being sure, she realized he wouldn't be who he was if it weren't for her and what she had done.

"But how did you know I was upset? Did you hear me?" She began to relax.

"It was the medallion, Mom. It started pulsating when I grabbed it, it was like I was looking right at you." He too was still trying to make sense of it.

"You are the one, my son, I promise you I'll be right here for you," she said, reassuring him they would do it together.

"I know, Mom," he said, looking down at the medallion. "What if you're not around when something happens that I don't understand?"

"Remember you never alone, son," she reminded him as she placed her hand over his heart. "It will never mislead or misguide you."

"You know what, I'm going to go get my stuff and come over here with you." He stood up and smiled. "Be right back."

"That would be great. Do you need help?" She rose to her feet.

"No, that's fine. I've got it, Mom," he said, heading back to get his stuff.

He knew this was the best thing to do after seeing the way his mother had been. He reached down and grabbed the medallion.

"Whoever or whatever is helping me through this time, I thank you." He took a breath. "As you watch over me, I ask the same for my mother, I couldn't imagine my life without her." He smiled, feeling secure.

As he began to grab everything, at the same time Saball could see him, being sure to keep his distance. He was not sure what was protecting him. Just as Rell was about to turn back, he heard some rustling coming from the trees. He turned in the direction of Saball and slowly began to look around, it made him curious where the noise had come from. Seeing nothing, he figured he must have been hearing things that weren't there. Saball noticed how he had looked in his direction, wondering how. He watched him turn back around and make his way down the trail. Saball decided to follow him but keep his distance.

Walking down the trail back to where his mother was, Rell heard it again. He stopped, knowing he had definitely heard something. He slowly turned around. Saball noticed as he stopped in his tracks, wondering how the boy knew he was there as he had kept himself cloaked. Rell knew he wasn't losing his mind, but at the same time he didn't know what was he hearing. Saball, unsure if he knew he was there, decided to change his direction and stay outside the tree line, when Rell heard it again. This time, it was coming from a different direction. Not sure what he was hearing and with all that had been going on, he began to pick up his pace; just wanting to get back to his mom was his priority. He made it to the clearing and finally see her, so he slowed down his pace. She waved at him; he could tell she was happy he was joining her and waved back. As he got closer, he noticed the medallion began to pulsate again. What was it this time, he wondered because he could see his mom. Slowly reaching down and grabbing it, he was not ready for what he was about to see. When he did, it had a silver shade and he was looking at his own back. Saball noticed that Rell had grabbed hold of something around his neck that stopped in his tracks. He continued to watch Rell looking in his direction, and started to feel frustrated. then it hit him; whatever he was holding was helping the boy. Knowing this, he knew he had to tell Shaydon but wanted to stay and know more.

"What is it, son?" she noticed him stop and look behind him.

"It's nothing," he said, releasing the medallion and hoping she had not seen. "I thought I dropped something, was just turning to see if I could see it." He did not want to bring any attention to whatever was following him.

"With all that has been going on, I wasn't sure if you saw something," she said as she helped him with his stuff.

"I'm sorry, Mom, didn't mean to worry you." He knew he wanted to investigate more. "I'm sure I left something. I'll be right back, Mom." He kissed her on the cheek.

"Please be careful, want me to go with you?" she asked, feeling there was more to it than he was willing to say.

"No, Mom, I'll be fine." He smiled and turned to head back in the direction he had seen the vision.

The entire time Saball stood in the distance watching them both, being sure this time to keep his distance. Knowing whatever he was wearing had to be helping him, maybe even protecting him with what he and Shaydon had discussed about Dawla.

Rell headed back in the direction of his spot. When he was out of her sight, he stopped and grabbed the medallion. He saw nothing this time, and you could see the look of confusion on his face. He decided to start looking around in the direction from where he saw the vision. In the distance, Saball was watching him getting closer to where he was. Being silent and not wanting his mom to be worried, he made his way through the trees. He began looking around for any sign of what it was but could see nothing. You could tell he was just trying to make sense of it. Just when he was about to give up and head back to his mother, he tripped. As he got up and he brushed himself off, there it was in front of him on the ground. This was nothing like he had seen before; this track in the ground was so large his foot couldn't even fill in half of it. A look of worry came over his face as he held the medallion, looking for a sign of what it was and saw nothing. Knowing what was important now was to get back to his mom to head home, not sure if what made that track was anywhere nearby, his mother's safety was more important.

Not taking this lightly with what happened at the willow, to the stories he had been told and the dreams. He could see his mom and waved at her, smiling; he just didn't want to say anything to her about this right now.

"Did you find what you lost?" she asked as he approached.

"No, Mom, sorry about that," he said, being sure to stay calm.

"Look what I got for us." She rose to her feet and walking over to the edge of the creek, she pulled up some fish she had caught.

"How do you do it, Mom? they look great. You always did say this was your spot." He smiled but in the back of his mind, he kept wondering what was following him. "You know I'm not feeling too good," he said, rubbing his stomach, trying anything to get them home.

"Come on then, son, let's get you back to the house so you can lie down." She knew there was a reason for this and agreed. Not saying anything to him, she gathered up the stuff.

"Thanks, Mom." He felt a little more secure they were heading back.

Saball could see now they were leaving as he continued to watch them. He noticed that unlike before, the boy had not looked in his direction and was curious why, he had done nothing different. Then he thought to himself, it must have to do with the distance, whatever the boy was holding seemed to make him aware of danger that was close to him. He watched them head back to their home and followed, keeping his distance.

"Are you feeling better, son?" Noticing he looked to be in a daze at times, she felt there was more to it than he was telling her.

"A little, Mom," he said, holding the medallion, "I just think with all that is going on, it finally is just getting to me." He did not want her to worry till he knew more himself. "You know, I am going to listen to what you said and lie down, maybe that will help."

Trying his best to have an excuse for his actions as they came to the clearing and could see the house, then he felt as if he was being watched by something. His mom was unaware he had stopped in his tracks. He turned around to look and you could see hadn't let go of the medallion. Then his mom noticed he had stopped as she turned. She approached him quietly, wondering to herself what was going on with her boy. Rell could still feel something was watching him, he had goosebumps shoot up his neck and down his arms, unaware of his mom approaching.

"What is it, son?" She reached out and touched his shoulder.

"Mom, you scared me." He jumped slightly, letting go of the medallion and grabbing at his heart.

"What are you not telling me?" She could see something had him worried.

"I don't know, Mom," he said as he looked around, "you ever have that feeling like something is watching you?"

"Is that what's been bothering you?" This had her a little worried as she began to look as well.

"I don't know, Mom." He shook his head. "I just know it's not a good feeling I have." He was concerned with what was going on.

"Come on, let's go," she said, grabbing his arm and trying to comfort him. He could see in her eyes she knew better and just wanted to get them inside.

With her getting his attention, both of them headed back to the house.

"Why don't you go in and lie down, I can get dinner ready," she said, thinking it would be best to try and get him to relax.

"Are you sure, Mom?" he asked, knowing she was aware.

"Yes, I'll be in shortly." She walked over to the garden as he went inside. After he was in, she looked to the sky. "Whatever this is, please watch over him and keep him safe. There is so much he still needs to learn. With all that is happening, it seems time is running out." She then gathered some greens for dinner and headed inside.

"Are you OK, son?" entering the house, she called out.

"Yes, Mom," he responded to her.

"Stay up there. I'll get dinner ready and bring it to you." She wanted him to rest for now.

Well, with him resting, she knew the day was coming to an end. She began to light the fire rocks around the bottom of the house, knowing the changes were coming, but to what extent? She began to prepare the food, cleaning the fish and prepping the vegetables. Upstairs, Rell was lying down like he said but looked far from relaxed. His mind was working nonstop, trying to figure out what was watching him, thinking what could make such a large track, and if it was coming back. Realizing the two most important things; it knew of him for the vision he saw but what worried him the most was it looking to bring harm his way. So much was happening, he was having trouble trying grasp that all he had heard, but he knew he had to try and figure out the answers. He lay back in bed he took a deep breath.

Lying there, he thought about the track; it was larger than anything he had seen or could have imagined, and knowing this made him wonder about the size of whatever made it. Looking around the room, you could see his mind working, trying to come up with any explanation. He started to sit up when something caught his eye; the medallion was beginning to pulse again like earlier. He hesitated, knowing what he saw earlier, wondering why was it doing it in the house so he grabbed a hold of it. It was like earlier; he saw a silver vision. He immediately let go of it and trembled slightly as he was nervous, but he needed answers and this could be the only chance.

He slowly put his hands back around it, trembling, knowing he couldn't let go no matter what he saw; this was his chance, to see who or what it was looking at him. Watching it pass through trees, it looked to be tall, noticing the angle, but what bothered him the most was what it was passing through looked very familiar to him. He took a deep breath, catching a sight of whatever it was, it had a large hand with four fingers and a large ring. He noticed it had scales as well, it pulled the branches back it passed. His breathing became more rapid because things were looking more familiar. He suddenly realized it had stopped and was somewhere outside the front of house. It began looking around the entire area and Rell wasn't sure what to do. The focus it had amazed him, it almost seemed to zoom in everywhere it looked. Holding on tight, Rell watched it focus in on his bedroom window. Knowing this was the chance he needed, he kept a hold of the medallion and slowly made his way to the window.

So feeling his way to the window not to letting go, wondering if he would be able to see himself. Reaching out for the window ledge, he stood up, seeing himself in the vision. Whatever it was, it saw him and turned, running away with such a great speed. the entire time this was going on, he had no idea his mother had made her way up the stairs and was watching him.

"What are you looking at?" she asked, leaning over his shoulder to see.

"Mom!" he cried, letting go of the medallion. "You scared me." He could see the beads of sweat and his breathing was irregular.

"What were you doing?" she asked, wiping his forehead and putting him back in bed. "Son, you're sweating!"

"I was thinking maybe the air might do me some good," he answered, not wanting to say anything to her right now; enough had already happened to them both.

"I brought you some food with the way you were feeling," she said, placing a plate next to him, "but I'm a little worried with you sweating." She paused, hoping he might give an explanation.

"I just think my mind is overloaded with everything." Grabbing the plate, he began to enjoy what she had made.

"You know if anything's bothering you, I'm here for you." She placed her hand on top of his head.

"I know," he said, looking up at her. "Mom, this tastes great!" You could tell he was trying to change the direction.

"You look to be enjoying that," she said, smiling.

"That's what I was missing, Mom." He handed her the plate.

"That was fast. Let me run this downstairs." She started toward the door then turned back. "You sure you're OK?" She could feel there was more to it.

"I am now," he said, leaning back in bed.

"I'll be right back. I need to clean up and put out the fire rocks," his mother said as she went downstairs.

With his mother out of sight. he sat back up in bed. He was still thinking about what he just saw. Noticing the medallion wasn't pulsating, he grabbed it anyway. He saw nothing and didn't understand why.

"Mom said this was to help and guide me," he said, talking out loud. "I see nothing. How do you work?" You could see he seemed frustrated and took a deep breath. "OK, let's try a different way. Please show me what I need," he said, grabbing a hold of the medallion and closing his eyes.

Then it happened; as he closed his eyes, the medallion began to engulf his body in a golden light. He was unaware of it. But the vision he saw wasn't silver like before, but instead a warm feeling came over him and it was the willow. He knew what he had to do.

"I knew it!" he said, opening his eyes and unaware of the glow that was gone. "I've got to go to the willow!" Speaking out loud, he was not aware that his mother had just entered the room.

"What about the willow?" his mother asked, standing there and looking at him.

"I just know that the willow might have the answers we are searching for, Mom." He was unaware she had heard him, but also didn't want to lie to her.

"Son, you know what happened the last time we went there," she said, sitting next to him bed. "You look like you're feeling better." She knew there was more to everything going on than he was telling her.

"Mom?" He was concerned she might be disappointed.

"Yes, son?" She had a slight grin.

"I haven't been honest with you," he said, grabbing a hold of her hand, "I wasn't feeling sick earlier at the creek."

"I'm proud of you," she said, hugging him.

"You knew there was more to it?" he asked, hugging her back.

"I'm your mother. With everything going on, I thought it might." She sat back. "But what had you so bothered earlier, is that why you were at the window as well?"

"I'm not sure how to say this," he started, taking a breath, "we weren't alone out there."

"Son, we are never alone, I've told you that," she said, thinking in a different direction.

"No, Mom, something was watching me."

She could see it had him worried.

"How do you know this?" She waited to hear his response, but was afraid she already knew the answer.

"The medallion, Mom, it showed me this vision," he said, holding it up, "unlike when I saw you, it had a silver tint to it."

"That's the reason you became sick all of the sudden?" She then realized he was looking out for her. "You said a silver tint?" she asked, standing up. He could see this was meaningful to her.

"I'm not sure," she turns toward him, "I remember some of those dreams." She then paused. "They warned me of the silver glare that would try and bring harm to us both," she said, sitting back down on his bed.

"Mom, why didn't you say anything about this to me?" He could see she was a little uneasy now as well.

"This all was happening so fast; it didn't cross my mind until you just said something."

She shook her head back and forth, this was really happening. "Can you remember anything else you saw in the vision?"

"Well, at the stream when I said I forgot something, that's not true. I went back to where I saw the vision was watching me from. I saw a track like I've never seen, Mom, it was twice as big as my two feet together."

"Was there anything else?" she listened as he continued.

"When you saw me in the window, I had another vision, but this time I saw its hand, Mom; it was big and covered in scales." Feeling better, he opened up. "It also had some sort of ring on."

"The vision of it was looking at the house?" She stood up and approached the window. "Is it still out there?"

"I don't think so, Mom, it took off in the opposite direction when I could see myself." He looked at her. "When you startled me, I let go of the medallion and lost the vision."

"This tells me whatever this is knows where we are," she said, sitting back down. "We need to be careful, especially now." She reached out and placed her hand on his face. "You said something about the willow?"

"I was getting frustrated, Mom, not having any answers to any of this," he said, looking at her, "so I grabbed the medallion and asked it to please show me what to do. When I did, it showed me the willow."

"Understand me, son, what you saw is not a friend or ally." He could hear how serious she was. "You need to careful in the days ahead."

"By the way you're talking, you think it might come back?" He was getting a little nervous.

"I don't know, son, but I know now we have to be aware of everything around us." She needed him to try and relax, knowing how hard it would be. "The vision you saw was in silver and then the vision of me had a golden tint?"

"Yes, I remember the willow was golden at first then it was clear, like when I saw you," he paused, "of course!"

"What is it, son?" She was curious.

"When I saw you, it was golden and the willow as well; these are things close to my heart, Mom." He smiled. "But that silver vision must be of the opposite, right?" He almost felt silly having not figured it out until now.

"You are getting wiser, but it takes time, OK?" she said, comforting him. "In time, I believe you will find all the answers that you search for, but wait to go to the willow until we know it's safe, OK?" She smiled and lay him down.

"OK, Mom. Sorry I didn't tell you earlier." You could see he felt bad.

"It's OK, no worries, we have each other." She placed a kiss on his forehead and smiled. "Now try and get some rest, it's late, we'll continue this on the new day." She headed over to her bed.

"Thanks, Mom, I don't know what I would do if I didn't have you." He felt so much better telling her, even with all that was happening.

With both of them in their beds, he heard a sigh of relief from his mother. A lot was happening to them but the new day was still ahead. She was curious and scared of what it would bring. She turns looking over at Rell and noticed he had already fallen asleep. She thought to herself how thankful she was for whatever was watching over him; her boy was growing and his father would be so proud. With the night so late, they both fell fast asleep and the day was behind them, but little did either one of them know this was only the beginning. Each new day that passed would only get harder to try and understand, for what he feared the most, and the question was, how would he deal with it?

Chapter Seven

Saball had been looking for answers and spying on the boy. As he made his way back, you could tell he was still wondering how was the boy able to look in his direction. It was important to fill Shaydon in on what he had discovered. He wanted him to know the boy had something around his neck he had never seen before. He believed there was a connection with Dawla and protecting the boy from harm, especially after what happened at the willow with Shaydon. Then he thought about this dragon; maybe he could follow him as well, to see if he could notice anything that would help them stop this from happening. He knew it would please Shaydon so he was off.

The suns had already risen over the mountains, shining brightly into HaVon's cave. Our young dragon was still resting from the day before. Ravin had still not returned from her journey she made to the Elders. He slowly began to stir about and opened his eyes, looking over to see she was not there.

"Hum." He let out a yawn combined with a small roar. *I wonder where she could be,* he thought. But he was not too worried as he knew they usually met up later.

Rising to his feet, he stretched his back. He then approached where she slept and was a bit alarmed as he noticed it looked as if she had not lain in it. He remembered her being there when he laid down, now he was becoming a bit concerned with all that was happening. He turned, stretching his wings, you could see he was ready to go and find her. He approached the entrance and was startled as she landed at the entrance.

"You had me a little worried when I woke up. You weren't here. Did you decide on an early flight?" You could see the look of concern in his eyes.

"No, young one, it wasn't an early flight." She still seemed winded from her flight.

"Ravin, are you OK? You look winded. You said it wasn't an early flight then where did you go?" The look of concern on his face said it all.

"Are you trying to tell me I'm getting old?" she asked, smiling up at him.

"No, I was just worried, but seriously, is everything OK?"

"Well, not exactly, young one." She had his full attention now as she made her way to the lake where she lay down.

"Wait up, what do you mean?" He followed her. "Not exactly?" He was curious, waiting patiently for a response.

As they both made their way over, sitting next to one another, she explained to him what she had been up to. The look on his face was of incredulity.

"Boy, I wish I could have gone with you," he said after she told him it was the Elders that she had gone to see. "I know, one day it will happen," he responded like she always had for him, or so he thought.

"They said your time is coming."

You could tell by his reaction that was not what he expected to hear.

She had thrown him off from what he expected to hear, she began tell him they knew about all that was going on. This was not like before, the tone in her voice was like nothing he had heard before as he listened to every word that she told him about what the Elders had said – the time was coming.

"Time for the beginning?" He could tell what this was about.

He had been raised on the stories of this and the part he would eventually take in it, he also knew of another one that would help him in this quest. Then, it was like something went off in his head.

"That's the visions I've been having, it's the boy?" He turned, looking at her. "He's the one, the boy I've been feeling?" He was anxious for a response.

"The Elders believe it is," she replied.

"Elders, you told them what was going on?" There was a slight excitement in his eyes. "What else did they tell you?" He hoped there was more.

She began to explain to him that this boy he was feeling a connection with would help him in this new beginning that Lanila had been waiting for. By his reaction, he didn't believe it at first, thinking it had to be much later than now, not so soon. Going on, she told him they believed that the time was upon them, and all that he had been feeling were signs that would help him later on.

"Later on?" He wasn't sure what she was saying.

She went on comforting him by wrapping her tail around him. This was what he had been preparing for, knowing about that someone that would join him.

"I remember you telling me of this someone that would be joining me, but I'll still have you?" He looked into her eyes, waiting for a response.

"My young one, only the Elders know of our futures," she said and smiled, "plus, I couldn't leave your side anyway, so you need not worry," she said, trying to ease and comfort him.

"I know, Ravin, but without you, my life wouldn't be the same." You could see how much he needed and loved her.

"Thank you," she said, looking back at him, "but remember what I have told you, no matter what my future holds, you must keep your focus on all that I have been teaching you." She reminded him how important it was to the land of Lanila. "I will always be with you no matter what, you know that."

"I'm sorry," he said, not meaning he couldn't handle it, but just the thought of being without her unsettled him. "I know you're always in my heart." He grinned.

"Your spirit as well," she replied, letting him know she felt the same. "Are you OK?" she then asked, knowing this was a lot to take in.

"I'm fine," he said. "Please go on."

"Good to hear and there is more you must know." She had his full attention. He was about to hear new information and was quite eager. But was he truly ready to hear about what would try and oppose him?

She reminded him of what happened when this darkness came, so this time it would want so badly to stop this new beginning that was to come. She let him know it was up to him and this boy; they would learn in time to become one. After hearing that, he looked confused.

"That's the part of this I don't understand," he said, hoping she could make it a little simpler for him.

"I understand how this may not make sense to you," she looked at him with a grin, "but I promise you in time, all these questions you have will be answered." This reassured him that she believed he would.

He smiled, agreeing and knowing she always had the answers, continuing on also letting him know of the ones that would try and bring pain to him. Our young dragon was silent not making one sound, holding on to every word she spoke, little did he know how important this would become helping guide him.

"Last night I left after you fell asleep, to see the Elders they told me there was a presence that's resurfaced," taking a breath, "they believe it to be Saball."

"What is Saball?" The look on his face showed he had never heard this name before.

She reminded him of the stories of the land before, how they worked with the people to keep it protected throughout. She explained what brought that all to an end was this darkness, but it was this creature Saball that tore the kingdom down from the inside. You could see the look of confusion on his face.

"How can something that was so terrible and threatening do this?" He sat up waiting for a response.

"It was the powers of Shaydon that gave him his strength, it had the features of both man and dragon. They were under the belief that he would bring no harm to them and was there to help." You could see how this seemed to be getting to her. "By the time they realized what his true intentions were, it was too late. He destroyed everything in his way, showing no mercy. His mission was to take it all from us."

"There was no one that could help?" He was trying to understand.

Comforting him with her tail, she could see him become uneasy and smiled, explaining to him for that reason, they were at this moment in life. For when this new beginning would happen, it would change everything. She told him how many cycles had passed for those that had survived waiting for this very moment, and it all began with him.

"So they knew of me before you did?" he asked, trying to understand how that was possible.

"They brought you to me before you were even hatched, my young one," she told him, smiling. "There is so much ahead of you that you will have to face, but remember all that I've taught you; never give up and stop believing in what you're doing is right." She looked at him with a serious look. "HaVon, you understand what I am saying?"

"I do, there may have been times I wondered but you always knew what was best for me." He smiled back.

"I'm so proud to hear that, seeing what you're becoming," she said, knowing deep down he would be OK.

"So it's up to me?" It was still hard for him to believe. "And this boy I'm feeling, do you or the Elders know who he is?"

She explained to him that together, they would bring Lanila back to its full beauty and stronger than it ever was before. As she spoke, you could see him hanging on to every word, being sure not to miss anything. You could see how happy she was that he was showing so much interest and was asking for more. She did just that, continuing on as the day passed by.

"Why don't you go and practice some lessons? We can continue this talk later," she said, making sure he knew she wasn't trying to put this off, but time was against them in a way.

She thought he still had so much he needed to learn and didn't have enough time, instead she would see how much he had learned and what he didn't know, time would help show him. Agreeing with what she said, he knew now that his lessons were more important than ever, and took to the air with power. Watching him take off, you could see it in her eyes; she knew he would be ready, admiring how big and wonderful he had become. She made her way to the cave, knowing he would be fine. She went inside to rest for she was still slightly tired from the night's events.

While she caught up on her sleep, HaVon had traveled some distance, and all they had just talked about was still on his mind as he flew through the air. Little did he know that he was being watched, observed from the shadows on the ground by who he had just heard about. Saball decided to follow this dragon on his own, hoping Shaydon would approve, to find out any information and the connection to this new beginning it had set in motion. He made his way with such an amazing speed, and looking up from the distance, he could see HaVon high in the sky, focusing in as if he was in front of him. One of the reasons HaVon had no idea he was there was because this was nothing he had ever had to worry about before flying through the clouds. As Saball watched HaVon, moving through the brush, he was camouflaged and blending in with his surroundings. He continued to follow him as he noticed he began to descend from the sky. Being careful, he wasn't sure if the dragon knew of his presence like the boy did and continued watching him from a distance.

While this was occurring here, on the other side of Lanila, at Rell's house shone under the moon that was still high in the sky. Something seemed to have him troubled, he began to move around in his sleep, mumbling something. Then he sat up and suddenly yelled out, "Be careful, he's there watching you!" He opened his eyes, confused, and began to look around.

He looked over at his mother, afraid he might have woken her, but she was still asleep. He took a breath of relief; it had seemed so real. Wiping the moisture from his forehead, he looked around and saw nothing. Little did he know, the eyes he was seeing through were that of HaVon's – they did have some sort of connection.

While Rell began to relax and fall back to sleep from what he thought was a dream, back on the other side, HaVon came to a rest in the clearing. Looking around, he seemed troubled by everything going on. He was almost frustrated, such an opposite from when he began his flight. He needed to relax, so he began to take deep breaths. While he was doing this, Saball had made his way closer, watching him while staying cloaked. He even seemed amazed by HaVon's size, then he noticed something got his attention.

"Be careful. He's there, watching you." HaVon heard a voice. Looking around, he seemed confused, not knowing where it came from.

Being careful not to move, Saball became worried, noticing he was looking around in his direction. Not making a sound, he waited for him to look away. He decided to move back slowly, not sure if HaVon knew of his presence or not. At the same time, he didn't want to take a chance; if they were protected, he didn't want to let Shaydon down.

HaVon remembered what he had been told. Was it possible the voice he just heard was that of the boy's? They had a connection and he started to believe it. Thinking this, he then began to slowly look around, but it was too late. Saball had made his way out of there. He focused in on his surroundings, thinking to himself, he could be losing his mind too with all that was going on. Still, he knew not to take it lightly when suddenly he saw Ravin, she was flying to him. She had noticed he had seen her but at the same time. he seemed distracted.

"What are you looking for?" Ravin asked, landing next to him.

"Well," he hesitated, looking around, "it was a voice." He looked at her, not sure how she might react.

"What did it say?" She showed interest and concern.

"It's weird," he said, shaking his head, "be careful, he's there watching you."

"When did you hear that?" She sat up and began to look around, smelling the air.

"When I landed here was when I heard it." He noticed the way she was looking around. "It was the boy?" He was eagerly waiting for a response.

"It's possible." She knew more than she was ready to say. "I don't see or smell anything, Let's head back and continue this at the cave." She tried to ease his mind and he agreed.

With that said, they took off, looking over at him climbing higher into the sky. She knew he was growing. This was still a lot for anyone to have to take in. She knew she needed to comfort him and try to ease his mind, and realized she needed to answer all the questions he might have; the time was closer than she could have anticipated.

Looking over at her and knowing she felt him, he could see the concern. They got closer to their lair as the suns began to descend further.

Chapter Eight

With the two got closer to the lair, Saball had made his way back to land of reflections. He had true speed traveling such a great distance in a short time. He would prove in time to be a great challenge for our young adventurers. Making his way through the lifeless valley, he came to the bottom of the one with the cave formation at the top. Looking up, he could see the formation seemed to be getting larger, so he began to climb the wall with ease. After approaching the top he just stood there, almost waiting for something.

Then suddenly, tremors could be felt as he stood there with a devilish grin. Then from out of the opening came this dark black mass. As it made its way up to him, it was all around him then like magic. Emerging from this dark black mass stood Shaydon.

"What did you find out?" his voice seemed to rumble through the walls of the valley.

"I followed like you asked both the boy and this dragon," he answered looking up at him.

"Did you find a way we can stop this?" He didn't want this to begin.

"No, my lord, but I have an idea." He looked back at the crystal formation.

"I believe they might be able to help," he said, grinning, "Let's get inside. I want to hear your idea, there's much we need to get ready for."

"As you wish, my lord."

Shaydon disappeared into the dark black mass and entered the cave, Saball followed close behind.

As they disappeared into the cave, only time will show us what they were up to; it seemed Saball had an idea for a method of success. Meanwhile, the dragons had made their way back to the cave.

Landing at the entrance, he looked over at Ravin. "This is really happening?" Knowing this, he still looked amazed.

"It will be OK, young one, you must believe in yourself as I do," she tried to ease him up a bit. "In time, it will all come to you," she said, letting him know to just be patient.

"I know." He could tell she was trying to ease the moment. "I just wish I knew what I am supposed to do when I hear the boy." You could see the frustration in his expressions. "But how am I supposed to know when he needs me?" You could tell he felt helpless.

"You are doing great. I promise you will know when you must do something, I believe this," she grinned. "Remember the Elders believe and support you as I do."

"Then why do they still choose not to see me and only you?"

He made a good point and she knew it, at the same time knew they had their reasons as well.

"It's not that they don't want to see you, they're always watching you and are very pleased with your progress. They just don't want to interrupt your lessons." Being wise with her words, she tried to ease his mind. She headed to the lake and he followed.

"I understand what you're saying. What about this thing you called Saball?"

She knew he wouldn't forget.

Following her to his favorite spot, they both lay down next to one another, and she proceeded to go further into the story about Saball. She let him know the voice was probably warning him; it wouldn't surprise her if it was because he was near trying to find out about this new beginning. She told he must understand that this creature would stop at nothing to please his leader, telling him she knew this from a previous encounter they had before Lanila had lost so much She knew of his power and informed him that he had probably only gotten stronger, it being so many cycles since their last encounter but with this new future, she knew in her heart and told him he was in store for great things and challenges he had never faced before.

"OK but how did this boy know if I was in trouble when I saw nothing?" You could see he was trying to understand.

"That's the connection that the two of you share," she paused before continuing, "it's a bond like no other."

"Like a family bond when someone close to you is in trouble, that's when you know they need you?" He looked at her for confirmation.

"I know it's hard, young one, but give it time; you will find all the answers you are seeking. I promise." She pointed out he had solved this problem all on his own.

She was trying to make him understand, to concentrate on what it was he needed to know, also how important it was that he believed in himself as well.

"Do you think this boy knows of his destiny?" he asked, looking over at her.

"Things are laid out for him and it is up to him to find them." She tried to explain how he knew of his destiny, but the boy was just now learning of his importance to it.

"What do you mean?" You could see he was confused.

"Only the Elders know of that," she continued, "this boy and your strength will have a power even I can't imagine."

"You said my strength so I'm curious what this boy has." He waited for a response.

"I'm curious to find out as well, but only time will answer that for you and me."

Looking at her, he just knew it would be OK. He asked, "Do you know how long I'm going to have to wait?" You could hear a tone of excitement in his voice.

"I'll tell you what," with what had happened, she knew what to do, "the time has come." She sat up and rose to her paws.

"Time for what?" His eyes lit up. "To meet the boy?"

"Not the boy," she smiled, "but what you have been waiting for. I will take you to the peaks with me."

He went silent; he'd waited so long to hear her say that.

"I'm going with you," He paused as if to take a breath, "to the Elders?" You could feel the excitement, knowing how long he had waited for this.

"It is time with all you have told me today and with what you have been feeling, they'll know what to do." Heading back to the opening of their cave, she looked back. "You might want to get some rest, we'll head out in the morning," knowing that was easier said with what he just heard.

"I will. I'm just going to stay out here a moment." You could see he was excited and needed to calm down.

"I understand, see you inside," she said, smiling as she entered the cave.

She disappeared into the cave. HaVon realized that finally the time had come, and his mind was going crazy. He had no idea how it would be, he seemed nervous but at the same time felt he was ready. He would be in store for something that was so important to Lanila; how much it would change his life forever, he thought looking to the sky.

"The time is finally here, I've waited for so long." Taking a deep breath, he looked back into the sky. "I feel the boy and promise to help him as you have done for me, we will learn to help and guide one another." HaVon rose to his paws and turned to head inside.

Then he stopped, as if he had one burst of energy he had to get out; he took to the skies. It being so dark, only the blue of the moon made it possible to see him. After he was done, he landed in front of their entrance. The smile and look on his face said it all – our young dragon was ready, but along with the joys that he would enjoy on the new day, there would be a change that would truly test our young dragon, there will be nothing he could do to change it because he would be too late to help.

We leave the two of them to rest for the new day ahead as we travel to the land of reflections; something in the cave was coming from the distance – it was Saball. The look on his evil face said he was out on a mission to do something again. As he turned back looking into the cave, he said, "I will stop this before it has a chance to start, I promise." Kneeling at the opening, he placed his hand to his chest. "I will do as you have told." He then turned and proceeded up to the top.

It seemed to draw a lot of his power from the ring, for the dark black mass seemed to surround him the more he used it. Was this a way to stop him and possibly the havoc that followed, only time would show any weaknesses and if he could evened be stopped. He made his way looking at this crystal formation. It seemed he agreed it might help by the way he smiled.

"He wants me to stop this new beginning from happening," he spoke to this formation, "he agrees with my idea about the boy being more vulnerable than the dragon. We can stop it before it begins." His evil tone could send chills up anyone's spine. It was obvious he was excited for he was allowed to be chaotic and forceful finally. "I will return when it is done."

They seemed certain they had found a way to stop this; it was to get to the boy first. The only problem was what they thought had not yet begun already had. The way he spoke to this formation would make you think that it was alive. He began to make his way out. It was clear he was up to something. He left at a steady pace and looked to be heading in the way of Rell's house again. With the moon casting its reflection, we could see both of the dragons resting well, then there was Saball coming to a clearing and looking into the sky, letting out a blood curling roar that seemed to almost shake the ground.

"I'm coming, boy," he began to laugh.

If this were true, our young adventurer was in store for more than he might be ready to handle, making his way to the horizon in the direction of the light. In time, Saball would find out that his journey wasn't going to be as easy as he first thought, he too would learn that he and Shaydon were in store for something that they had never faced before. Nor could they have imagined the power they would face, finding out what they were trying to stop was a powerful force, it was true this would be a battle of the ages. The question is, would Rell be able to stay safe long enough for the two to be united; only the Elders and time knew the answer to that question.

Chapter Nine

Rell had no idea of the danger that was headed his way. The suns had barely broken the horizon, the rays started to shine on his home. Rell began to stir in his bed. Stretching out, he noticed his mother was still asleep. Letting her rest, he tried being careful not to wake her. Suddenly, his medallion got his attention as it began to glow. Grabbing a hold of it, he closed his eyes and saw a golden light at first. Then, it became clearer, where he could see and it was the great willow he was looking at. He knew seeing it that there must be a connection. Looking over his mother, he saw she had still not woken up. He thought to himself what she had said about going to the willow, but deep down he knew he had to.

Being careful, he moved to get up, so he would not wake her, and gathered his stuff together. He didn't think she would understand why he needed do this. He made his way down the stairs and headed toward the table. He decided to leave a note for her to let her know he went out for a walk; not saying where, just letting her know he would be safe and return soon. Heading to the door, he stopped and looked toward the stairs.

"Please watch over my mother and keep our house safe from all the dangers," he said and smiled.

Closing the door carefully, he made his way on to the porch. He had no idea what lay ahead. Approaching the first hill, he looked back at his house, unaware that when he would return, so much would have changed. After standing there for a moment, he continued on his way to the willow, but unlike the other times to relax, this would prove to be a good idea. He was about to find out all that was headed in his direction. So much was about to be taken from him, would he be able to handle what would happen to him? But he remembered he was never alone. Picking up his pace, he had almost a spring in his step, he seemed excited due to the vision from earlier. He was getting closer to the willow while Saball was getting closer to his house, unaware the boy was gone having left his mother there alone. Could it be that the medallion knew of the danger that was coming, and got Rell to leave for his safety to the willow?

Rell approached the fourth hill knowing he had only one more to go. Coming to the bottom of the hill, he noticed a bright light coming from the top. He ran, curious about what he was seeing, then stopped as he saw it was the willow glowing. In all his time, he had never seen this before. The glow covered the entire tree. The medallion began to glow as well and he realized there was a connection. He slowly approached the tree, amazed by what he was seeing. He noticed the branches had begun to open up to him. He felt a slight hesitation, not knowing what would happen.

He entered and the branches closed behind him, then it was like something in his head told him to grab the medallion. He began to see a vision; it was the trunk of the tree showing behind it a carving close to the roots. When he opened his eyes, he began to make his way to what he had seen. There it was. Kneeling down, looking closely, he noticed it was similar to the medallion. He thought to himself how all the times he had been here, he never saw this before. He was confused, not knowing what it was he was supposed to do, then the medallion began to glow again. Grabbing a hold of it, he saw a vision of the medallion being placed into the carving. Opening his eyes, he realized that medallion was trying to help him with his question. He had no idea how all of this was happening but knew he needed to do this. As he removed it and placed it into the carving, the tree began to glow brightly. He looked around when suddenly, the trunk of the tree opened up, revealing a book inside. He reached down to grab it, and when he did, the warmth and energy he felt was overwhelming. It made him smile.

Then the tree closed back up as he sat at the base like he always did, looking at what he had just found. He noticed he couldn't just open it up, then he realized that like the willow it had the same marking on it. The cover looked to made out of some kind of gold that resembled scales. He thought it worked on the tree why not this? When he placed the medallion in it, what happened next both confused and amazed him; the willow began to glow again. Opening it, he realized it was a journal. He started to read it, amazed at how it explained things that were happening. Then a tear appeared to roll down his face. He realized his father had written this and it seemed to be left here for him. He felt really confused as he had never heard of this before.

My son, if you're reading this, you have found what we have kept hidden; the time has come for you to understand your destiny to Lanila.

He continued to read about the power of one's mind and the strength of another's, these two are the new beginning that the land had been waiting for. These two powers were to find the each other that have been waiting; with their help, it would help bring Lanila a power it had never seen.

"It's true what Mom was telling me." He leaned back he took a deep breath. "Who are these others it speaks of?" It seemed to confuse him more as he read on.

You're probably thinking this isn't possible and I understand, but believe me when I tell you, it is very real, my son. I know and believe in my heart it will all make sense. In time, it will show you the answers in ways you could only imagine.

Looking at his expression, you could see he was mesmerized with all he was reading. It told him about the medallion's purpose. It would guide him and the powers it had were like no other.

The entire time this was going on, with Rell reading and learning of his destiny, there was an evil that he had not seen yet but felt that was getting ever so close to his home, where his mother was totally unaware and was doing chores around the house. Having seen the letter he had left, she thought nothing of it. She knew this was common for him to do. But she still seemed a little worried with all that was going on, there was still so much she wanted to help him with.

When Saball reached the last hill, he stood there looking around, totally unaware that Rell wasn't even home. He was still at the tree reading the journal and learning more. It seemed not only did the medallion take him to the willow to show him the journal but it took him to a place where he would be safe from this evil that was coming.

"This new beginning that is spreading through the land is going to come to an end before it even has a chance to begin," said Saball in an evil tone that would send chills up your spine as he snickered.

He approached the house, thinking that no one had seen him. Ruthanna was doing like she always did and was around the back of the house. When suddenly out of nowhere, a chill came over her body, giving her an uneasy feeling. She began to look around when she saw something coming. She needed to hide; you could see in her eyes how worried she was. It was big and getting closer. Saball approached, unaware he had already been spotted by Rell's mother. He stepped onto the porch and as he slowly opened the door, he stopped and turned, smelling the air. Something had his attention and it was coming from around the back of the house, but it wasn't the boy's scent he was picking up. She had moved, staying hidden and thinking whatever it was had gone into the house, but it was the opposite. He had picked up her scent. Walking toward the back, he looked carefully and spotted her. He did not want her to know so he walked right by where she was hiding. You could see how quiet she was trying to be, thinking it had worked, watching this creature as he continued past her down the path. He knew what he was doing, and let her think she was safe. He walked into the trees toward the creek, out of sight, and cloaked himself, as he watched her assuming he was gone.

She took off toward the house as fast as she could go. He watched her with a grin thinking she would lead him to the boy. She got to the front door and you could see her shaking as she opened it, how afraid she was running upstairs. Praying for her and Rell's safety as she hid in the closet, staying quiet and shaking when suddenly, she heard the front door opening.

"Son, is that you?" You could hear the crackle in her voice. "Rell?" she called out again and there was no answer. She then realized it was coming up the stairs.

What was about to happen next was something she could have never imagined. As the closet doors were ripped open, there stood Saball, blocking all light with his size. She lets out a terrifying scream.

"Where is the boy?" He grabbed her and threw her to the floor. "I won't ask again." He put his hand through the wall as he leaned over her with his muscular structure, he could see the fear in her eyes and grinned. He seemed to be enjoying this.

When he said that, you could see the relief in her eyes and heart; he had not seen or found her son. Tears of relief began to run down her face.

"What boy?" She struggled to take a breath as he hovered above her. "I live here alone." She had no idea he knew better and was trying to protect her son.

"You lie!" He grabbed her and picked up from the floor by the neck and threw her against the wall with such force.

"He's...safe...from...whatever you...are!" she was struggling to say a single word; he had hurt her and it could be seen by the blood that was coming from her mouth. "You won't...find him. He's smarter than...that." She coughed up more blood and was barely able to lift her head. "You...won't be...able to stop...it from...happening." She was in so much pain yet a smile appeared on her face.

He leaned over her and placed his ring to her head. It seemed to be scanning her memories, looking for an answer to where the boy might be.

"I told you...already," she said as he releases her, "you...won't be able...to stop this...this new...beginning from...ha-happening. We've b-been waiting for too...long," she continued with a bloody smile, "my s-son will stop...you..." She then took her last breath, closing her eyes for the last time.

"Stupid human, you think we can be stopped," he said, looking over her lifeless body, "by a boy!" He began to laugh. "Too bad you won't be around to see him fail."

Then with no respect, he began to trash everything, looking for any sign of where he might find the boy. He knew Shaydon would not be pleased knowing he had survived. Saball's rage was evident as he threw stuff around, even on the lifeless body of Rell's mother. He continued to tear the house from the inside, looking for anything that might lead him to the boy. Rell was completely unaware of what was going on back at the house as he continued to read on into the journal.

The further he got into the journal; the clearer things got. He tried to understand and make sense of all he was reading, being sure he didn't forget anything, as if it was all being sketched into his brain. He was taking it all in knowing the importance it had on his future. It seemed at times he looked to be in a trance as the information was being taken in. He was learning about this dragon that had so much power, about the chaos and destruction that this darkness had brought to Lanila. When he seemed to come out of this trance, looking down he noticed the medallion was pulsating and in a way he had not seen before. He closed his eyes and grabbed a hold of it. when he did, what he saw next brought tears to his eyes. It was his mother and she wasn't moving in his vision. looking around the room, he saw it was all destroyed. He let out a scream of anguish.

He opened his eyes; you could see the pain in them. He knew what he had to do; he needed to get back to the house as fast as he could. The tears began to fall from his face, he didn't know what to think, but he was worried because all the visions he had had turned out to true. He placed the journal back into the tree and it closed back up, hiding the journal. You could see how shook up he seemed by what he had just seen. He wiped the tears from his eyes so he could see better. He would soon learn that unfortunately the vision was true and he would be too late to help her. He did not know of Saball or that he was behind this, but that would soon change as he headed toward the branches and they opened for him. Walking through, he then stopped in his tracks as he looked up, noticing smoke coming from the direction of his house. The look of panic and concern came over him, and he began to run in the direction of his house from where the smoke was coming. By this time, Saball had already caused havoc on the inside of the entire house, setting it on fire that explained the smoke that could be seen. Saball knew if he was close, this would bring the boy to him, so he decided to lay low and wait to see if indeed it would.

"It can't be Mom!" he let out a scream.

Then it was like a light bulb went off; he began to remember what he had been reading. So he grabbed a hold of the medallion, and a golden glow came over his entire body. Suddenly, he took off quicker than the wind blew. So fast that even Saball who was hiding and waiting didn't even see him enter the house. Rell did not let go of the medallion, hoping it would keep him safe from whatever or whoever did this and all that was burning around him. When he approached the top of the stairs, it was still working; he didn't feel any of the heat that was around him. Then he saw what he was afraid of – his mother lying there lifeless. The walls were beginning to burn around her. He worried they would collapse. Rushing over to her, he leaned down and reached out to pick her up when he suddenly heard a voice he had never heard before.

"I have no idea how you got in here, but I hope you said your goodbyes." Saball had felt him inside the house and towered in the doorway, not concerned by the heat as if it didn't bother him at all. "Your time is over before it could even have a chance to begin." His evil voice sent chills down Rell's back.

He made his way toward Rell who was holding his mother tightly in his arms, then the medallion began to pulse again and Saball noticed it as he lunged without hesitation. But as he did, right before his eyes the boy and mother vanished in a bright golden light, leaving him crashing through the burning wall. He let out a roar of frustration. It had transported Rell and his mother back to the willow tree.

Rell opened his eyes, knowing the powers of the medallion had helped him, with his mother still in his arms. He placed her gently on to the ground. He couldn't fight the emotions anymore; he laid his head on her chest and began to cry out loud.

Meanwhile, at the same time all this was going on, HaVon was very restless. At times, he almost looked like he was having a bad dream as he tossed and turned in his sleep.

"I'll come for you, stay there!" HaVon spoke out loud as he woke up. He began looking around and at that exact time, with Rell's head lying on his mother, sobbing, he heard, "I'll come for you, stay there!" Rell raised his head up off his mom. His eyes were so red from crying, he wiped them to see where that voice had come from.

Saball had no idea what had happened to the boy and where he went, as he watched the house burn, looking around for any sign of him. He knew what he saw was the same as Shaydon had referred to; that golden light. He knew now it was there to protect him. He continued to look around to see where he went.

Rell, being safe, was still wondering where the voice he had heard came from, when suddenly, he noticed the tree's branches were coming to life. He watched as they reached down toward his mother. He stood back, watching, wiping the tears, as he kept apologizing for not being there for her. The branches began to glow again as they became golden, they carefully wrapped around his mom, picking her up off the ground. He wasn't sure what was happening, but in his heart, something told him not to worry. He watched as she became completely wrapped up, until nothing but her head was showing then suddenly, he heard a familiar voice,

"Don't be sad, son," she spoke out and opened her eyes but they were golden.

"Mom?" The tears began again. "How is this happening, I saw what that creature had done to you," he said, fighting the tears.

"My sweet son, it is the powers that you will learn more of, they protect all that is good in the land," she spoke.

"Protect how? You're not here anymore!" You could hear the frustration in his voice.

"But, son, you are and that's so important for all of Lanila." A smile came over her face as her golden eyes looked at him. "Right now, things are going to be hard to understand, but please remember your heart and to believe in yourself like I do, and I'm never too far from you." Her hand came out from the branches and touched his heart.

"But, Mom, what do you mean?"

Then before another word could be spoken, her eyes closed and her breath was gone. The trees' branches began to cover her head to a point where nothing could be seen and he watched, as the golden glow became so bright and warm. Rell was still fighting the tears. Having no idea what was happening, when suddenly a golden flash occurred so bright he had to cover his eyes. He removed his hands to see what that bright light was and she was gone. He looked around, wondering what had happened; the tree was still glowing but his mom was gone.

"What did you do with her?" He looked up, talking to the tree.

As if it understood, his medallion began to pulse gently. He grabbed it and closed his eyes. All he could see was gold then he suddenly heard her.

"I'll always be with you, my son, and remember how proud I am of what you're becoming. But the most important thing to never forget is how much I love you."

He opened his eyes realizing what had just happened to her and fell to his knees with his hands over his face.

While Rell was still dealing with all he had lost, on the opposite side, HaVon had no idea what he had just done, so he decided to lay back down seeing he had not woken up Ravin and to try to get some rest for the new day; it would be upon him soon and so much was about to change. He hoped the Elders would shed some light on what was happening and the dreams he was having. Little did he know they would tell him that his time was coming sooner than he realized.

Meanwhile, back at the willow, Rell rose to his feet, wiping his eyes. Taking his mind off what had happened, he decided to get the journal to read. He comes upon a part of the journal that talked about his father's disappearance. He had no idea how this was possible that the journal had this information; he had found out about it himself just recently.

Back at the house, the flames had almost gone out, leaving very little left standing, Saball still watched it slowly burn. He smiled with an evil grin, showing no regards for what he had just done as he looked to the sky.

"You may have been able to save him this time with that golden light," he snarled, "but I have taken something special from him that he will never be able to replace." His evil laugh penetrated the air.

With that said, he turned as if his work was done here, but you could see the rage in his eyes for not getting the boy. He took off, every once in a while knocking trees down randomly, knowing Shaydon would not be happy with his report on what happened. He headed back toward the land of reflections.

Rell was still lost in the journal back at the willow when he stopped reading and looked up into the branches. You could see he was wondering if it was safe to return to the house. He remembered that voice telling him he would come and get him, but who was he? He thought to himself maybe the medallion might be able to help with his question. So he grabbed a hold of it and closed his eyes. Nothing happened. He then remembered what his dad had written in the journal about believing in what you asked.

"Show me my house. Let me know if the danger is gone." He closed his eyes and saw the vision of his house. He noticed there seemed to be hardly anything left and was clear of whatever he had seen that did this to his mom.

Realizing the danger was gone, he stood to his feet. He turned toward the branches and they opened for him. As he walked through, he turned back and said to the tree that he would return. As if it understood, the branches closed behind him. He started making his way to what was left of his home, his eyes still red from all the emotions he had gone through after losing his mom. With each hill passing, he looked to see very little smoke coming from what was left of his house. When he approached the last hill, he could finally see what was left. The look on his face as he thought what would he do now, everything was gone and he had no one. For the very first time, he was alone. Approaching the bottom of the hill, he couldn't believe it was all gone, everything his father had built. Only parts of the fireplace still stood. Everything around it was still smoldering as he walked toward what used to be the porch. He fell to his knees, the emotions taking over. It was all gone, everything that he had loved and enjoyed.

"I have no idea what kind of creature you are," he spoke out, "but I will not stop till I find you and I promise you this for my mother." He wiped a tear. "I will have my day when we meet again." His tone changed and you could hear the anger in his voice.

This was such a dramatic change for him to have to go through, and he was left to face it alone, but even after such a loss he stood to his feet. Wiping the tears away, he began to look around for any memories that might have survived. He began putting out what small flames that still burned, when suddenly he saw something that got his attention. Kneeling down, he found something special and dear to him; it was his mother's necklace. He cleaned it off, amazed how it had survived the fire. Looking at it closely, a tear formed, reminding him of how she was taken. For anyone to have to go through such a horrific tragedy before taking their last breath, it was unimaginable. He had lost so much yet the anger could be seen in his eyes, so he began to gather larger rocks from around the area, making a memorial for her. In the middle of it, he placed the necklace as a center piece and stayed kneeled to the ground.

"I already miss you so much, Mom," he cried, looking at her necklace, "may the Elders watch over you. Not one day will pass when you will not missed," he wiped the tears, "like you have taught me that I will never forget you will always be here." He choked up, placing his hand over his heart. "Whatever did this to you and our home, I promise I'll find it."

Raising to his feet, he wiped the tears from his face. A lot of time had passed, as he noticed the blue moon was rising higher and the night was coming. Having no house left to lay his head and recover from the tragedies of the day, he knew there was only place for him to go where he would be safe – back at the willow. When he approached the top of the hill, he stopped and looked back one last time. He remembered how it used to be and a smile began to appear on his face.

"I love you both and you will be forever close to my heart," he said looking to the sky one last time, then turned and headed in the direction of the willow.

Saball had made his way back to the valley of reflections. He approached the valley with the cave when he noticed the crystal formation; it was no longer clear as a mass of nothing but black had covered it. Still bothered by the fact he wasn't able to get the boy, he climbed to the top with such ease and just stood in front of the formation. Suddenly, this black mass began to come off the crystal formation in front of him. As Shaydon appeared from it, Saball kneeled before him looking to the ground.

"I wasn't able to get the boy, but I took the mother from him hoping he might come back." He hesitated, not knowing the reaction he would get.

"Did he?" his voice rumbled the walls, showing his aggravation.

"He did, my lord, I had him right there in front of me," a slight pause, "then he was overcome with that golden light. When I reacted and lunged, they were both gone, so I burned the house and returned." He kept looking down.

Then the frustration showed as he picked Saball, who was quite large, off the ground with ease, and raised him to eye level.

"This has to stop!" he growled. "Whatever is protecting him, its powers seem to being getting stronger." He threw Saball to the ground. "This golden light and flash, it has the Elders and Dawla all over it." He let out a roar that echoed off the valley wall.

"What do we do?" Saball asked as he picked himself up off the ground. This was nothing new to him when Shaydon got angry.

"We'll show them there is no stopping us." Shaydon looked at the crystal formation. "The more they try, the more pain and damage we will bring to them all," he snickered evilly, "unlike anything they have ever seen."

Meanwhile, Rell had reached the hill where the willow stood. His mind and heart had gone through so much. Looking up at the massive tree, he realized this was all he had left. He approached it and like before, the branches opened to him to let him enter. Then the willow became luminated in a golden glow, he could feel the warmth and a smile appeared on his face.

"If you do understand me, thank you," he said as he approached the trunk to sit against it.

"Why is this happening to me? I'm losing everything I care about." You could hear how tired and drained he was from all that he had been through.

His eyes began to get heavy and you could see him fighting back, but it wasn't working. He grabbed a hold of the medallion and began to slowly fall asleep. His mind and body were drained from all the emotions, needing the rest, and finally, he had some security from the willow and the golden glow that surrounded him. It seemed to let him know that he wasn't alone. When he would wake from his sleep, he would realize that he was truly far from being alone. He would see someone that had been waiting for him. Finally the time for the two of them to meet was here. This new beginning that Lanila had been waiting for was finally here – it was time they met and for their journey to start.

Chapter Ten

In the land of reflections, for the first time there seemed to be nothing going on; the mass that surrounded the formation was not there and Saball was nowhere to be seen. But the same could not be said for the land that HaVon called home. The suns are rose as Ravin was waking up to an empty cave. She stretched and looked around. She closed her eyes and seemed to go into a trance, then opened them, smiling, and made her way to the opening of the cave. There in the distance she found him as he sat by the lake. She approached him and noticed he was staring off into the sky.

"What is it, young one?" she asked as she sat down next to him.

"I feel as if something terrible has happened." She could hear clearly how upset and sad he seemed.

"What do you mean?" she began to look around.

"No, Ravin, not here." He saw she had her guard up. "I think something terrible has happened to the boy." She could see the concern in his eyes.

"The boy?" he had her full attention.

"I believe so," he paused, "it's this feeling I'm having a problem with."

"I'm listening, just take a breath," she said, trying to calm him down.

"It's this feeling in my heart, like he's lost something very close to him." You could hear how confused he was.

"You're fine, my young one. That's what is so special about the two of you, the bond you share." She knew she could help. "The Elders will have the answers you seek, I promise." She believed they could help him.

Like a snap of the fingers, the sadness did seem to be lifted for the moment. Hearing her speak of them reminded him it would only be a short time before he would be standing before them. All these questions that had been troubling him would hopefully be answered. At the same time, he would find about so much more – this was the day he had been waiting for. Without another word spoken, he turned to her with a grin and took to the air. Now it might seem as if his mind had forgotten what he was feeling. But just the opposite; he felt this pain in his heart, needing help to understand it, and the answer was the Elders. The higher he climbed into the air, she realized finally the time was upon them, and she took to the air behind him. The two dragons looked truly magnificent as they flew, with each stroke of their wings getting closer to the peaks that penetrated the clouds.

It was so beautiful the way the suns shone off of them both as they flew through the clouds. At times when the light hit him, his scales nearly made him invisible. Then there in the distance, the tall peaks came into sight. It seemed to be more than what he expected as he looked over to Ravin,

"I always figured it would look different being so close, yet it has a menacing look to it." He was referring to how dark it seemed around.

All she could do was smile at him and took the lead, understanding what he could see, but she knew of the incredible beauty ahead and he was about to discover for the first time. As they passed over some of the dark ravines, he could finally see what looked to be the base of the peaks in the distance. She landed and he did the same. He stared at the walls that lead to the peaks that penetrated the clouds.

"Do they end?" he asked, looking at how high they went. He was a large dragon for his age, but standing there, he didn't seem so big.

"These help protect the peaks, young one, we must pass through the ravine to get to them and then we can fly." Taking to the air, she entered the ravine.

"That makes sense," he said, talking to himself as he followed her.

The further they went, he began to notice truly how tall the walls were. You could see how amazed he was, barely making it through some of the openings. He yelled out to Ravin, "Glad I didn't eat before we left." He continued to follow close.

"Don't be worried by the walls, you're doing great," she said, flying close to him at times with a smile.

As they flew, you could see how much he admired her, like a snake on the ground going from side to side having no problems with the walls. He had always been amazed by her abilities, but these ravines seemed to go on forever in his mind. Noticing the further they went, the darker it seemed to get. He was thinking to himself when a chill came over his body as something got his attention in the distance.

"Ravin, do you see that, what is it?" he asked, speaking of the light that he saw ahead.

She turned and smiled then took off with such a great speed, knowing how much he would enjoy the challenge as he followed. Catching up, he began to notice that the light was getting brighter, as if the suns were suddenly turned on. At the same time, he was overcome with a warm feeling it seemed to have. Then his eyes widened; he was amazed at what was in front of him.

"We're here, young one." They had broken through the darkness and were surrounded by a golden light.

He couldn't believe it, he was finally here and what he saw, he could have never imagined it to be so beautiful and mesmerizing at the same time. He had thought of it in so many ways different ways, but nothing like he was seeing, you could tell by his expression. It looked as if everything around them was so alive. Taking a moment, he just stood there, admiring all that was before him, not saying a word.

"I've imagined this place in a lot of ways, Ravin, but being here now I'm just so amazed by all that I'm seeing and feeling." He smiled looking over at her.

"This is what the lands were like before they were split and divided." She explained what he felt was the power of the Elders.

"This is so great." He stood erect looking over at her. "I promise to help Lanila return to this again."

"I know that, young one, but you will make it better than this in time," she said, knowing what was about to begin, she knew how much greater it would be.

They continued toward the peaks. Getting closer, he noticed the one in the middle was larger. They came to a stop as she pointed a path out to him, it seemed to go up through the peak itself.

"Is that where we go up?" he asked, referring to what he saw.

"Even though we can fly, you must respect the Elders and journey your way to the top through that way," she said as she looked over at him.

"If that is what they ask of me," he smiled.

He wasn't bothered by the climb he had before him, he had waited too long for this moment and would do whatever it took. He made his way to the start and began to walk up it, when he suddenly stopped as she approached next to him.

"It's only a matter of time before some light will be shed on all the answers that you seek." She smiled and walked on.

"I know," he hesitated. "I'm just nervous. I didn't think I would be." Being his first time seeing them, he did not want to disappoint them.

"You need not be so worried, everything is going to be OK," she smiled seeing how worried he seemed. "Remember they know of you and have watched over you." She always knew what to say. He smiled.

She led the way up, looking back every so often, noticing how he seemed amazed by the size of the path. Even as he walked on it, there still was so much room and the view as well, it was so beautiful how high these peaks were going into the clouds.

"Did you imagine the peaks to be this big?" She looked back at him.

"I would have never thought they would be this large," he answered as he looked around. "They make me feel so small," he said, smiling at her.

She was so happy to see him enjoying all that was around, knowing how much he appreciated it as well. Continuing up the peak, he followed close. He kept looking over the area the higher they climbed, admiring the color and beauty he saw in everything. Each step they took to the top the closer they were to this new beginning.

Meanwhile, in the land of reflections, a movement was occurring again. There seemed to be something coming from the cave. As it got closer to the opening, it appeared to be Saball. He stopped and waited. Then in the distance, a large body seemed to be following him. It was Shaydon. He approached his side and looked down at him – they were up to something again.

"I will not fail with this, I promise," he said as he clutched his fist to his chest. "The boy may have gotten away, but his mother didn't." An evil grin appeared on his face. "Today, I will take something important from the dragon," he paused. "It's been such a long time since we've seen one another." He looked to the ring. "We'll see if it can start without their hearts." His laughter filled the air.

He spoke as if whoever this was, they had met before, but who was he speaking of. As he jumped to the ground and Shaydon jumped with him, the ground trembled.

"Don't fail me again, the time is upon us and they will have no idea what is coming," said Shaydon, looking up at the crystal formation again with a grin.

"I will not." Saball knew it was important to try and stay ahead of this new beginning.

With that said, he had his orders and began to make his way out of the valley. But where was he going as he spoke of meeting again? It was someone that knew of him and he had met as well. It was certain he felt confident he wouldn't fail doing as planned, but what was it? He left in an entirely new direction.

Meanwhile, HaVon and Ravin were halfway up over the peak. He noticed the higher they climbed, the thicker the clouds seemed to be getting, making it harder to see.

"Are you OK, Ravin? I can barely see anything, it's crazy how thick these clouds have become." You could hear the amazement in his voice.

"I am, young one, it's not much further," she said, knowing if he could hear her, he would be fine.

She knew in a matter of moments they would be at the top and then he would be truly amazed by all that he would see. It was at that moment he began to notice the clouds seemed to be getting lighter. Suddenly, he saw a bright light was coming from just ahead. Seeing the eagerness in his eyes, this was what he had been training and waiting for. He noticed they started to clear the higher they walked up the peak. Looking to the side, he noticed they were above the clouds and the ground seemed so far away. Then like a snap of the fingers, the clouds seemed to vanish. They had come to the end as it opened up. Looking down, he noticed they were standing on top of them, it was like an entirely new world up here. He saw everything had a golden light to it along with a feel of warmth, he noticed a path that led off in the distance. On each side of it were large pillars that looked to be made of marble. They seemed to follow the path all the way down both sides.

"How's it we're on top of the clouds?" You could tell he was having trouble understanding.

"The power of the Elders, young one, they call it a world on a world," she said as she grinned.

"This is unbelievable! it seems to have so much life. I see in the distance this path leads to some large structures." He was very observant of all his surroundings.

"Come on, young one, it's time," she said and took to the air.

"I thought we didn't fly," he was confused, taking off behind her.

He admired the clouds as he flew above them. This was nothing like he had seen before or could have imagined. The way the gold lined with the clouds it was beautiful, the pillars were so large and did look to be solid marble with hints of gold as well. He saw how they all continued ahead and seemed to make a circle. As they got closer, she approached the base of the pillars landing in between them. He did as well, amazed by the size of everything around and how it made him feel so small. As they walked to the end of the pillars, it opened up to a large circle, spread throughout as well were large golden statues of dragons. In the middle of these was a large pool that seemed to be made of what looked like golden water.

"Who are they?" he started toward the large statues.

"They are the Elders, my young one." She too looked up at them admiring each one. "This is what you have been training for and I am so proud of this moment," she said, smiling at him.

He began to look at them closely, fascinated by all the details he was seeing in each one. He noticed there were five dragons; the large one in the middle with two on each side that seemed a bit smaller. Out of the corner of his eye, he noticed Ravin approached the larger one, bowing before it. Knowing how important this was, he followed suit. A grin appeared on her face seeing what he was doing, following her lead. He was a large dragon but seeing him before these statues and kneeling was a different story. With them both kneeling, he suddenly began to notice the golden light was beginning to pulsate and get brighter. Saying nothing, he just watched as the statues began to pulse as well.

Then suddenly, he heard Ravin as if she was speaking to them, "I'm afraid it has begun," she spoke out loud. "We believe the boy might be in danger."

"Who are you talking to?" HaVon lowered his head to whisper to her and what happened next answered that question.

"My son, how we have waited for this moment to come, watching you grow, knowing you are part of what this land has been waiting for," the voice seemed to be coming from all around him. He was mesmerized as he listened.

"Ravin, what do I do?" he didn't exactly know what to say.

"Relax, it's OK," she smiled at him.

Letting him know everything was going to be fine and he was about to learn so much more about these statues. A moment was about to occur that the young dragon would remember forever. It was just as he asked, right before his eyes the magic would be shown, for this large golden statue began to move and come to life. She smiled as she saw the look of disbelief on his face.

"We see Ravin has done a great job guiding and keeping you protected, as we too have been watching over you," it spoke. "Please rise, young one, there's no need to kneel any longer."

As they both rose, the smile on her face showed how excited she was for him, and the dumbfounded look on his face, by what he was seeing remained.

"There is so much you will learn, young one, but it will take time. So be patient, we will help you along the way as much as we can, for all of Lanila has been waiting many cycles for this day to come."

HaVon was eager to hear more.

"How much I too have waited to be called before you," he said as he looked up to him.

"You said something about the boy?" he asked, looking over at Ravin.

"Well, I brought it to her attention, it was these dreams I've been having," HaVon answered, looking down. They could tell it still had him troubled.

"It's the bond that the two of you share," the statue directed his attention back to him.

"What do you mean? I had a pain that I have never felt before, he seemed sad and scared at the same time." The statue could see he seemed troubled and worried.

"It has to be Shaydon and Saball." He looked to the other statues, as they too began to move. "It is time we must get to the boy before they do and something happens to him."

HaVon's eyes were amazed by what he was seeing as all the statues came to life, surrounding this pool of gold.

One of them spoke out to the larger one, "It's time, Cliffon, for the two to meet."

"Cliffon?" HaVon looked at the larger one. "That's your name?"

"Yes, young one, it is," he answered looking down at him. "I think you may be right," he said, turning to the smaller ones.

"I'm sorry, hold on, please help me understand." HaVon was trying to put this all together. "You all are the Elders?"

"Yes, we are, my name is Cliffon, the father of all dragons. To the left of me stand the dragons of earth and seas," then turning to the right, "these are the dragons of the skies and of Middle Lanila."

"Middle Lanila?" He looked over at Ravin who was smiling, he could tell she was enjoying every minute of this.

"I promise, in time," Cliffon said, trying to ease his mind, knowing that it was easier said than done. "Right now, we need to concentrate on what you said about the boy." HaVon could hear the importance of what he was saying. "It is time for you to meet."

His excitement was evident, finally the day he had waited so long for was finally here and he couldn't wait to get started. All the statues had come to life and were looking at him. Suddenly, he remembered all the terrible stories that Ravin shared with him, he had always felt frustrated that he wasn't around to help them fight this evil.

"I see the frustration in your expressions, young one," Cliffon said, looking at him, "remember what she has taught you, that's why this is so important for you to know, you're not alone. We are behind you and the boy as well, it's time to change Lanila forever."

Knowing he had so many questions that he wanted to ask them, at the same time he knew time would fill the voids in. The boy's safety was more important to them all at this time, you could see the eagerness knowing he was going to finally meet him. He was hanging on to every word that Cliffon spoke, who went on telling him the reason he called him son. Explaining he was the beginning to all of the dragons that were taken and how they all led to him, explaining to him like he had heard from Ravin about her raising him from an egg, that she had received from Cliffon and that brought them to this very moment in time.

"Lanila has been waiting so long for you and the boy to come together, giving them," suddenly all the dragons finished his sentence by speaking all at once, "hope."

"Whatever it is you ask of me, I'm more than willing to do knowing how important it is to Lanila." HaVon got Ravin's attention with what he said.

"To hear you speak like this makes us all very proud and the willingness to get the boy." They all could feel the warmth that he seemed to have for the boy having not even met him yet. "We understand you've been hearing and feeling the boy?" as they waited for his response, but they all already knew.

"I believe I have been by what Ravin has been explaining to me," he paused to take a breath, "but this last time wasn't like the ones before. I felt a horrible pain and loss for him." He looked up this was what he was hoping they would be able to help him with.

"We can see how bothered this has you, we too have felt the boy might be in danger." They look over at Ravin. "We think it's Saball?"

"That's the Saball you spoke of?" HaVon's attention turned to her.

"He is the evil behind the havoc that destroyed all that we had. His leader's name is Shaydon." She went on to explain the prior encounter they had with each other, she had escaped the fight and fled as they told her to.

"So this Saball and Shaydon were here when all this happened before, why have they started causing damage again?" He looks at the Elders and her. "Why would they go after the boy?"

"That's what we're all wondering," They all looked at one another, then almost at the same time, said, "They must know how important he is, that's why we have felt trouble from him. We believe they're trying to get to him and stop this new beginning." You could hear the seriousness of this in the tone of their voices. "For some reason, we're having trouble keeping an eye on his location, and we're sure that's because of Shaydon's power, especially if he knows that we're so close to it starting."

He went on to explain all they knew and agreed that it was time for HaVon to go and get the boy. They told him of this great willow on the opposite side that covered a hilltop, how it was put there for protection for the boy. There was a look of confusion on his face about this tree. They also told him a little about Dawla and explained how she was the Lady of Lanila, telling him in time he would learn all he would need of this Dawla and her purpose, but now the importance was to fly toward the sun and never let it set, knowing he would see the willow if he did and they were sure the boy would be found there.

"This is what you've been training and waiting for, young one." They could see a look in his eyes. "You need not worry, just trust your heart and bring him back to us."

Then one of the Elders spoke out, "Make sure he brings the journal as well."

"Journal?" he asked, making sure he had heard them correctly.

"Yes, this is what has been given to him, to try and help teach him of this new way." They could see how they had his full attention. "It was put together for this very moment," he said, as he nodded to what they said.

"I will do as you ask and return with the boy." He paused a moment. "Do we know his name?" That was one thing they hadn't mentioned.

"That we don't know, but we believe he will know in his heart you mean no harm."

Then they all said at once, "Trust us." Hearing that, you could see the confidence building inside him.

"I hear your confidence in me, from that alone I know I'll be OK." He bowed before them all. "We will return soon."

"Young one, you have developed into more than we could have imagined, you truly are a magnificent dragon." Even Cliffon was amazed by the presence that he brought.

He went further into the specifics of exactly where he would find the boy, explaining before the willow he would come upon five boulders and explained the house that was set at the bottom of them. It was after that there would be some hills and at the top of the last one, he would find the willow, letting him know if the boy was not at the house then more than likely he would find him there.

"This boy you speak of, he won't be afraid to see me?" he asked, referring to the fact that he was a dragon.

"He will feel you before you even see him. Remember, we've asked you to trust us." Cliffon grinned slightly, easing his mind. "Be safe with a strong and quick return."

"I will." You could see the confidence and excitement, but at the same time, he knew how important this was as he bowed before them all.

He stood tall and erect, knowing what he had to do. He turns to Ravin and thanked her for all she had done for him.

"I know, HaVon, and I thank you for being there for me as well, but it's your time now. You must go and bring the boy back to us, where he'll be safe from both Saball and Shaydon." She smiled, very proud of this moment, knowing that this was the new beginning for them all.

"Ravin, you be careful while I'm gone." He cared a great deal for her. "I will return as soon as possible," he said, smiling.

"I will patiently wait for your return. I must return to the lair and soon as I'm done, I'll be back." She tried reassuring him that she would be fine.

"Why don't you wait till I return and I will go with you?" With all that was happening, he just wanted her to be careful.

"Young one, I'll be fine," she grinned loving the way he cared, "remember who taught you what you know."

"I know but like the one that has always told me, even the great ones must always be ready and careful for the unexpected."

Hearing him say that, she knew he had listened well.

"I'm so very proud of you," responding to what he had said. "You must go and help the boy; I promise to be here when you return."

He turned and instead of walking all the way back down the peak, they pointed out an opening that he could see between the pillars. He knew the suns were in the direction he was told to go as he looked back at Ravin and the Elders. Wasting no more time, he took to the air with such power and force, his wings with each stroke seemed to blanket the sky the higher he got. He looked back and noticed the peaks shrinking in size the further away he got. This entire time while they were at the Elders and preparing for the boy, Saball had made his way to the ravines that stood before the great peaks. He seemed to be hiding, knowing he couldn't get any closer than he was, not with the magic and power of the Elders, they would know of his presence and he wasn't that stupid.

"You may have gotten away from me before, but this time, you won't have a chance." He began to snicker, saying this in an evil tone as he waited.

It was clear now, seeing his direction and hearing him. With HaVon not around to help, what would become of Ravin, as Saball was hiding and waiting for her. How would she have a chance against him now; he was filled with so much rage and anger and all he wanted to do was destroy anything and everything that stood in their way. As she descended down the peaks, totally unaware of who was waiting for her, you could see her thinking to herself of how proud she was of HaVon. He was on his way and she knew when he returned, he would have gained a new ally, but little did he know of what was waiting for Ravin and what would happen to her causing so much pain.

Chapter Eleven

Now that HaVon was on his way to finally meet Rell and return to the Elders, Saball was on a mission of his own. He wanted to bring pain to all that were rising against them, it was certain so much was about to change on this new day. Rell was at the willow and he was still out, resting his mind, even though the suns had begun to rise into the sky, bringing a new day. The tree still had the golden glow to it as he slept, you could feel the warmth and security it gave him, knowing he was safe here. As our adventurer still slept with all that he has gone through, it was nothing in comparison to what he would wake up and see for the first time. As he remained in a deep sleep, the land HaVon came from had grown a bit darker. Ravin had finally made her way down the peaks and was about to enter the ravine. She was totally unaware of the danger that was waiting for her. This day was about to bring more changes than anyone could have imagined or wanted.

HaVon had been flying, following the sun as the Elders had instructed, then in the distance he saw some large boulders and wondered if they were the ones the Elders spoke of. If they were, it wouldn't be much further before the willow was in sight, so he began to speed up as the boulders became clearer the closer he got. He knew that just beyond that was a house, he approached the boulders and saw what looked to be a house still smoldering. He brought himself in to land next to it, becoming worried, looking around and hoping to see any sign of life. He began to realize what he was feeling before with the boy had to be this, seeing that there was nothing, but a little bit of the fireplace left, of what seemed to be at one time a beautiful home.

He continued to look around when he saw a make-shift memorial that got his attention, it was at that very moment he knew the boy was OK and had to be the one that did this. He focused in on the necklace that hung in the middle, he then realized the boy had lost more than just the house. HaVon bowed his head in respect. When he raised his head, out of the corner of his eye he noticed some tracks in the distance. These were like nothing he had seen before as he noticed the size of them. They were large. Suddenly, he realized it must be those of the creature they called Saball. The Elders were right about him being after the boy and his priorities went back to finding him, he had to make sure he was safe as he scanned the area. Then without hesitation, he took to the air with even more power and force. He started to worry and knew he had to get to this willow they had spoken of. So he flew straight up into the air and began to hover above the house, looking over the area. The way the suns hit his scales was mesmerizing, the color of him was truly magnificent.

Suddenly in the distance, a golden light got his attention. He knew in his heart this must be what they were speaking of. He headed toward it with good speed, worried of the boy's safety.

At the same time this was going on, Ravin was making her way through the ravine. She wanted to hurry and be sure to have enough time to return to the peaks, she spread her wings and took to the air. Beginning her way back to the lair, she was totally unaware that Saball had moved into place. He stayed hidden, waiting patiently to see her. The question is why and what was he planning for her, it was like he knew there would be no one there to help. The further she flew into the ravine, the darker it became, the walls seemed to be so close at times as if they could reach out and grab her. It was at that very moment when she avoided the walls to look back, he lunged out of the shadows with such a force, and hit her in the side, causing her to crash into the wall. The impact it caused forced her to tumble to the ground, even some of the walls themselves fell down around her. She lay there having trouble moving.

She tried to raise up with the debris all around. You could see the pain in her eyes as she fell back to the ground, letting out a small moan. She tried to focus in on what just happened. She gasped for each breath as her pain increased with each movement. Then an evil laugh began to fill the air. She then understood what had happened.

"I should have known by the stench that filled the air," she spoke through gritted teeth.

As he approached her, you could see his true size; she wasn't much bigger than he was. He walked up next to her and knelt at her side with that evil smile of his.

"You're too late, Saball," a smile came over her pain-stricken face.

"Why would you say that?" he asked, placing his muscular and large paws to her neck. "I think I'm right on time."

"Do as you wish!" she gasped. "But soon the boy and HaVon will be together," she then smiles. "Tell Shaydon he has failed to stop it from beginning."

He held her life in his hands and by the look on his face, you could see he was enjoying every bit of it, as he moved his head from side to side and then leaned in close to her.

"What makes you think this time is different?" he grinned, shaking his head and squeezing her neck tighter. "This is our land now, you're never getting it back and there is nothing that can stop us," he chuckled, "especially a boy and this dragon."

You could see the satisfaction in his eyes with what he was doing as he released her and rose to his feet. She grasped for breath as she watched him. What he did next even had her attention as she saw him hold the ring into the air, when suddenly, above them a dark mass appeared. As it began to rotate, it was if this mass was giving him even more power.

"Saball! It doesn't matter what you do to me." You could see she was in pain.

"You might think that," an evil grin appeared on his face, "but we disagree."

Then holding his ring into the air, a force of black energy shot from this dark mass, then he held it against her. She let out a roar. It was clear whatever he was doing was causing a great deal of pain to her. This ring let out some sort of power, and she started to decompose as if she had no life. You could see the pain in her eyes as she struggled and Saball was enjoying every bit of it, seeing there was nothing she could do to fight back.

She lifted her head up at him. "You may have got me," her body disappeared slowly with every word, "but he will avenge me." A last smile appeared on her face and she laughed. "You're too late!" She lay her head back down.

"You won't know what happens!" You could see how mad he became at her, reminding him of the boy's mother and her last words. At last, she became completely consumed with this dark mass and was gone.

It was clear now that like Rell's mother, they wanted to hurt someone close to HaVon this time. Saball had done as he was told. The look of satisfaction appeared on his face as he looked above at the mass.

"I will return, my lord." Then the mass above him began to disappear. "From both of them I have taken something very special and meaningful to their weak hearts." He laughed out loud. "I won't stop until it's their turn." You could see how confident he was.

He turned toward the land of reflections; his work here was done. How would they handle this once the word got out of this terrible tragedy? He took off with such speed and it was clear they had thought the way to stop this new beginning was to try and weaken them by taking something close to their hearts, but in time, they would find out it would do so much more than that.

Meanwhile, HaVon had approached the golden glow he had seen in the distance. When he got closer, he realized it was the willow that the Elders had spoken of. He had no idea how big this tree was going to be as it covered the entire hill. He was amazed and at the same time remembered he didn't want to scare the boy. He was sure this would be a lot for anyone to handle, especially a boy, but Rell had been reading the journal that was left for him and when he wasn't, it was always feeding information into his mind. HaVon landed close to the tree. Looking at it, he understood why the boy felt safe here. He could even feel it in a way, looking around for any sight of him, but was unable to see through the branches and the golden light.

While he was outside trying to see through the branches, Rell was still sleeping having no idea what was going on. Then the medallion woke him up as it began to pulsate and vibrate. This was unlike anything it had never done before. Slowly, he sat up and just looked, then he closed his eyes, and holding the medallion, he saw a golden glow as it slowly disappeared. Amazed, he was looking at the outside of the willow and what he saw confused him. He let go of the medallion and stood up. He began to look around and thought to himself, *What a strange vision.* Then he felt a small tremor as HaVon was walking around the outside of tree, trying to see in; that's when he knew he wasn't alone. Not sure if what he saw was real, he tried being extra quiet. He began to think to himself about the vision he had just seen, the warmth that came with what he was seeing when suddenly he heard a deep voice.

"Please don't be alarmed, I told you I would come for you."

Hearing that voice sent goosebumps down Rell's spine. He remembered the voice that he had heard earlier and realized it was the same. So, very carefully, he approached the edge of the tree's branches as they slowly opened up. You could see how nervous he was, not knowing what would happen next. He walked through being very cautious and holding onto the medallion, he knew it would protect him. When he came through the branches, he released the medallion. His eyes and mouth fell wide open at amazement over what he was seeing standing before him. His eyes opened as wide as anyone's could, he simply gazed at the most majestic black dragon he could have ever imagined in all his dreams. He just stood there looking up at him as HaVon slowly approached him. He wasn't worried, but then, he fell to his knees as a tear appeared in his eye. This was really happening; all that he had been told by his mother, all the bedtime stories and what he had been reading in the journal, it was all true. HaVon then kneeled in front of him, seeing the tear, He wanted him to know he was not in danger and safe.

"My name is HaVon, young one, I'm not here to harm you," he said as he lowered his head. "Are you OK?" he asked showing concern for him, feeling he had been through so much.

"I'm fine," Rell replied, without thinking as he wiped the tears from his eyes, when he suddenly realized he had just heard the dragon speak. "I can hear you! You're a dragon and you just spoke to me." He was astonished.

"Yes, I am, and yes, I did," HaVon said as he chuckled under his breath and smiled, seeing the boy was not alarmed.

"Amazing!" Rell just stood there staring at up at him. "Hello, HaVon, my name is Rell and I'm sorry, this is so hard to believe that this is happening." He was clearly excited about what he was seeing.

"Now I know your name, Rell." He could see the boy wasn't scared at all. "We were worried after the dream I had, and especially after what I saw at the house, that you might have been harmed." It was then that he realized by his reaction Rell had lost something very special.

"No, I'm fine, but my heart isn't," Rell replied as he bowed his head.

"Forgive me, Rell, for asking, but that was your home that was burned down, wasn't it?" He could tell the Rell was clearly still upset.

"It's OK." Rell took a breath and collected himself. "It used to be my home until some creature came and destroyed it. This thing also took my mother's life from me." He then looked up at HaVon.

"Rell, I'm so sorry for your loss," HaVon said as he lowered his head to him, "I know this is hard for you, but did you see what it was?" He hoped Rell could shed some light on what happened.

"It was big," he paused, then continued, "it was like a cross between a man and what looked like a dragon, it had these dead black eyes and so much hate and anger toward me."

"It sounds like this creature is who the Elders call Saball," as he said this, HaVon shook his head. "I haven't seen this creature myself, but have been told of how dangerous it is." HaVon wanted to share as much information as he could.

"I saw him briefly when I went to help my mother." Rell explained to him what he tried to do.

"But what I've heard if this creature, how did you get away if he saw you?" You could hear the concern in HaVon's voice.

"I think this helped me," Rell said and held the medallion up for him to see. "I was holding my mom in my arms then it lunged at me." He stopped to take a breath. "Then somehow, it transferred me and my mom back here at the willow. She had always told me this place would keep me safe." A small smile appeared on his face.

"That is amazing; looking at it and by what you have just told me, it also seems pretty powerful too." You could hear how glad he was that it protected him and to see him safe.

HaVon went on to try and explain as much as he could to him, letting him know that where he came from in Lanila, they knew of him. He told him of the willow and how it also acted as a place where they hoped to find him, knowing when the time was right and by all they were encountering, it would seem to be now. As soon as he said that, the biggest grin appeared on Rell's face; you could see the relief on his face.

"So you're like my teacher, HaVon?" Having heard what he said, it just felt right in his heart.

"I thank you for saying that." He too felt the warmth in his heart. "I will help you in any way I can, but something is telling me this is something that we will learn together." He could feel the connection with Rell that the Elders had spoken of.

He went on to try and explain what this Saball was trying to do, letting Rell know he had heard that there was another that was behind it. He explained that it gave him even more power and strength, but there was still so much that he didn't know as well.

"This darkness that you're speaking of, I've heard and read about, it took them all from us and caused the splitting of Lanila."

HaVon was surprised Rell had some knowledge of what was occurring.

"Its name from what I've been told is Shaydon, but you're right about what he has done." HaVon smiled. "You've been taught well about that past of Lanila." You could see HaVon was pleased he was hearing that.

HaVon wasn't sure at first how the boy would react when he saw him, but now after seeing and listening to him, Rell carried himself well. Also knowing he had been through so much, yet the way they asked each other questions, you could see a bond forming which led them to this very moment. They two went on for a while, like two friends that hadn't seen one another in a long time and had just been reunited. This was going to be a special bond, stronger than the Elders may have first thought.

"This is so hard to believe at times," Rell was referring to all the changes that had happened to him.

"It truly has, I see why they feel you're such a special boy," HaVon tried to show compassion for him; it was clear that these two were meant for this destiny together.

They continued talking to one another, showing interest in all they discussed, then HaVon stood up and looked down at him.

"I'm not trying to cut you off, but we might want to think about heading out of here." He knew he needed to return with the boy. "I know the Elders are just as anxious to meet you as I was, they mentioned that you needed to bring a journal."

"It's inside, HaVon, like me go get it." You could see he was excited by the smile. He turned toward the willow's branches as they opened for him and he entered. "You were right, Mom," he said as he looked up while retrieving the journal.

HaVon waited outside amazed by what he was seeing as the tree's branches opened for him, confirming indeed how amazing and important this boy was to Lanila. HaVon kept his eyes on the surroundings, being sure he didn't see anything that might be a danger. Rell made his way back out of the tree and he was carrying this journal to his side.

"Did you get everything you'll need?" He knew from this time on, everything would be new to them both.

"Well, I got the journal," Rell answered as he showed him.

"It must be important if the Elders have asked you to bring it." He smiled; you could see how happy he was.

"My father wrote this and left it here for me."

Hearing that, HaVon understood the importance of it.

"I do have one question, though; how do we get there? Magic?" Rell asked.

"No," HaVon smiled, amused by what he had said. "We're going to fly there."

"You said fly?" You could hear a slight tremor in his voice, it seemed he didn't care much for heights.

"Don't worry Rell, I promise everything will be fine." HaVon could see how uneasy he seemed. "I promise you from this time forward, I'll never allow you ever to be harmed in any way, not as long as I'm around." He placed his hand to his heart.

Hearing that, Rell looked up at him; he knew in his heart he would be fine and that his new friend had his best interest in his heart. He looked down noticing the medallion was pulsating so he grabbed a hold of it and closed his eyes. This had HaVon's attention and curiosity as he watched, not really sure what was going on but feeling he was in no danger, he just watched, waiting patiently as Rell came out of the trance and opened his eyes.

"What's that you were doing?" he was wondering what he just saw.

"Well, this medallion," Rell answered as he looked at it, "it seems to show me things."

"Show you things?" HaVon was confused.

"Things that are good and bad as well, I believe along with you, it was sent to protect and guide me." Rell was still amazed by all his experiences.

"What did it show you?" HaVon asked.

"I saw a bunch of clouds and just a feeling of security," said Rell and looked up at him with a smile.

"I'm glad to hear that." He looked back at him with a smile.

"So, how do we do this?" He began to look where he might sit.

HaVon just smiled, lowering his body close to the ground. Seeing the look on Rell's face, he noticed that he still might need some help. So, carefully, he helped him onto his back where he sat in between his wings. Rell was tall for his age like HaVon but on his back, he seemed much smaller.

"Wow!" was the reaction on Rell's face.

"What is it?" HaVon turned and looked at him.

"This is amazing! I can see everywhere." At this is a moment, you could hear the boy in him come out.

"If you like this view, just wait, you're about to see so much more." HaVon could see how excited he was. "Hold on now, OK?" he said as he looked back at him again. "Now remember, don't worry, I've got you."

"Promise I won't," Rell said and lowered his body as close to HaVon's as he could. He then looked up at him and nodded, letting him know he was ready.

Then with a graceful stroke of HaVon's wings, the two were airborne. Remembering how Rell felt about heights, he climbed into the air slowly. When he looked back, remembering his first reaction about flying, he was concerned, but Rell was looking around with not a worry at all and a big smile on his face.

"Can you hear me, HaVon?" He didn't know if they could talk while he was flying.

"Yes, I can," he answered as he looked back at him.

"This is unlike anything I could have imagined," he said as he looked from side to side. "Unbelievable!" Suddenly, he let out a cry of excitement.

HaVon could hear and see how much Rell was enjoying the ride without a look of fear in his eyes, as they flew in the opposite direction of the suns on their way back to the Elders. As the wind blew in Rell's face, you could see with all that had happened to him, this was good therapy for him as it seemed for the moment he had forgotten all the pain he had been feeling moments before. There was a smile on his face.

"You still OK back there?" HaVon asked as he turned his head back to notice Rell was just looking all around and smiling.

All Rell could do was look at him and nod his head up and down. HaVon could see this had his full attention as he just continued to look at all that they flew over.

"I've never been able to travel this far." He was in a trance. "If only Mom could see me now." He smiled, raising his hands into the air and hooting into the wind.

"I'm sorry for what has happened to you, Rell," he said, looking back.

"Thank you, HaVon. It's OK, I still hurt inside but this really helps," he said as he wiped a tear.

"You know, you must never forget that those we lose are never far from our hearts." You could see how much HaVon was trying to help Rell, to ease his pain.

"That's funny you said that." A smile came over Rell's face.

"Why do you say that?" HaVon asked, curious as he continued to fly.

"My mother was always sure to tell me that all the time, it was like she knew this would happen." He began to shake his head thinking of the possibility.

"She sounds like an amazing and smart woman, must have been great to have such a wonderful person raising and caring for you so much." HaVon tried to bring the good things to his attention and also knowing how hard it must be at the same time.

"She truly was," said Rell, holding his hand to his heart. "You're right, she will always be with me." He saw that he was trying to help, which made him feel even more secure with what was happening.

He smiled back at him then focused back on the direction of the peaks, getting closer with each stroke of his wings.

Meanwhile, Saball had finally returned back to the land of reflections. He wore an evil-hearted grin on his face as he walked into the valley, knowing this time he had not failed, his reflection casting off the walls. He looked up, noticing the formation seemed darker than before. Lunging to the top, he just stood there. It seemed as if his powers were growing as well. It wasn't much long before Shaydon appeared.

"I did as you asked, my lord," said Saball, kneeling before him. "She said I was too late and it would be only a matter of time before the two would be together." You could see him waiting anxiously for a response.

"You don't think I already know that?" He struck him out of anger after hearing that, once again showing how ruthless he truly was. "I don't care, we'll be ready for them both," he said as he looked at the formation.

"I know we will," he said as he pulled himself off the ground.

"They have no idea what's going to happen to them." He turned to Saball, his voice echoing through the walls. "Let them think this boy and dragon can stop all that I have taken from Lanila." He began to laugh. "Because of them, if any of those that have survived decide to rise and stand against us, we will destroy them all. No one has the power to stand against us!" You could hear the anger in his voice as it bellowed across the walls.

"We will be ready, my lord," Saball said as he knelt before him. "Forgive me for what I said." He lowered his head.

"Now go and cause havoc on Lanila, there is nothing that will help them," Shaydon went silent for a moment, "remind those who have forgotten about us or believe in this false new beginning."

So now with his new orders comes, an evil laugh followed a grin. This was what he liked the most; cause harm and pain to others. Lanila was unaware of what was coming, he would soon remind them all of who they were, but what they didn't understand was that a word of hope had already started to spread.

Chapter Twelve

With Saball obviously excited by what he was told to do, the two new adventures made their way to the where the mountains sat just on the horizon.

"We're close, you see up ahead those mountains in the distance?" HaVon asked as he smiled. "That's where I call home. Are you still doing OK back there?" HaVon wanted to be sure Rell still felt safe and secure with his flying.

"I'm doing great, this is so beautiful!" Rell continued to look around. "I had no idea mountains could get so tall; I've only heard stories of them." It was his first time seeing anything like this and he was speechless at times, just staring off.

"You think those are tall? These are only the beginning of the things that will amaze you," HaVon smiled wider, seeing how much he was enjoying himself.

"Everything has so much color and life in it." Rell kept turning his head from side to side, taking in all the beauty they were flying over.

"You know, Rell, most people have forgotten that." He knew why he had waited for this boy; his heart and mind were pure.

"Mom raised me to appreciate all that was around, also everything you see has life," said Rell, looking up and smiling, "she reminded me of that every day."

"Like I told you before, she sounds wonderful and wise." Rell had been raised well and he could see that.

"Thanks, she was amazing," Rell replied, smiling big as he continued to admire the scenery.

"Rell, do me a favor and hold on, OK?" HaVon looked back at him with a big grin.

"Why, what's wrong?" asked Rell, hoping he was OK.

"It's nothing bad, I was just thinking if you like this view, wait till I get you closer to the ground if that's OK?" he waited for his approval.

"I'm holding on, let's do it!" Rell grinned from ear to ear, and you could hear the excitement in his voice.

Hearing that, HaVon dove toward the ground, looking back to make sure he was fine. The look on his Rell's face showed he was fully enjoying himself. As they flew close enough to the trees, he reached out and touched them. As they approached the lake, they were so close that Rell leaned out to see his reflection in the water. As he did, HaVon lowered his front paw far enough into the water that caused the water to spray over them, getting them both a little wet. They both laughed out loud, you could really see how much they were enjoying this moment. HaVon did notice how wet Rell was and told him to hold on tight. He then smiled and took off with such a force, it was fast enough to dry him completely. HaVon then slowed down, looking back to a big smile.

"Now that's what I call speed drying." Rell began laughing out loud, forgetting for the moment about all that had happened.

"I hoped you would enjoy that," HaVon laughed as well.

"That was great! I can't believe all this view!" The mountains seemed to go on with no end in sight.

"Hold on," HaVon called again, seeing he enjoyed going fast, so he decided to fly in between the trees and mountains, showing the true beauty of them up close.

Seeing he was enjoying all that was around, HaVon decided to show him more by climbing high into the air. They were above the clouds and in every direction Rell looked, all he could see was a blue sky. Every once in a while a mountain would poke through the clouds. He continued seeing how much Rell was enjoying it, but he also knew at the same time they were getting closer to the Elders. Rell got his attention and he looked back.

"Thank you for this, I thought I've seen things in my life, but what you've shown me today I will never forget." He just wanted him to know he appreciated what he had done.

"You're more than welcome," HaVon said as he grinned at him, "but you know they say this is only the beginning of things we'll see together."

"I'm glad we were brought together, you're an amazing dragon and fast as well." They smiled; you could see this would be a friendship of legends.

"I couldn't have said it any better, Rell," he could also feel in his heart how right this was.

He seemed to pick speed up a bit flying over the clouds, you could see the clouds were going by a little faster. Rell held on a little tighter, noticing they had picked up speed, but that smile wouldn't leave his face when at one time he had been afraid of heights. The speed they were going didn't seem to bother him at all, then HaVon began to slow down as the clouds became thicker. Rell couldn't see anything in front of him now.

"I'm glad you know where you're going, I can't see a thing," Rell said as he squinted, trying his best to see what was ahead of them.

"Be patient, we're going to be completely through them in a little while." Then as quickly as he said, it became clear. He had known they would soon pass to where he could see again.

The clouds were gone and Rell could see again, he was even more amazed of how they seemed to be on top of the clouds now. Every once in a while, a mountain peak could be made out just barely breaking through. Looking around, he seemed to be just a young boy having the time of his life as he smiled, looking in every direction.

"Do you live near here, HaVon?" Rell asked, wondering if that was where they were going.

"Not too far from here," he answered as he looked back, "but for now, we're heading to the Elders." HaVon paused for a bit. "Tell you what, after they meet you and we have the time, I promise to show you."

"Sounds great," Rell replied, knowing how important it was to see the Elders first.

"Plus, I can't wait till you meet Ravin." You could see he cared for her.

"Who's that?" It was the first time Rell had heard that name.

"She raised me," a smile appeared while talking about her, "taught me everything I know." HaVon was a proud of her.

"She sounds great! I can't wait to meet her." Rell could tell he cared for her by the way he spoke.

"She really is."

They continued to get closer to their destination.

Flying above the clouds toward the Elders with each stroke of his wings, HaVon was unaware of what had happened to Ravin while he was gone. Having done the same to Rell by taking his mother from him, it was clear they were out to cause pain to their hearts and minds. But instead of weakening them like they hoped, it would only bring these two closer and stronger than anyone could have imagined. It would show an entirely new side to them both, truly proving to be a task to overcome. Being there for one another would teach them both that they're no longer alone and having each other would bring Lanila the peace and hope it had waited so long for.

"Wow, what's that?" Rell asked, pointing in the distance at some formation he could swear was on top of the clouds. "Am I seeing things?" You could hear the confusion in his voice.

"No, you're not, that's where we're heading," HaVon replied as he chuckled. "Yes, they're on top of the clouds, this is the peak of the Elders."

"How beautiful is this!" Rell's eyes widened as the golden glow reminded him of the willow. "It's so hard to believe this is real, but I can feel it my heart," he paused, "we're going to succeed, HaVon; for Lanila!"

"I understand what you're saying," said HaVon as he looked back. "I feel the same." He approached the ledge and landed, lowering himself for Rell to get off.

"Wow!" He stumbled slightly. "My legs are numb," he said as he smiled, rubbing them, trying to bring them back to life. "Look at this place!" All he could do was stare at everything.

"Are you OK, Rell?" HaVon asked, seeing him rub his legs.

"I'll be fine," Rell smiles at him, "they're coming back to life. They just fell asleep; it was a long ride." He then stared at the pillars and the detail work on them.

"It truly is something amazing to see. To think, all the cycles I've been through and the stories I've heard, I still could have never imagined any place like this!" You could hear the boy in him coming out. "Look at all the detail work and it doesn't seem to end," he said, taking a note of how far he could see.

"It is like a whole different part of Lanila and I'm a part of it," he then paused for a moment. "Wow! this is exciting!"

"Hearing you speak, I see why the Elders have brought us together." He could see and feel the excitement and energy Rell was emanating. "Come on, Rell, this way." He led him down the path in between the pillars.

"Where are we going now?" Rell asked as he continued to admire all the detailed work.

"You see there in the distance where the pillars come to a circle?" he asked as he pointed ahead. "That's where we're going."

"I'm following you, just lead the way." He noticed how truly big HaVon was walking next to him, and you could see the twinkle in his eyes.

He followed him, looking all around and at times closely at the pillars, at the detailed work, when he noticed they had symbols on them as well. Some of them he had seen before in the journal. He could do nothing but shake his head, he was amazed and lost for words. He saw the circle of pillars were getting closer, along with the golden glow that seemed to be getting brighter as well. Then, Rell noticed the medallion started to glow. He pointed it out to HaVon. The smile and look on his face showed he knew that there was a connection with the Elders. As Rell began to focus on what he was seeing, looking at what he thought were statues, but he wasn't sure if that was indeed what he was seeing.

"Who are they, HaVon, and what's that in the middle?" he noticed the large pool. "Is that gold water?" he asked, looking up at him.

"Not exactly." He got a response but it wasn't from HaVon.

Rell turned to see where the voice had come from.

"It guides and helps us in protecting you two."

"Oh my!" Before his eyes, he saw the larger golden statue of a dragon come to life. "You're seeing this, right?" Rell asked, looking up at HaVon.

"Yes, I see him too," HaVon chuckled, amused by what he had said, "that's the great Elder, Rell."

"So, your name is Rell?" The golden dragon approached closer and lowered himself down a bit. "We are glad to see you're safe and welcome you to the peak of the Elders. My name is Cliffon."

"Nice to meet you, Cliffon," Rell replied, not sure exactly how he should respond.

He stood there just staring at the size and how detailed they all were, his eyes grew even larger as he saw every one of the dragon statues come to life. HaVon was enjoying every reaction he could see on his face, as Rell just turned looking at each one of them, he could see the twinkle in his eyes and his smile won them all over.

"You all are so amazing," said Rell and turned looking at HaVon. "I can't believe this is happening!" He was lost for words.

They all went on to introduce themselves, letting him know of how each was a part of Lanila, and all Rell could do was listen as they spoke and HaVon as well, as they stood side by side. The Elders let them know of how this all had come to be. As Rell had read the journal, it helped him a bit in understanding and they knew it as well. His reactions were so mature for his age, even with what he was seeing around him. the Elders could feel the power the two were emanating between them.

"So, you're all the Elders of Lanila?" asked Rell, looking at each of them.

"Yes, we are," they all spoke at one time.

"Rell, you have only begun to find out how important the both of you are to what is happening," said Cliffon.

"They might be right, Rell. You see, I've been raised and trained knowing of what I'll become," HaVon said as he looked down at him.

"So you knew of me and what's happening?" Rell asked, looking up at him.

"Well, not exactly. I knew there would be another just not who," HaVon answered, hoping that made it a little easier for him to understand.

"I remember something about that I read in here," said Rell, pointing to the journal.

"We're so happy to see you brought that with you." Cliffon knew of its importance to everything that would happen.

"It's so amazing; it keeps filling my mind with information," said Rell, looking up at Cliffon, "even if I'm not reading it." He didn't know how that was possible.

"It is one of the keys to it all, Rell," Cliffon also tried to help with his questions, as the Elders looked at one another.

"You said one of the keys?" This even had HaVon curious.

"Yes, our young adventurers." Both of them were holding on to every word they spoke. "We see you're wearing the medallion as well."

"It was given to me by my mother. This is important as well, isn't it?" Like the journal, he felt it had its place.

"It is," Cliffon smiled. "Let me try and help with any doubts you two might have."

Looking down at them both, he began to explain how they were the new start that Lanila had been waiting for. But hearing that they were to be the ones to help Lanila, they patiently listened to what he was saying as he went on. Cliffon could see the look on their faces, promising them it would all make a little more sense to them before they left. He went on to tell them both that they had been here since the beginning, and what happened to them all was the biggest loss that Lanila had gone through.

"You're speaking about the great battle?" Rell remembered the stories his mother had told him.

"That's right." You could see how impressed Cliffon was to hear that. "Back then, we had both dragon riders that helped and dragons that flew next to men on horses."

"But it still wasn't enough to stop them," another one of the Elders spoke up.

"No, the two of them were too strong," he answered, speaking of Shaydon and Saball.

"OK, you're telling me all that was not enough," Rell looked up at HaVon, "but we are?" he pointed at them both.

"Yes, Rell, I believe we are," HaVon said as he looked down at him with a smile.

"I'm glad to hear you say that and you're right, always believe in your heart and yourself."

Hearing HaVon, it helped, but he thought about all those that had failed; it kind of had him scared a bit.

"It's OK, I understand after hearing what they said, but this time there is a difference. I have your back."

The Elders listened to them and began to smile, they could feel them getting stronger already.

You could see how both young adventures were more excited than worried. The Elders could see right before their eyes the bond growing between them. But in time, HaVon would find out of a terrible tragedy that had occurred while he was gone, and how important Rell would prove to be helping him through this great loss, letting him know they would do it together, as one.

Chapter Thirteen

The two of them continued taking in all this information from the Elders, holding on to every word they spoke, when HaVon began to look around.

"What is it?" He got Rell's attention.

"Cliffon, where is Ravin?" HaVon had just realized she wasn't there and hadn't seen her since his return.

"She's the one you mentioned to me on our way here?" Rell remembered he spoke of her highly and could see he looked worried.

"She was going back to our lair when I left." Rell could hear a little worry in his voice. "She never returned?" HaVon asked as he looked up at Cliffon.

"No, she hasn't."

HaVon looked at the Elders.

"I'm sure she's on her way here now," said Rell, seeing he was worried, trying to help him in any way he could.

"I have to go find her," said HaVon as he looked at them all. "I'm sorry, I have to make sure she's OK. She should've been back by now." He was becoming more worried with each word he spoke.

"We can't feel her anywhere." The Elders became worried too. "Return to the lair and check to see if she's there."

"You want me to go with you?" Rell asked.

"Thank you, Rell, but you stay here and I'll return as soon as I find her." HaVon knew he meant well, but at the same time, he did not want anything to happen to him.

"You can stay here with us while he's is gone." Cliffon knew this was the best thing for them both, especially if something were to happen, they could help keep him safe.

"I will return as quick as I can." HaVon knew how important this was for the two of them, but he was just as worried for Ravin too.

"You go and find her, HaVon, I'll be fine," he looked back up at the Elders with a smile, "be careful though."

"We'll watch over him," they all spoke out, feeling the connection they had, at the same time they seemed very afraid of what he might find.

With that said, he kneeled before the Elders, smiling to Rell, then he headed toward the opening where they had landed. You could see how worried he was becoming with each step he took, then he spread his wings and took to the air with a great force. Rell made himself comfortable as he talked with the Elders, looking around and asking questions as he did. While HaVon, instead of continuing in the air, decided to fly directly to the ground, toward the base of the peaks so he could track her steps all the way to their lair. He made sure to go the same way she had brought him earlier, hoping he would find her or a clue of where she might be along the way.

He approached the bottom of the peaks, gliding slowly, and scanning over the area, hoping to find any sign of her. Then suddenly something seemed to be drawing him to a certain area; this was where she had disappeared from. As he came up to it and looked around, you could see he was uneasy, wondering why here. He felt something was not right here but he had no know idea what. He was becoming frustrated and worried; you could see it in his face. Not seeing anything around but knowing something just felt wrong, he took to the air, this time moving at a faster pace and scanning in every direction for a sign. As he saw the lair in the distance, he used his vision to scan the area, but there was still no sign of her and that's when he became more worried, with each stroke of his wings that drew him near. When he got to the opening of the lair, he landed, but unlike the times before, he did so with a force and a purpose, and he began looking around and entered the cave.

"Ravin, are you in here?" You could hear in his voice the concern as he called out for her. "Ravin?" he shouted her name but saw no sign of her anywhere, he was worried now, unlike before, thinking the worst with all that was happening around. Then suddenly, he heard a familiar voice.

"Young one!"

A sense of relief came over him after hearing her voice.

"I'm so glad to hear your voice, you had me worried something happened." He turned with a big smile but saw nothing. "Ravin, where are you?"

"Listen to me, young one, you must return to the boy." HaVon continued to scan the cave but did not see her, although he could hear her voice.

"But I want you to come with me, he wants to meet you." The look on his face showed he was starting to panic, not knowing where she was at.

"They will stop at nothing to get to you both."

He still no idea where she was saying this from.

"Who won't stop, this Saball or Shaydon?" Then it hit him; he realized what was going on. "Oh no, Ravin?" Tears began to form in his eyes.

"Yes, young one. I'm sorry, Saball got to me when I left the base of the peaks, he was hiding and waiting."

"That's where I landed when I was looking for you, I felt as if something terrible had happened." You could see how upset he was becoming.

"What did he do to you?" he was starting to feel the anger over what Saball had done.

"That's not important right now," she said as she knew it wouldn't help.

"But how am I hearing you and not seeing you?"

Suddenly, a vision of her appeared before him; it had the same golden glow as Rell's mother, confirming his worst fear. She was gone.

"Oh no!" HaVon fell to his knees. "I should've been here to protect you and this would not have happened." He began hitting the ground with anger and it shook.

"HaVon, no!" The spirit of her reached out to get him to raise his head. "Then all this wouldn't be happening."

He began to straighten up and listen to her.

"You and this boy are what we all have been waiting for, this very moment is what Lanila needs."

"His name is Rell," as he wipes his eyes, to clear his vision from the tears.

"Well, that sounds like a strong name, I can feel the bond you two share already." She smiled. "You know how important this is to us all, we can't let anyone or anything stop this from happening." It really helped him to finally see her. "You must return to the Elders, fulfill this destiny that has been laid out for the two of you and remember how proud I am of you."

"It going to be so hard not having you here." He already missed her so much.

"Young one, I always am." Smiling, the spirit reaches out and touched his heart; as if he had absorbed her, she vanished.

While all this was going on, back at the peaks Rell and the Elders were talking, then suddenly the medallion pulsated as he grabbed it, they noticed Rell's expression changed.

"I can feel HaVon, this pain he's feeling, I've felt this once before." A tear fell from his eyes as he looked up at the Elders. "Oh no, something terrible has happened to her!" This was what they had feared.

HaVon was still recovering from seeing the spirit of Ravin; it had disappeared when she touched his heart. He now needed to get back to Rell as she had wished.

"I promise you to return and fulfill the destiny," he spoke to the air hoping she could hear him. "I will forever miss you." He raised to his paws and headed out of the lair on his way back to the Elders and Rell.

With each stroke of his wings, he climbed higher into the sky. He looked over the area, remembering all the memories he had with Ravin and all she had taught him. Deep down, he knew this couldn't be changed, he knew his life was in store for all new memories with Rell. But you could see it still hurt, remembering what her spirit had told him, how important this was to them all. The way he traveled, picking up speed so quickly, was unlike anything he had done before – he had a purpose and it showed.

It wasn't long after that before Rell and the Elders looked up and could see HaVon as he approached the ledge, landing with such grace. They could see the way he carried his head that something was wrong. He walked in between the columns and looked up at the Elders and Rell. They all could see how troubled he looked while heading toward them.

"She's gone," he looked down taking a breath, "Ravin's spirit appeared to me while I was at the cave, she told me Saball had gotten to her and did this while I was gone." A tear appeared on his face.

"I am so sorry." Rell could feel his pain in his heart. "It's all my fault, if you didn't have had to come and get me," he lowered his head as he spoke, "you would've been able to help her." They could hear the anger in Rell's voice as he felt at fault for what had happened.

"No, Rell, it's not, she told me they would try and stop us any way they possibly can." He really needed him to understand he wasn't to blame for this. "Both of us have lost someone very important to our hearts, but that's what will feed us and make us stronger together." Rell lifted his head hearing that. "Neither one of us will ever be alone again because we have each other now."

The Elders, hearing how they talked amongst the two of them, had them looking at one another. They knew this bond the two were showing could not be broken and knew indeed this was the beginning of something special. With that said, they both turned and walked toward the Elders.

"We're sorry for what you've lost, the both of you," Cliffon said as the other Elders looked at them both. "We're afraid this is only the beginning of the encounters that you will face along the way."

"They explained a lot to me while you were gone," Rell said as he looked up at HaVon. "They even told me of there being others, they could help us and, from what I've heard, are needed as well."

"Others?" Even though his heart was hurting, this got HaVon's attention.

"Yeah, others, but they're hiding and waiting, we have to find them." Rell was about to tell him more about all he had heard when Cliffon spoke up.

"HaVon, lower your head down to Rell." They looked at each other in surprise, but HaVon did as he was told. "Now, Rell, reach out and place your hand to his mind."

"You want me to put my hand to his head?" Rell looked at him and touched his head knowing they knew best.

Just as he did, something amazing happened. As they watched, suddenly a golden glow came over them both. The Elders smiled.

"What just happened?" they both said at the same time.

"You transferred all your thoughts you have, Rell, that we have talked about, into HaVon," the Elders continued to smile, "you two share a bond, more than anyone could imagine. It can never be broken."

"Do you feel different?" Rell asked as he looked up to HaVon as he raised his head.

"He's right, I know now of the others." He looked back down at him. "We do share the same pain, Rell; I'm so sorry for your loss. I can feel it more now." Having that happen, they now shared one another's thoughts along with feelings.

This was only the beginning of the changes that were to come to our young adventurers. It was clear that Shaydon was trying to stop this from happening by trying to attack their hearts. But unlike the times before when everyone had lost, this would be different; they could see it now. With what had happened and what the two of them had gone through, it would only make them so much stronger.

Chapter Fourteen

The two of them had lost such a big part of their hearts, yet there was still so much more they had to learn. As they all approached the pool of gold that stood in the middle, at the exact same time all this was happening, Saball looked to be heading in a new direction. It was a place people had come to call the old land; it was clear he was there for a reason and only time would show us what it was. He was on another one of his personal quests; meanwhile, back at the peaks of the Elders, the two had begun to learn more of this new beginning.

"This is so beautiful!" said Rell, speaking of the pool of gold and noticing all the detail work on the sides.

"It really is," said HaVon as he looked down at him.

"What purpose does this serve?" They said it almost at the same time.

"This is the pool of power and knowledge." Cliffon was glad to see their curiosity. "This is very important to the beginning, which you both will see shortly."

After all that had happened to try and discourage them both from continuing, for the moment they had forgotten the pain and were eager to hear more of this.

"What do you mean power? This is the beginning?" Rell asked.

"The key to it is the journal that was left for you, plus the medallion you wear proudly, Rell," Cliffon looked down at him, smiling.

"Now I'm understanding why you wanted me to make sure he brought the journal," said HaVon.

"Those are the keys?" Rell asked as he looked at them both. "These are the keys to what and how do they work?" You could hear and see the look of confusion on Rell's face.

Cliffon went on to explain that Rell should place the medallion into the journal, but instead of opening and reading it, he should then place it into the golden pool. Rell looked up at HaVon and you could see he was confused, but this was the Elders and so he did as he was told by placing it in the journal.

"OK, now you want me to place it into the pool?" he looked up at Cliffon.

"Trust us, you'll see," all the Elders spoke at one time, you could see the excitement they felt as they smiled.

"Go ahead, Rell, I'm right here with you." HaVon was just as eager to see what would happen.

With all of them watching closely, he lowered the journal into the golden pool. HaVon happened to look up and saw they were all smiling, they seemed very excited this was happening and he would soon realize why. As soon as Rell placed them in the pool of gold, it began to pulsate as this gold began to climb up his arms, working its way over his body.

"What's it doing to my body?" Rell asked; you could hear the concern in his voice.

"Don't be alarmed, Rell," Cliffon assured him, "all it's doing is bonding with you. Be patient."

"Don't worry, I'm right here with you," said HaVon as he could also sense it in his voice, but knew the Elders would do nothing to put either of them in harm's way.

The more it was consumed by the pool, the more it began to spread throughout his body. Looking closely, it resembled what looked like golden dragon scales that covered the journal. Everyone watched in amazement as it covered his arms and his eyes grew even larger in wonder as it began to cover his body too. Holding his arms out, Rell started turning them, he admired the way they completely covered his arm. He watched as his entire body was now covered all the way up to his neck, it looked like his body had these gold scales all over and they worked as protection similar to armor.

"Wow! Look at this!" You could hear excitement in Rell's voice.

"The way it completely covers you," said HaVon, lowering his head to get a closer look, "they look like my scales, just smaller."

"It will always protect you. Now that you have bonded< you're one with it." Cliffon and the Elders smiled at them, knowing its purpose.

"So, OK, it's like armor?" Rell asked, looking at them.

"Similar purpose, yes, but it's a part of you now," Cliffon tried to explain it was more than just armor.

"Well, I think this is awesome," Rell grinned. Looking it over, he saw something on his right shoulder and arm. "Hey, this looks like the medallion, but look how it spreads from here to the end of my arm." He pointed to his shoulder, looking at the design.

"You're right about that, Rell, it is." The Elders were pleased to see how aware he was.

He looked at it closely, seeing how it had spread out, noticing the dragon head was on his shoulder now. Then he saw the four different colors of crystals, that once surrounded the head, were now spread out along the top and bottom of his forearm. They seemed to be connected to each other by wavy thick lines, that all led back to the head of the dragon at the top. He also noticed that this new armor he was wearing had no weight to it at all, but it was hard as a rock. Rell smiled at HaVon, amazed by what had just witnessed.

"OK, I now have this on to protect me," he said as he looked at HaVon. "So, do I ride him with this on?" You could see they both still needed guidance.

"Well, not exactly, young ones." They both seemed even more confused hearing that. "We did tell you of the dragon riders, plus the men and dragons that fought side by side," then the Elders looked at one another with a smile.

They went on to explain how this was so different from what they had heard of in the past, telling them how this suit was the key. They told them that it would merge the two of them together, and then, what Lanila had been missing would be begin.

"We're going to merge together?" they responded at the same time as they looked at one another.

"This suit is amazing to see on Rell, but Elders, you're telling me that this will merge us into one?" HaVon asked, trying to understand how this was possible.

"We agree, this all has been so magical and unbelievable at the same time, but if that's what it does, how do we get it to work?" Rell knew anything was possible and was eager to hear how while the Elders smiled.

Cliffon began to explain why this time would be different and special for Lanila, the joining of those two was the reason for the conflict they were encountering from Shaydon and Saball. That's why they were trying to stop it before it began, they didn't exactly know how but had heard of the power it's supposed to have. They explained that once Rell and HaVon merged together, they will be a power and force that had never been seen before and once they do merge, all of Lanila, including Shaydon and Saball, will know it has begun.

"I'm ready, how about you?" said Rell, looking up at HaVon.

"I am as well, it's time for Lanila to stop hiding."

A smile came over the Elders, they were excited by what they were hearing.

"So how do we do this?" both of them asked at once, showing they were ready.

The Elders began to explain how they would get it to work and merge together; they looked at one another, listening to every word they spoke.

"I just have to touch him?" Rell looked confused. "Hold on, I touched him earlier and nothing happened," he said, referring to when their minds were joined.

"You're right, Rell, but that was before you were bonded with the journal and medallion." Hearing that, Rell was eager to hear more.

They did tell them though when they do touch each other from this time forward, it would happen, and that's when they would see something amazing happen that they could have only imagined. Holding on to every word the Elders were speaking, finding out how they would have unlimited power when they did, they were also explained that in time, they would learn more of their abilities and what they could do as one.

"That's what Mom meant when she told me that," said Rell, remembering how much she would say that to him.

"You know, Rell, Ravin would tell me the same thing," said HaVon as he looked down at him.

"The power of one's mind and the power of one's strength," continued Rell, looking up at HaVon.

"That's right, Rell, exactly what I was told." All of the sudden, everything that they had learned seemed to click.

"So I'm the strength and you're the mind?" A big smile of sarcasm came over Rell's face and they both began to laugh. "Just kidding, I know it's my mind and his strength," he said, then reached out and touched him.

This is when it all began, for as soon as he reached out to touch HaVon, they were all blinded by a golden light as it engulfed both Rell and HaVon. the Elders couldn't see what was happening. Then the light diminished and it became clearer to see, as everyone just stood there in amazement at what stood in front of them. Rell was nowhere in sight but as they looked at HaVon, his entire body was covered in the suit that Rell had been wearing. Instead of being solid gold though like his suit, it seemed to have highlighted all his scales throughout his body. His leg and feet were covered completely, along with his head, which seemed to give him more protection. Each shoulder also looked to have extra protection as well, making him seem broader. The truth was that they had merged into one as HaVon's eyes had changed from yellow to a deep blue.

"Hold on, where did Rell go?" HaVon looked worried, then he noticed his body was covered with the suit. He was astonished to say the least.

"I'm right here, HaVon."

Hearing his voice, HaVon looked from side to side.

"Where's here, I hear you but I don't see you?"

The Elders were enjoying what they were witnessing.

"This might be hard for you to imagine, HaVon, but like they said, I think we're one now," Rell responded.

"Did you just say we're one?" He looked to the Elders who were smiling.

"That's correct, Rell, you two are," they answered them both.

"OK, hold on, so you're telling me from this time forward this is how we'll always be?" You could hear concern in Rell's voice as if he was standing in front of them.

"Relax, young ones, not all the time," Cliffon answered, hearing the panic in Rell's voice, "HaVon, if you look on your shoulder, you'll see the mark."

"Wow, there it is, I see it and it looks like your mark, Rell," HaVon said, looking at it.

"HaVon, reach over and touch it." A smile came over the Elders' faces.

Doing as he was told, like before everyone was overcome again by this bright golden light, then just as it did before when it was gone, standing there next to him was Rell. There he was wearing the suit again, and HaVon's eyes too had changed back to yellow.

"That's amazing!" said Rell, seeing now they could separate. "I'm sorry to ask about that, I was just a little worried at first we were stuck like that," he said, looking up at HaVon.

"Hey, don't worry about it, I was as well." You could see the relief in his eyes.

"This is so unbelievable that this is happening to us!" Like a kid, Rell was still amazed by all the changes.

"You're right about that, so when we're joined like that, what do we call ourselves?" You could see the both of them starting to think.

"Whatever you decide in time, young ones. What's important is when you're merged, you are the hope that Lanila has needed." You could see how happy the Elders were that they both were beginning to understand.

They went on to tell them how they would learn more of their powers and abilities as time passed, also letting them know it would be up to them to find these others. How they would assist and help them in bringing Lanila this new beginning, but at the same time, they needed to be careful for the evil that was Shaydon. How he would bring all of his powers and forces to oppose this, telling them how he would try and stop them in any way he can.

With the two of them learning more of how much things were about to change, we come upon an entirely new area of the Lanila we haven't seen before. It was warm and so colorful, everything seemed to have a sparkle to it. Then coming from the distance was a creature with very long ears that stood tall, half the size of a horse, with long fur and it seemed very peaceful as well. As it scurried into the land, moving through all the tall flowers and plants, it approached this enormous and amazing waterfall that shone like nothing we've seen. This part of Lanila had so many types of furry creatures, and the animals seemed to roam around in peace.

This creature approached the bottom of the waterfall. It started to get wet by the spray, but it didn't seem bothered by it at all. Suddenly, it was overcome by a bright green light. As it appeared in front of it, this creature suddenly kneeled. Appearing from this green light and standing in front of the creature was a tall beautiful woman, her hair was copper colored and her eyes were as green as the light she came from. Her entire body was covered in what looked to have some similarity to Rell's suit, but it was green with gold highlights throughout it. She carried a staff in her hand that was gold, it looked to be topped with a dragon's head that also had green eyes.

"Ranforray, please stand." Her voice was so soft and inviting as she spoke to this creature.

"My lady!" This creature then transformed into what looked to be of a medium-size person; it had large ears, eyes and was hairy as well with a deep voice.

"He has bonded with him," the woman said, knowing of our young adventurers and what had just happened.

"You felt them, my lady?" Ranforray asked as he started walking with her.

"That I did." She smiled, looking down at him. "He has come along so well."

"Do you want me to go to them?" He looked at her.

"Not yet, Ranforray," she answered with a smile. "We've waited too long for this," her voice was so comforting as she said this. "What have you learned of Saball?"

"He seems to be searching for something, I'm just not sure what," he paused, looking down, "you know he took the boy's mother and the dragon's teacher? I'm sorry I couldn't do anything to help either of them."

"There's nothing you could've done, Ranforray, it's OK." She reached out, placing her fingers under his chin to lift his head up. "I need you to continue to watch over Saball for me, we need to be sure he stays away from him and if he doesn't, you let me know." She smiled again. "I'll keep my eye on Shaydon," she said, looking at the staff in her hand, "just in case they need any help."

"As you ask of me, Dawla." He knelt before her then transformed back into the creature. He then headed off in the direction he had last seen Saball.

"In time, I promise our paths will cross," she whispered into the air, "I'm so proud to feel your growth and the beginning of a new time for Lanila."

So this was the lady of Lanila, known as Dawla; her presence and beauty were breathtaking. She smiled to herself and disappeared back into the green light. What the Elders had mentioned about the land knowing of the joining was true. Dawla was pleased with what had happened. The way she referred to one of them, it seemed as if she had already been watching over them. Meanwhile, the young adventurers continued to learn more about these others, who they needed to find that would help, as we see them still talking. They were totally unaware of the surfacing of Dawla and her intentions to help them, that she would be there if they might be in trouble along the way.

Meanwhile, Rell and HaVon were still curious about the suit.

"Having this suit on is so amazing," said Rell as he looked at the Elders. "So this will never come off?"

"You need not worry. Just like you do when you two are together, touch your arm and it will not be seen." The Elders knew this would ease his mind.

"Look at that, HaVon!" said Rell, doing as they had told. "Where did the suit go?" as he saw he had his clothes back on.

"Pull up your sleeve," Cliffon spoke.

"Look at that!" Rell now had a permanent mark on his shoulder resembling the one on the suit. "Oh my, it covers my entire arm!" he exclaimed, staring at all the detail it had.

"Now you know, for when you want to keep it from the sight of others, you need only to touch it, but remember the bond you share." The Elders could see the astonished look on both of their faces.

"So this is a magical mark?" Just as before, he touched it again, which was followed by the blinding gold flash and he was back in the suit.

"OK, so where do we find these others you've spoken of?" HaVon asked, curious. "Do they know that we'll be coming?"

"Right, will they be waiting for us?" Rell asked, adding to the questions.

"We're glad to hear your questions have direction," the Elders smiled, looking at them, "they know of this new beginning and have been waiting for a sign," they said as they looked at each other, "but many cycles have passed and you need to understand, but also know that you have merged together. In time, all of Lanila will feel and know." They all smiled.

"So do we at least know in what direction we should start?" Rell asked, looking at them.

"I understand. It does seem that we have all the answers, but to us this is all for you to find." They paused. "From this time forward, it's not written, it's up to the both of you to find and bring them together."

"I understand, Elders, but do you have an idea where we can start?" HaVon asked, hoping they could give some sort of direction for them to go.

"We all feel the willow or your home, Rell, would be a good place to start," said Cliffon and they all agreed.

"My house or the willow?" He was silent for a moment. "I guess that makes sense, that's where it all started for me."

"Then that's where we go." HaVon looked down at him and smiled.

By the time they had decided where to head, the day had grown long, HaVon could see the wear it had put on Rell as he looked at him and saw him yawning.

"But first, let's head back to my lair," said HaVon, seeing Rell yawn again. "He needs his rest."

Hearing this, the Elders knew even more they would be there for one another.

"Thanks, HaVon, that would be nice," said Rell, yawning again, "but are you sure you're OK with that?" he asked, knowing it was a place of memories; he still hadn't forgotten what had happened.

"I am," he looked down at him, knowing what he meant. "I told you I wanted to take you there, and I would be honored if you stayed; it's close and you'll enjoy the spring," said HaVon, smiling, knowing how much he himself enjoyed it.

"The spring?" he asked, curious.

"You'll see," he said as he smiled.

"That sounds like a great idea, HaVon. You two go rest and first thing in the morning, head back to your home," Cliffon said and looked at the other Elders and they agreed. "We hope there you will find the answers you search for to begin your quest for the others."

"Thank you, Elders, we will," they both answered.

They all agreed that rest was important for what was ahead, and they should wait till the new day. They suggested Rell's home might have the answers for their quest to begin. It seemed maybe the Elders might know more than they were willing to tell them at that time, letting them know this was where they needed to go to find the answers they searched for. The two of them had already joined together and were heading back to HaVon's cave. You could see the excitement among the Elders; they had finally witnessed this new beginning they all had been waiting for.

"This is so amazing and hard to believe at the same time; it's us that all of Lanila has been waiting for," Rell spoke to HaVon as they flew.

"I know what you mean, I'm excited as well." Even though they had known one another for such a short time, you couldn't tell; it seemed they had been together a lifetime.

In the distance, HaVon could see his lair and told him they were close.

"There it is in the distance," he said, letting Rell know.

"I thought it was," he replied, forgetting when they were merged, he could see through HaVon's eyes.

They approached the opening to the cave. The blue moon was high in the sky. Landing so gracefully as he did, HaVon touched the mark on his shoulder and they became two.

"Thanks for bringing me here," said Rell, smiling up at him while yawning. "I know it brings back memories."

"You're welcome, Rell, you really need your rest." He knew he was thankful.

"Remember, I feel what you do." He winked at him and headed into the cave. HaVon just shook his head, smiling as he followed him in.

When they entered the cave, Rell noticed how well-lit it was by a blue glow; the further he got into the cave, the brighter it seemed to get.

"It's so much bigger inside here than you would think." Rell was looking in every direction as if it had no end. "Is there an opening for the moon, that's what's keeping it so bright in here, right?"

"Not exactly," HaVon answered, "you'll see where it comes from."

"Wow, this is so beautiful. Now I see," said Rell, finally understanding where the light was coming from. "It's the spring?"

"It is." He could tell Rell was enjoying all he saw.

"This place is awesome!" His energy may have been low, but the boy in him was coming out as he ran and jumped into the spring.

"Rell!" HaVon shouted, but it was too late.

Seeing him jump like he did into the spring brought a big smile to his face. Shaking his head and grinning, he did the same, causing a big wave and splash and they both began to laugh. For at this very moment, all the worries and heartache were gone; the two were truly enjoying themselves. Laughing and splashing one another, even at times Rell would climb on him to jump off into the spring.

"I can see why you mentioned this earlier," he smiled, "it's so warm and relaxing," he said as he floated by.

"I'm so glad to hear you say that, you know it's magical as well," he said, looking down at him.

"What do you mean?" Rell asked, looking at him as he floated by.

"I'm not sure exactly how but it heals my wounds, and energizes me every time I have gotten into it." It was like a light went off in his head, "You know, I now believe this spring was intended for me."

"You're probably right," said Rell as he climbed out.

"I think so," following him out. "Did you even get wet?" HaVon asked, noticing only his hair seemed to be.

"Wow, you're right," he said, looking over his body, "it must be the suit." He reached over, touching his shoulder. It was followed by a gold flash. "Look at my clothes, they're dry!" You could hear how amazed he was.

"They really are." He shook his head with a smile. "Rell, you can rest here," he said, leading him to where Ravin used to rest.

"HaVon, are you sure?" Having the connection, Rell also knew this was where she rested.

"I am, it would mean a lot to me." He was not saying it, but you could feel the bond he had for him.

"OK then," said Rell and reached out touching him.

"Rell!" he reacted as he touched him.

"Remember, no suit." He nudged him, followed by a wink and a smile, as he lay down.

"Sleep well, young one." He shook his head and smiled. *This is going to be a fun relationship,* he thought. "Thanks again for coming."

"You as well, HaVon," Rell replied as he watched him lay down not too far away.

This was proving to be a bond you could only wish for in your dreams, seeing as how they were connecting together already. This was going to be an adventure where they would only get closer and watch out for one another. The day had finally caught up to them and they began to fall asleep.

Chapter Fifteen

Rell and HaVon rested from all the events they had encountered, waiting for the new day. By now, Saball has made his way to the land of the forgotten when he suddenly stopped in his tracks. For some reason, he turned back in the direction he had just come from. By the way he was scanning the area, it appeared he had seen something.

"Hmm," he growled under his breath in frustration.

Suddenly, he saw the ring begin to let out a pulse over and over; it was a way for Shaydon to let him know he was needed. Saball looking into the sky.

"I'll be there soon, my lord." He took off with great speed in the direction of the land of reflections.

Leaving that menacing black streak, he disappeared into the distance. Then, from the direction that had got his attention earlier that he kept staring at, Ranforray came out from hiding and was still in his creature form.

"My lady," he said, transforming back into himself, "he's taking off with great speed, what should I do?" he asked, speaking into the air as if she were there.

Suddenly from behind, as he watched Saball disappear into the distance, he noticed a bright green light travel toward him. He wasn't alarmed as he knew it was Dawla. She walked out of it and approached him.

"He looks to be heading back to Shaydon," she said, placing her hand on his shoulder. "I need you to do me a favor and follow him, but not into the valley. Keep your distance and just let me know if you see what they're planning."

"As you wish," he said, looking up at her with a smile then transformed back into the creature. He took off in the same direction as Saball.

"Don't worry," Dawla spoke to herself, "they won't stop you. I promise." Once again smiling and speaking of the two, there was an obvious connection showing that she would be a great ally and they didn't even know of her help yet. She then turned and vanished into the green light.

The new day was slowly starting to begin back at the cave. Rell was up before HaVon, trying to be careful not to wake him or so he thought. He made his way out of the cave when he noticed the lake surrounded by the trees. He approached it, not knowing this was the exact same spot that HaVon would come to. He sat down and just gazed into the water, thinking.

"I wish you could see me now, Mom," he whispered, wiping a tear from his eye, "I miss you so much."

He sat there missing and thinking of her, having no idea that HaVon had watched him leave. HaVon saw where he was sitting by the lake, at times just speaking into the air, and instead of approaching him he decided to hang back and just watch over him. If anything he understood Rell needed some time alone to think, so this is what he did. Then suddenly, he noticed something amazing was happening.

"I know you'd be so proud of me," Rell was still speaking into the air.

Totally unaware that HaVon was watching from a distance, he looked up, when he noticed something coming toward him. It had a golden glow that he could see, it was getting ever so close to him but he didn't seem alarmed. Instead, he felt security and warmth from whatever this was. The closer it got, the clearer it became, and then he heard a familiar voice.

"I am proud of you, my son." It was his mom.

"Mom!" Tears poured from his eyes. "Is it really you?" He was amazed and happy to see her standing in front of him.

"Yes, my son." It was the energy of his mother's spirit he was seeing.

"How's this happening?" You could see how happy he was, but also confused at the same time. "Is this real?"

"It's as real as you believe, son," she smiled.

"I miss you so much." Real or not, he was relieved to see her.

"I've missed you as well, I'm so very proud of what you're becoming." She was so close he could reach out and touch her.

"You were so right about dragons, Mom. HaVon is the greatest," he was so excited to tell her she was right.

"I'm so glad to hear that and he truly seems to be." At that moment, Rell knew she had been watching over him. "I need you to listen to me, son. When you return to our home, search the top of the fireplace," she had his attention, "you will find something to help with what you're looking for."

"How did you know that's where we're heading?" he looked at her.

"I will always be watching over you," she said. He could see a twinkle in her eye as she smiled.

"What is it I'm looking for, Mom?" he asked, hoping she could give him a little more detail.

"You'll know when you see it, I promise," she said, speaking as if she knew what they had to do.

"OK, thanks, Mom." He smiled. "When will I see you again?"

"You'll always be able to see me, son." He looked confused, so she said, "Remember what I've always told you, I'm right here." She reached out and touched his heart and then vanished right before him.

He could still feel her warmth as a tear rolled down his face, he placed his hand to his heart with a big smile and wiped his face. From the distance, HaVon had been watching. He walked up next to him and sat down.

"Are you OK, Rell?" he asked as he looked down at him.

"You've been there watching, I could feel you," Rell replied, looking up at him. "You know I miss her so much." Then he stood up, brushing himself off.

"I know you do, Rell, and she misses you." At that moment, he looked up. "I miss Ravin too."

"I'm so sorry, HaVon, I wasn't trying to be thoughtless about your feelings at all," Rell immediately apologized.

"I know that, Rell, they were both very important to us." He let him know he was fine. "Sometimes, we all need time and that I do understand." He smiled. "What did she say?"

"She mentioned the house like the Elders, and when we get there, to look at the top of the fireplace." They looked at one another.

"Then that's where we will head." It was clear they agreed this was indeed the place to start.

Unlike before, instead of riding him they merged together, as Rell reached out touching the mark on his shoulder and then HaVon. They just stood there looking at their reflection. They were truly breathtaking, the way they seemed to glisten off the water.

"Wow, look at that!" They continued to look at themselves. "It's still so hard to believe that's us," Rell spoke up.

"It's even crazier how we can hear each other talk." HaVon found it amazing how they communicated to one another.

"That too, HaVon," Rell agreed.

With the suns beginning to climb even further, the new day was finally upon them. They knew where they needed to go as they took to the air; with each stroke of the wings, they head back in the direction where this all began.

"I see you've become more at ease with being in the air," said HaVon, remembering when they first met.

"Does it seem that way?" asked Rell as he chuckled. "Let's just say I'm getting more comfortable with each flight we take."

"It just takes time." HaVon laughed, gliding through the clouds.

While the young adventurers, knowing Rell's home was the place they needed to look for answers to these others, made their way to that land, Saball had made his way back to the land of reflections. Entering the valley walls, he was curious why Shaydon had called for him. Ranforray too had caught up to him. Watching from a distance remembering what Dawla had said to him, he hid from being seen in the tall grass. The look of frustration could be seen on Saball's face. His breathing picked up as he approached the cliff with the formation at the top.

"What is he doing?" Saball wondered, noticing Shaydon holding something in his hand, it was putting out a red glow. "My lord, you called for me?" he asked once he had climbed the wall, getting his attention.

"I felt it," Shaydon said, looking back at his hand. "This will help us slow him down."

"Felt what, my lord?" he looked up at him.

"They've merged," Shaydon let out a roar, you could see he was frustrated.

"Merged?" Saball paused for a moment, then realized. "You're talking about the boy and dragon?"

"Yes." The glow stops as he turned to him. "You need to go back to his home and use this on the boy." Shaydon handed him the disc he had been holding.

"You want me to return to the boy's?" Not sure why, but he knew not to question him further and knelt before him.

"Yes, and the disc I gave you. When you see him, throw it in his direction," Shaydon instructed.

"You want me to throw this at the boy?" Saball stood there looking at it. "Not that I question you, my lord, but how is this going to help us?"

"Saball, it will trap him in the same crystal that you see around us." A smile appeared on Saball's face upon hearing that. "He won't be able to move. It will be easier for you to bring him to me."

"I will do as you ask, my lord." Saball knew if anything, it was not to question what he had been told. "I will not fail you."

"Be sure you don't." You could see how important he felt this was to getting an advantage on them both.

With nothing else said and by the look in Shaydon's eyes, he knew not to fail him. Saball leapt from the top of the valley wall, leaving a crack in the ground as he took off. Heading in the same direction as our young adventurers, he left the valley with such great speed while Ranforray watched him. He could tell whatever it was, it seemed urgent by the way he had left. Knowing he needed to follow so he stayed in the creature form. He left with such great speed, showing his abilities as well, it was amazing how he stayed hidden from Saball's sight while traveling so fast.

Having no idea what was headed in their direction, the adventures had finally reached the willow.

"You know, HaVon, I spent a lot of my time there," said Rell as they flew right above of it.

"It seemed that way," replied HaVon, remembering when they first met. "I remember what I saw it could do, I knew it was a place where you felt safe."

In the distance what remained of the house could also be seen.

"Are you OK?" HaVon asked as he could feel the pain in Rell's heart.

"With you here with me, I will be." Rell knew HaVon was concerned for him, seeing how it brought back memories.

They approached the house and could see a clearing ahead, as they landed and became separated, he just stood by his side. Rell began looking around as a tear rolled down his face. He did not say anything to him but HaVon could feel his emotions. He decided to walk away to give him a moment by himself, thinking it might help.

"You know, Mom always told me Dad was particular about where he wanted to build this." HaVon stopped as he looked back at him. "She mentioned a name Dawla, I'm starting to believe she's part of some stronger force out there, that's here to help" You could tell by both of their reactions it was possible, considering all they had found out already.

"I believe, Rell, that we are all guided in one way or another, while still being protected at the same time." Rell agreed. "We just don't think about it."

"Isn't that the truth!" Rell smiled as they both began to look around.

"Hey, Rell, look over here," HaVon came across what remained of the house.

"That looks like what Mom was talking about." He walked through the debris, amazed at what they were seeing. This hadn't been visible to him until the fireplace had fallen. Suddenly, his hand began pulsating along with the design they were looking at. "You're seeing this, right?" Rell asked, looking up at HaVon.

"There has to be a connection." They both noticed it began pulsating more. "This has to be the reason we're here, the way it's reacting more being so close." HaVon looked at Rell. "What are you going to do?"

"I think, I'm going to touch it, I guess." You could tell he was slightly timid.

"If that's what you think is the answer, I'm right here," said HaVon, letting him know he wouldn't let anything harm him.

"I know you are." There was a slight tremble in his voice; he was not sure what would happen when he did.

With HaVon watching over him, he approached it with his hand out. When he did, they noticed the pulsating suddenly stopped and he could see it had the same design as the medallion.

"All the cycles of growing up here, I never knew this was on here." He was so amazed it took the fireplace falling for him to know it was even there.

"Looks like the same design that was on the medallion you used to wear." HaVon saw the similarity.

"You're right, it does," said Rell as he reached out and touched it.

When he did, the ground around them began to shake and tremble, they looked at one another and HaVon went into a protection mode, not sure what was happening. Then, Rell's attention got diverted as they watched the five boulders that stood behind the house begin to rise from the ground. As they rose, the taller they became. They both stood there watching, the look on both their faces was that of amazement at what they were seeing. They noticed from a distance each one of them had a particular spot on them, then he noticed one began to pulsate. The closer they approached, the clearer it became they all had the same marking as the medallion.

"Look at that!" Rell said as they got closer. "It's the same." He shook his head and had a smile on his face. "I know now Dad was guided to this spot."

"You may be right." HaVon approached his side, he seemed small standing next to the boulders. "So I take it you're going to touch that as well?"

"I need to." Rell slowly approached it as HaVon watched over him. "Look at that, each one of them has the same mark." They knew this was the connection they needed to find, but had no idea what would happen next.

"But why is this the only mark that is pulsating." HaVon could see the others had the mark, but this was the only one getting their attention.

"That I don't know." He was right though, as Rell looked at the rest of them. "Hopefully we'll soon find out." He leaned out and placed his hand to the mark.

They both watched as it was overcome with a glow, then suddenly, it began to open up and they could see a bright light coming from within. As they looked at one another, Rell decided to lead the way. HaVon looked around really quick then followed him close behind. You could see when they entered how amazed they were, they both looked around seeing how large it was on the inside. HaVon had more than enough room. They noticed the walls; the closer they approached them they could see something. It became clearer to them seeing it had drawings all over them, and were very detailed as well.

"You know, I think this is the land of Lanila we're looking at." Rell noticed how much area it covered.

"You know, I'm not sure, Rell, but it must be," answered HaVon, looking down at him.

"This is amazing, look at all the detail and how much of the wall it covers. Just think, there is so much of Lanila we have not seen!" Then, Rell saw something that was written on the wall. He looked closer. "It says the land of the forever trees."

"Wonder why it says that," said HaVon and started looking around.

"Look at the size of those trees," Rell said as he reached out and touched it. Suddenly, a charge of energy shot through the room.

"What was that, are you OK?" HaVon looked back at Rell.

"I'm fine, it came from the wall when I touched it." He was also confused with what he had just seen.

They both just stood there, looking at one another, wondering what's next, then suddenly from the middle of the room it began to glow. They looked at each other, startled. They realized it was the drawings they had seen on the wall. They approached them and realized they were able to walk through as if it were a mirage.

"Look at the size of these!" Rell now understood why it said the forever trees. "They have no top to them, it's as if they keep going," he said, looking up.

"You think this is where we're supposed to go?" HaVon walked through the image.

"Maybe, I don't know," Rell replied, still gazing at the size of them. "In all your time, have you ever seen a place like this?" he asked, looking up at him.

"No, I never have, not like these. I'd remember trees this size." HaVon had seen a lot but this was new even to him.

"That drawing on the wall covered a large area," said Rell.

"So, Rell, you're thinking this is where we can find one of the others that the Elders spoke of?" He made a great point as Rell looked at him.

"It must be, that makes sense, but where in Lanila is this place? Where do we begin to look for it?" He walked through the image searching for any clue.

"Maybe the Elders will know where it is," HaVon replied, looking down at him.

"OK, let's find out if they know." He agreed with his idea, then suddenly, something got his attention from above.

He was looking at three visible white lights and it even got HaVon's attention, they watched them go in out of the trees and work their way down closer to them both.

"What do you think those are?" HaVon asked, watching them getting closer.

"I don't know." Suddenly, Rell noticed the white gem on his right arm began to pulsate. "But this would make you think there is a connection."

"Hey, they're getting closer, Rell!" They both stood watching.

Then without a warning, they picked up speed and were heading in their direction faster. Passing by HaVon, they headed for Rell. By the look on his face, it appeared he wasn't worried as they hit him. When they did, they seemed to merge with him and he began glowing in a bright white light. Seeing Rell not panic brought ease to HaVon but he couldn't believe what he just saw. Then as quick as it happened, it was gone, along with the vision of the trees that they had been looking at.

"Hey are you still OK? What was that all about?" HaVon asked.

"I'm fine, HaVon. I really don't know, maybe it just merged with me like the journal and medallion did," Rell replied, shaking his head at what had just happened. "Hey, look at this mark," he said, pointing out the white gem stone that led up his arm to the dragon mark; they were both glowing with the same white light they had just seen.

"Seeing that now you might be right," said HaVon, still amazed at what he had just seen. "Plus, the image is gone as well."

"Let's get back to the Elders and tell them what we have found. Hopefully they can help us." Rell then smiled. "This is all so amazing!" he exclaimed, looking up at him.

"I agree, it's amazing and if anyone will know, it's the Elders."

They both turned to head out.

While they had been searching for answers to help them in their journey to find the others, Saball had made his way to the willow. He began to look around for any sign of the boy. Then suddenly, he began looking in every direction, it seemed as if he was looking for more just than the boy. He wasn't able to see Ranforray who had finally caught up to him, he was looking in his direction and lay very still, blending in with his surroundings. Saball used his vision to scan the area when he noticed some activity at the boy's house. Thinking this had to be the boy, he decided to get closer to see. Ranforray saw that something else had gotten his attention and was afraid it may be the boy, so he decided to follow him closely, being sure to stay hidden.

"I hope it's the boy," said Saball, speaking to himself as he got closer to the house. "Those seem different from the last time I was here," he said, noticing how much taller and bigger the boulders seemed to be, then he noticed Rell and HaVon coming out from one of them. "There he is!" Saball decided to stay low so he could get closer with the disc in his hand.

"This all has been amazing what we have found, I can't wait to tell the Elders," said Rell as he walked out first with HaVon close behind.

"It truly has been, it's exciting!" replied HaVon looking down at him when he suddenly stopped in his tracks.

"What is it, HaVon?" Rell asked, noticing he had stopped and began to look around.

"I don't know," he replied, looking over the area as he smells the air. "Something's not right." He stood in front of Rell in a stance of protection.

Saball could see the dragon begin to look around, wondering if he had been spotted, so he crept up closer, unaware this entire time Ranforray had made his way in between them both. Ranforray watched Saball getting closer as he stayed hidden between him and our adventurers, the two having no idea of the danger that was approaching them.

"Stay here, Rell," said HaVon; he wanted to check out the area.

It was at that moment Saball thought he had his chance, seeing the boy was alone. He made himself visible and when Rell saw him, he yelled out for HaVon.

"You're ours finally, boy!" Saball sneered, taking the disc and throwing it in the direction of Rell.

"HaVon, help!" Rell shouted, noticing he had thrown something at him.

"Rell!" HaVon called out his name. As he turned and saw Saball, he let out a roar.

The disc he had thrown was getting close to hitting him, then suddenly from where Ranforray was hiding, he jumped out in between the disc and Rell making himself the target. He yelled out, "My lady!" As the disc hit him, it caused a bright flash. Ranforray fell to the ground covered in the crystal, not moving and looking lifeless.

"What just happened, who was that?" Rell had no idea what he had just seen.

It was then at that moment everything was suddenly frozen in time; nothing was moving. Rell and HaVon were both motionless but not the same could be said for Saball. He just stood there, he had no idea why everything wasn't moving, and started looking around, confused. He knew the disc he had thrown had hit some creature and not the boy, but he did notice for some reason whatever it was threw itself in the way. For some reason, the boy and dragon were not moving and he knew it wasn't because of him, but also he knew how important it was to bring the boy back, so he started to walk toward him. Suddenly, he was blinded by a bright green light and he let a roar; it shook the ground. Suddenly, he knew what was going on.

"You're not thinking, Saball," from the green light walked out Dawla, "both of you should know by now, I've been watching over him and won't let anything happen to them," she said as she walked toward him, smiling.

"Dawla!" Saball growled. "You won't be able to stop us, like you couldn't do before."

"You were lucky the last time. You just tell him we're taking Lanila back," she spoke as she walked toward him. "You won't have a chance this time, he's stronger than you two realize."

"We will destroy everyone this time!" he let out another thunderous roar and she just shook her head, smiling.

Just as he let out that roar, the grounds around them began to shake and tremble, even getting his attention, He did not know where it was coming from. Dawla smiled at his reaction.

"It's OK, calm down," she said, looking to the ground, "I've got this." It was as if she was talking to something. "Now, Saball, be sure to tell Shaydon he won't stop this." she winked.

"I'm not going to let you stop me from getting the boy, I need him!" he lunged in his direction.

She just shook her head, almost amazed by what he was trying to attempt. She hit her staff into the ground, causing a blinding green light and then he was gone. Whatever she had just done to him, he was now gone, nowhere in sight. She then turned and saw Ranforray lying there, lifeless, and walked up to him. Kneeling down by his side, she reached out and touched him. It instantly freed him of the crystal, bringing him back to life.

"Thank you, my lady," he said, thankful for what she had just done. "I'm so sorry!" You could see he felt bad for what happened.

"It's OK, Ranforray," she replied, touching his face, "you did good."

"Are they going to be OK?" he noticed that Rell and HaVon were still not moving.

"They'll be as soon as we leave and won't even know what happened," she looked at him.

"You're not going to let them know you helped?" he asked as he looked back.

"For now, it's important they do this on their own and we only help when they need it," she said, smiling. He knew she had her reasons.

"What about Saball, where did he go?" Ranforray asked, noticing he was nowhere in sight.

"Let's go, OK?" she did not answer him but smiled. "Let's just say he won't be bothering him anytime soon." She placed the staff into the air and as the green light appeared, they went to walk through it. She turned once and smiled, you could tell how important they were to her and Lanila.

The entire time this was going on between her and Saball, she thought since they were motionless neither one of them could see what was happening. She had no idea, but would soon learn, how strong Rell's mind really was. He may have been frozen, but he was able to see all that was happening, including seeing her and what she just did. Just as the green light disappeared, both Rell and HaVon were able to move again.

"Where did he go?" HaVon roared again as he looked around.

"You didn't see what just happened?" Rell asked, looking up at him. "Who was that woman and where did she go?" He walked toward where he had seen her, looking in every direction.

"What woman?" asked HaVon, following him as he was looking around. "I didn't see anyone but that creature, then there was that furry thing that jumped out of nowhere and somehow became frozen." He saw it was gone as well and then he wondered if he had seen what he thought.

"She was standing right here, that furry thing moved when she touched it, then it turned into what kind of looked like a person, then they both went into a green light." Then Rell began to wonder if indeed he saw what he thought. They were both very confused by what had just happened.

"I don't know, Rell, I wasn't able to see anything until I could move," said HaVon, looking around. "Tell you what, we need to head to the Elders before anything else happens." HaVon looked down at him, not having any explanation for what they had seen.

Suddenly, they noticed the boulders that rose out of the ground for them to enter started to receded back into Lanila like they were before. So much was changing as they both looked at one another, realizing it, they knew this was what they needed to find. It was the beginning to all that was about to change around them. They merged together and took to the air with force, heading back in the direction of the Elders.

The young adventures went on their way back to let the Elders know what they had discovered, they had so many questions of what they had seen and encountered as well. They hoped the Elders would be able to help guide them, after seeing these forever trees they just needed to know which way to go.

In the part of the land where we were first introduced to Dawla, the green light appeared and out of it walked both her and Ranforray.

"I can't thank you enough for coming when I called out for you," said Ranforray as he looked at her. "So what did happen to Saball, where did you send him?"

"I'll always be there for you, my friend," she said as she smiled. "As for Saball, let's just say I sent him back to where he belongs." She snickered. "Shaydon will know now that I'm watching over them."

"Because of what Saball tried to do and with what he had to do?" You could see he still felt somewhat responsible for what happened.

"Ranforray, I said you're fine. It was only a matter of time before they would have figured it out." She seemed not worried. "It's good in a way this happened, because they might think twice before trying anything like that again. It lets them know they're being watched and they will not go unchecked," she said as they walked next to one another.

Dawla mentioned he was back from where he started and she was right. Saball lay in the land of reflections, still not awake from what she had done to him. But that wouldn't last for long for Shaydon had seen him from the formation at the top. He let out a roar that shook the grounds around him, waking Saball. He slowly sat up, rubbing and shaking his head. Finally able to focus in, he began to look around and saw where he was. He knew this wouldn't be good as he looked up and saw Shaydon. He slowly rose to his feet, still drained from whatever she had done and slowly started to walk in his direction.

"Saball!" Shaydon roared his name as he landed at his feet. "Where's the boy?" his voice was deeper, showing his anger.

"My lord, it was Dawla, she was there," he said, rubbing his neck that was still sore from the encounter.

"What do you mean Dawla was there?" hearing her name upset him even more.

"I had the boy there in my sights and I did as you told me, I threw the disc at him," he said, looking down, "then this creature who I've never seen before jumped in front of it, crystalizing it and not the boy." Shaydon wasn't happy and Saball could see it. "Then everything including the boy and dragon were frozen in time when she appeared."

"I knew she was involved; from what happened at the willow, it all makes even more sense now." Shaydon turned, with Saball following him.

"Also, my lord, it seemed as if there was something else there with us. I couldn't see anything but the grounds began to tremble and when she said something, it suddenly stopped."

"Something else?" He stopped and looked at Saball. "You said the grounds were trembling?"

"Yes, my lord, then I went to lunge at him and was blinded by this bright green flash and woke up here." He lowered his head. "I failed you, this I know, but I promise it won't happen again."

"Dawla, you may think you are ahead of us, but you'll soon find out you're not." He then looked down at Saball. "I know you won't, it's time everyone prepares." An evil smirk appeared on his face.

"You want me to go?" It was if he knew what was next. "I'll return as soon I can, let them know that the time will soon be upon us." He turned to leave the valley.

"Hold on, Saball!" He stops in his tracks. "Be warned, we know now that they're watching, tell them soon."

"I will." He knelt before him then took off.

It's clear they seemed to have a plan to stay ahead of her, they must have considered possibly failing to be able to stop this new beginning. Saball was now heading off to let someone or something know about how it won't be much longer till they would be needed. After hearing about Dawla, you could see the aggravation in the way Shaydon walked, heading back to the formation on the cliff. This looked to be an important part of what they needed, the attention he gave to it; but the question was how. As we leave Shaydon seeing that there are so many changes happening, finally our young adventures were getting closer to the Elders.

"Hey, Rell, what do you think happened to that creature? It was there one minute then gone," said HaVon, as they flew.

"I really don't know," Rell hesitated a bit before answering him.

"Who's the woman you keep thinking about, you're convinced she had something to do with it." Rell had forgotten about their connection, so this surprised him.

"I don't understand, HaVon, how I saw her and you didn't, it makes me wonder what I saw." He was confused. "The one thing I do remember is that creature took my mom. It was there and then she did something and he wasn't." He seemed bothered.

"Hey, don't worry, I believe you saw what you're saying and know the Elders will be able to help with this." He was trying to ease his mind.

"Thanks, HaVon, that means a lot," he said, knowing he was trying to help.

When they finally realized they were at the peaks, they sped up to the ledge. You could see the relief they felt when they landed, separating as they did. They could see the Elders up ahead by the pool, and it looked as if Rell couldn't stop thinking about the woman he'd seen. When they got closer to Cliffon and the Elders, they could tell something had happened to them.

"Young ones, we're glad to see you've returned." They knew there was more as Rell seemed to be thinking hard about something. "Whatever happened seems to have you troubled," Cliffon said, looking at Rell.

"We went back as you suggested, hoping it might help us and it did show us something." HaVon spoke up as he knew what was on Rell's mind.

"I'm sorry about that." Rell looked at them hesitatingly. "HaVon's right, we did find something, but all it did was give us so many more questions that have us wondering."

"What do you mean even more questions?" Cliffon responded.

Rell looked up at HaVon who nodded with a smile; it seemed to relax him, so he went on to tell them about what they had found on the fireplace. How it opened the boulders that were behind his home. Looking up at them, he saw he had their full attention. As he went on, they could see he seemed troubled, he told them of what they had found inside one of the boulders. Telling them how it showed a place called the land of the forever trees.

"It's speaking of the Ludes," they all answered at one time, smiling.

"So, Elders, you do know of this place?" HaVon felt certain they would have the answers.

"We do, the Ludes live where the trees are the size of mountains and are allies to the new beginning," Cliffon spoke up.

"They did seem large," Rell responded. "So you know where we can find them? I believe that we are connected."

"Rell, why do you say connected?" Cliffon looked at him.

"Show them your arm," HaVon knew once they saw what happened they would understand.

"Cliffon, it's one of the others." One of the Elders took note of what they could see, the way it was connected with the dragon, and they all began to smile.

"It truly is!" Cliffon could feel the excitement in the air after seeing it. "What it showed you are the Ludes; they're led by King Edbow and we know the direction they can be found in."

"That's great!" they both answered at the same time.

"We're glad to see you're excited about this," the Elders all looked at one another as Cliffon looked at Rell, "but what are you not telling us?"

"I saw that creature that took my mother, he was there again," said Rell as he looked up at him.

"That's Saball, we have spoken of him," they all looked at one another. "When you saw him, this took place at your home?"

"That was Saball, he's the one Ravin told me took her life?" You could see how angry HaVon had become, having been so close. "I wish I had known."

"I feel the same," Rell looked up at him, "but we know now they are trying to stop us, I promise you we'll have our chance." He then smiled sadly. "But both mom and Ravin would want us not to stop, they both lost their life for this new beginning."

"You're right, Rell, we'll see him again." He felt the same but finding the others was important. "I saw him after we came out of the boulder, he must have been waiting for us." HaVon looked over at Cliffon.

"What did he do?" Cliffon seemed a bit worried hearing this.

"I don't know, all I can remember is he was there and then we couldn't move. When we finally could, he was gone." HaVon knew how crazy that seemed.

"I'm telling you, HaVon, it was that woman I saw, she helped us," Rell spoke up.

"You said a woman helped you?" the Elders all looked at one another.

"Yes, for some reason when we were motionless, I could see her." He took a deep breath. "By what I saw looked like she was there to help," he said, waiting to hear their response.

"Do you remember, Rell, what she looked like?" You could see they seemed eager to find out.

"She had long copper hair, also seemed to be wearing a suit that almost looked like mine, it was mostly green but had some gold in it as well," he was trying to remember even the smallest details as he answered.

"Can you remember if she was caring a gold staff?" Cliffon looked at him with a grin.

"Yes, she was." Looking up at HaVon, Rell asked, "Do you know who she is?"

"I believe we do. Hearing you speak of her brings a great joy to us all." They were all smiling. "You're right about thinking she was there helping you; not only that, it seems to be she's also watching over you as well."

"Who is she though, why would she be watching over us?" Rell was still eager to find out who the mysterious woman was that had helped them.

"Her name is Dawla," the Elders spoke at one time.

"That was the lady of the Lanila?" Rell remembered all the stories he had heard, plus what the journal had said about her as well.

"Told you they would be able to help us." HaVon could see the relief on Rell's face. "But why was Rell the only one that could see her?"

"Were the two of you merged together when this happened?" Cliffon asked.

"No, we weren't, we had just come out of the first boulder," HaVon responded.

"Then that's why, HaVon. It was his mind that gave him the ability to see through her powers." You could tell HaVon now understood.

"How did we get frozen where we couldn't move?" They both were curious to find this out.

"She had to have known about Saball's presence, then did that to keep you protected." Hearing this relaxed them both.

"So she probably wasn't aware I could see her?" Rell was curious why.

"We're sure there's a possibility she might have known." This just confused Rell even more. "What's good to know is that she's OK, it pleases us to know we're not the only ones watching over you both," Cliffon said, trying to ease their mind and letting them know it would be alright. "Now you see this new beginning is so important for all of Lanila?" He smiled at them.

"So much around us is changing, to think this is only the beginning," HaVon spoke up, looking down at Rell.

"You're right, it is," Rell agreed. "So, Elders, which way do we go to find these Ludes and the land of the forever trees?" He knew there were so many more questions he wanted to ask, but at the same time how important it was to find out more about the others first. "I know in time all that we wonder will be answered and become much clearer to us."

"I agree with that," HaVon looked at him. "In fact, I know it will," he responded with a big smile, "so which way do we head?" They both wanted to get this journey started.

"We are so very proud and honored to have you standing before us," Cliffon spoke up, letting them know where they would find their next journey.

He went on to tell them it would be a distance that they would have to travel, letting them know to be cautious while flying with what had happened. He explained that they'll come upon the trees of land that they seek and will need to land. Looking at one another, they were slightly confused why that was. So Cliffon told them that they wouldn't be able to fly above them, now that Saball and Shaydon had showed that they were out to stop this new beginning and it would be safer for them both.

"We hope you both understand, it's going to take some time for you to understand all your abilities as one." the two listened carefully. "Right now, what's important is to help you find the others that will assist you." The Elders looked at one another. "We believe that's why Dawla helped you, she too knows how important it is for Lanila."

They continued telling them about some of the landmarks they would see, letting them know what they needed to avoid as well. They explained it would take time for Lanila to be safe all over like it was before, letting them know even when it's all completed and restored, they were sure there would always be something out there, especially when they see what Rell and HaVon are capable of, they would try and bring it all back down.

"You know, my mother used to tell me something similar," Rell smiled, "for everything positive you do to rise up, there would be a negative that would try and bring you further down." He placed his hand to his heart.

"She sounds like an amazing woman." Cliffon could see he cared a great deal for her.

"She really was. Every new day, I thank her for all I've become." Rell looked up at HaVon. "From what I've heard, the same can be said for Ravin as well." A big smile came over HaVon's face as well.

Hearing this just brought a great feeling to the Elders; they could see this bond these two were beginning to have between one another was strengthening. They smiled.

"The blue moon is rising, young ones," Cliffon pointed out how much time has passed.

"It is." They both wanted to learn so much more, but they had their directions and this was important.

"HaVon, let's go back to your cave and rest for the new day's adventure," Rell suggested, looking up at him.

"Then that's where we'll go, Rell. Thank you, Elders, for helping us in the direction we need to go." They both kneeled.

"Hopefully the next time we see you, the questions we're searching for will finally be answered," Rell spoke up. He hoped that this new direction would lead them to one of the others.

They now had the direction to head and what they needed to look for, they were also advised to be careful while traveling to the land of the forever trees. As the two headed toward the ledge, the Elders just watched them. You could see in their expressions how pleased they all were and how happy they were to hear of Dawla's return. It was now only a matter of time till they would be joined by another that would help in their journey, they also knew that there would be challenges ahead that would truly test them both.

"What a day! I can't wait to jump into the spring," Rell looked up at HaVon with a big smile.

"I knew you would enjoy it," he snickered in a playful manner. "Are you ready?" He looked down and Rell nodded.

Rell reached over, touching him, and they merged.

Now the young adventurers had the direction of where they needed to head, they needed to find out if there was a connection with one of these others they were searching for. They might have some of their questions answered that they were wondering about, but there would be so many more that would be revealed as well. Watching them taking off into the blue moon light was truly amazing, the way it seemed to glow off of them.

"You know, I'm excited about all the journeys we're going to take, we're going to see places that I could only imagine in my mind," Rell spoke up.

"By the way the Elders talked, I have to agree I look forward to that as well." You could tell HaVon was just as ready.

"You know this is the first time we've flown at night. See the way the moonlight shines off of the lake?" He could see through HaVon's eyes.

"Well, I'm glad you're enjoying this." HaVon had flown over these lakes many times before, hearing that he realized he never took in the true beauty.

So he dove down to where he was flying right over the lake, seeing their reflection he could feel how much Rell was enjoying it. They finally could see the cave in the distance. Speeding up, they came to the landing and as they touched the ground, HaVon reached over to the mark on his leg and they separated.

"You know this flying is getting so much easier for me, plus that was awesome flying over the lake," Rell's smile said it all.

"I can feel you are becoming more at ease. Tell you what, how about we race to the spring?" HaVon smiled, taking off, thinking he didn't have a chance to catch him.

For the first time he was about to see something that Rell had only done once before. Just as it seemed he was going to beat him, a blur of a gold passed by him. He stopped in his tracks, wondering how Rell did what he just saw.

"What just happened, how did you do that?" he saw Rell smiling from the spring at him.

"I might have a few tricks of my own I haven't shared," he started laughing at seeing the look of confusion on HaVon's face.

"I see that, but how?" HaVon was trying to figure it out. "It's the suit that helped you?"

"Well, not exactly, I've done that once before and thought why not try it again," he smiled. "Mom always told me if I believe in my mind then anything is possible."

"She's right, I just saw it myself. That was amazing." He smiled and jumped into the spring, causing a large wave that overcame Rell and resurfaced. "It makes me wonder when we're one, do you think we're able to do that?"

"We might just have to find that out one day," Rell smiled then splashed him for the wave he caused.

"You know, Rell, I'm glad you're here and that we've been brought together," HaVon said, followed by a big smile.

"I was just thinking the same thing," said Rell, splashing him again. "So what they said about the Ludes and their king…"

"About how the mark will help us, at the same time letting them know who we are?" he finished as he floated by Rell. "I guess we'll soon find out."

"You're right, we'll see, I just feel this is going to answer a lot of questions," said Rell, wiping the water from his eyes, "but I wonder what will come after this journey." He then dove under the water.

HaVon followed his lead and did the same, making a good point they may know the way to head now. But where would the journey take them to find the rest of these others, the two didn't worry for now but enjoyed the spring together.

The last time we had heard of Saball, he was sent to somewhere new, while at the land of reflection the crystal formation that stood at the top was no longer there. Then, something could be seen coming out of the cave; by the size of the shadows, it appeared to be Shaydon.

"It's time we do as before." He jumped down with an evil grin on his face and walked toward the opening of the valley. "It's time I let the valley warriors know the time is coming." It was clear he had a destination in mind but who were these warriors he spoke of?

As Shaydon was leaving the valley, he became engulfed in a black mass, he did something we haven't seen yet; he changed his appearance. He looked almost like a man but was four times larger than one, his body covered in something similar to armor. It was black and silver with a large double-bladed axe to his side, his eyes hadn't changed though, still solid silver an earie look.

"OK, Dawla, they may have help of their own," his evil laugh was echoing off the walls, "but you'll soon learn that they're not the only ones." He took off in a new direction and it seemed like always he was up to no good.

There was so much change happening for the young adventurers, and by the looks of things, they had many more surprises ahead of them. Seeing Shaydon being able to change his appearance showed us his true power, but what we just saw him do has no limits. With our young adventurers finally resting for the new day ahead, we see back at the Grelands, Dawla had been busy as well. They seemed to have help of their own, and they looked like they were created by the land around.

"Ranforray, they should be of great help to all of us; it's so amazing what they can do." You could see how happy she seemed to be.

"My lady!" they all put their hands to their chest. "We thank you for waking us, we will do anything to help you and this new beginning we all have been waiting for," one of them spoke out.

They were called the Gramudds and had always been there for her.

"You're very welcome and the same to all of you." Her smile just brought happiness to them all.

"So you believe it will help them?" Ranforray looked at her.

"I know it will." Then, it was like a thought came over her as she stopped and looked at him. "I have an idea of how they can start helping him and it would mean so much as well."

"My lady, what is it?" he could see she seemed excited.

"I remember when you called me when they first needed help—" she had something on her mind.

"I'm sorry for that again," he still felt a little shame for what happened.

"No, not that, Ranforray," she said, placing her hand to his face. "The way it was around his house, there was nothing left of his home." She smiled big, looking at him and the Gramudds.

"What are you thinking?" he could see her reaction.

"We should take the Gramudds back to his home or what's left of it," she smiled, "clean it all up and rebuild it for him. I know they won't be around there and we should have the time."

"Are you sure, my lady?" he knew she didn't want them to know of her help right now.

"I'm certain when the new day is here for them, they'll be on their way to the forever trees. It would give us the time we need and it would give him a home to come back to. This could be the difference he needs but this time with a few changes to be sure it never happens again." It was clear how important this was for her and they all agreed.

"We shall do as you wish," said Ranforray as he placed his hand to his chest.

"Thank you, Ranforray, this will be great surprise!" She wanted this to be a priority and was very excited. "You know if you need me…"

"I know." He turned to the Gramudds and told them of what they were to do.

"We shall make it better than ever, Lady Dawla, we promise you that," they all placed their hands to their chest.

"I thank you all for this, it will make a difference in helping the new beginning." She held the staff to the air. "Are you ready?"

"We are!" they all spoke at one time.

She placed the staff into the ground and a green light appeared. The Gramudds disappeared into it. Then just, as Ranforray went to walk through too, she stopped him by placing her hand to his head. It seemed she was transferring a vision to him, the memories of some things she wanted to stay that was important. He nodded and walked into the green light. The smile on her face said it all, so many changes were happening in Lanila; seeing Shaydon change his appearance, Dawla sending Ranforray, and the Gramudds building back Rell's home. With all this going on, Saball was in a place where the land had no color and the rain never stopped.

"I can't stand this place; it drives me crazy!" One could hear the frustration in his voice as he wiped the water from his face.

He continued walking, knowing now this wasn't a place he enjoyed. You could see a castle in the distance; like the surrounding, it had no color and was just gray everywhere you looked. When he approached what looked to be a draw bridge, you could see there was life here. From the shadows, two large figures, not quite as tall as Saball or as muscular, approached him.

"What are you doing here, Saball?" one of them spoke in a deep voice.

"You know better," said Saball, looking at the one that spoke out. "Lower this bridge." You could hear in the tone of his voice he had no respect for them.

With that said, the one that spoke whistled and the bridge began to be lowered. Looking around, it was gray all around, nothing had color. You could see it was built for strength though. The ones that seemed to call this their home were called the Harbsides and were grayish in color. They all seemed to have triangular marks under their eyes and were twice the size of a regular man.

"Shalcox will want to know you're here," the one that had spoken out led the way.

"Why do you think I'm here, to see you?" Saball walked past them. You could tell he wasn't worried by them at all. "Come on, let's go."

The look on both of their faces when he bullied past them showed they felt the same for him. The walls inside were very tall, and seemed to be made out of nothing other than large gray stones. Saball looked around as they made their way through the castle, he passed up what looked to be the women and even some that resembled children. It seemed by the look on their faces they also seemed not too pleased to see him. He snarled at them as he approached a staircase that led up even higher.

"See, we all still feel the same for one another," his evil tone was followed by a laugh that filled the air.

"Why should we be?" one spoke out. "We have no choice, but I guess you remember that." Whatever had happened, it was clear they didn't care for him.

"But you did," Saball grinned evilly, "You're just smarter than that knowing what Shaydon would have done. I have had enough of this talk." There was certainly more to it than what appeared from Saball's words.

The closer they got to the top, the more it opened up, it was so opposite of what it was like below. Everywhere you looked, it was colorful and had gold laying all over. There were fancy tapestry hanging all around with a throne in the middle. Sitting on the throne was what looked to be a man of sorts; he was a third of everyone else's size and had gray hair. On his left hand and arm, he was wearing what looked like some sort of glove and covered his entire arm. It was black and silver. It looked to have some similarity to Saball's ring. For a small individual, he seemed very muscular.

"Saball!" unlike the others he greeted him with open arms. "I have missed my old friend." He stood up and approached him with his hand extended.

"Unlike the others, I see," said Saball as he extended his hand as well.

"Never mind them, they don't respect true power like I do." He smiled. "Come on, let us sit down and catch up. Get us drinks now," he yelled out as they approached a large table and sat down, one at each end. "Seeing you must only mean thing, this new beginning has finally begun." From the stairway, one of the Harbsides brought them drinks in large gold mugs.

Seeing how they acted different to one another, then hearing what Shalcox had said, it appeared he must have known of this new beginning. By his reaction, you could see he was one of them that was against the changes. It was now clear that Saball was sent here for a reason. They looked to be talking about him being ready for when they needed him. With Shaydon heading in a new direction and Saball here, it was clear they were preparing for what they would do ahead.

"Tell Shaydon I can't thank him enough for all I have." Looking around, it now made sense how this part of the castle seemed so different from the rest. "What does he need me to do?"

"Looking around here, are you sure they'll listen?" Saball questioned as he sipped his drink.

"Trust me, they know better," he smirked looking at the glove he wore. "Let's just say this helped those that questioned me. Thank him for this as well, they listen so much better now," he said laughing out loud.

This explained why all the Harbsides seemed to act the way they did. Without this glove and whatever power it had, Shalcox probably wouldn't have the control he did, seeing his size against the Harbsides. This meant that he more than likely abused those that didn't listen; it was clear he had no respect for them at all. It looked like they had no choice and had to listen, especially having Shaydon and Saball on his side made it even harder for them.

With the two of them talking here, the young adventurers were still resting for the new day ahead. Totally unaware of the surprise Dawla was planning for him, the green light appeared at Rell's home as the Gramudds and Ranforray walked through.

"What happened here, Ranforray?" the Gramudds looked at all the havoc that was caused and could tell someone had lost a lot.

"It was a terrible creature, he tried to get this boy and stop him from his future; this new beginning we've been waiting for," answered Ranforray, shaking his head seeing it all in the light. There was nothing left. "It took his mother's life as well."

"His mother too?" this got the attention of them all. "This poor boy to lose so much." Even though they did not know him, you could still hear the compassion in their voices.

"It truly is, that's why Dawla has sent all of us here," he looked at them with a smile, "she wants to help him by giving him a home to come back to." Suddenly, they were distracted by the green light as Dawla walked through. "My lady, I thought you were going to stay in Grelands?"

"I was, then I started thinking and changed my mind," she said as she looked around and smiled, knowing how much this would help him. "Other than coming here to help with Saball," she paused, "it's been sometime since I've been here."

"You've been here before?" This got Ranforray's attention. "Why didn't you say anything about this before?" They may have shared a lot but this was new to him.

"Many cycles have passed and I have had my reasons," she smiled and that was enough for him to understand.

They began to clean up the area of all the debris.

Seeing what she had planned to do, this would be a great surprise for Rell the next time he returned. They had great intentions, knowing when it's all done, it would be a great improvement. With everyone working so hard cleaning the area, she had walked in the direction of the back of the house as Ranforray smiled. You could see how hard it was at times, looking at what was left as she walked through the debris toward the fireplace, looking for the mark on it.

"Ranforray?" calling out for him, she kneeled down, picking it up. "I need you to save this," she said, handing it to him.

"As you wish, my lady." He put it in a special place and got back to work.

This was so important to her as she made her way to the front of the house, you could see how happy she was that they were doing this for him. She smiled watching how everyone was helping, then turned and headed in the way of the willow. We can see why they call her the Lady of Lanila; the way she cared for everyone and everything that was around.

While all this was going on here, Shaydon was headed into a new direction. He had transformed his appearance, showing more of his abilities and power. He walked in a place similar to his. But these valley walls were brown and ridged with a dry appearance to them, seeing this place and where Saball was, it really makes one wonder how much the great battle had taken from the land, perhaps these were the repercussions of it. He entered this valley, when he did suddenly, he could hear grunting and it was becoming even louder. It even caused the ground to tremble a bit, then you could see movement coming from the caves. When they became more visible, they resembled the form he had taken, unlike where Saball had gone, they all came out grunting with their hands to their chest and kneeled as he passed. They appeared to be allies.

"Our lord!" From the distance, an even larger figure approached. "We're always ready when we see you, we all have been waiting for your return." Maybe Shaydon knew if he tried to stop the boy from this new beginning, he might possibly fail and had been already preparing for it just in case.

"Jadard, I wasn't able to stop him and they have joined, I need you to be ready like we have planned." They approached one another and extended their arms. "All your valley warriors look strong; I need them to be ready for what's ahead." Unlike the Harbsides where Saball was, these warriors seemed more welcoming and eager to help.

Jadard's skin was tanned like the grounds around them, showing they spent a lot of their time in the suns. To his sides were large double-sided axes, compared to his height it wasn't even close to touching the ground. He was very muscular like the rest but they seemed a bit shorter, as they all began to walk toward what looked to be a large fire pit. It was surrounded by large stumps that made a circle as they all sat down.

"It's been many cycles, my lord, we thought we might not have to worry about this," Jadard said, as they all looked at one another.

"Jadard, I as well. It seems they have some protection and guidance of their own," Shaydon replied, looking at him. "It looks as if Dawla has resurfaced and wants to interfere to help them."

"My lord, did you say Dawla?" They all looked at one another. "Never thought we would hear her name again." You could tell they didn't want to hear her name.

"Don't worry about Dawla." He saw the reaction they had. "I'll take care of her." He paused, a bit frustrated. "I want you and the valley warriors to be ready for when I need you."

It was clear they seemed troubled hearing her name, but he needed them to concentrate on the plans he had for them. They began to talk among themselves.

While Shaydon had been on a quest of his own, Dawla had finally reached the willow. Knowing this was a place where Rell had spent a lot of his time, she stood there looking at it. She smiled from ear to ear.

"My, you have grown so much, my dear," she whispered, walking up to it. A golden glow came over the willow; it looked as if the branches reached out for her. "Thank you, you have done so well keeping him safe." This had been a present to Rell's father from her. "We're doing something special for him that I know he'll love," the branches let go, "thank you for this." She smiled then turned to head back in the direction of the house. Looking down in her hand, she had taken some of the tree branches with her. "This will help so much; I'll plant you closer to keep what we're doing safe from harm."

Heading back, she saw the day was getting longer. Coming to the last hill, she stopped and looked at where Rell's home used to be. She noticed they had already cleared and cleaned the entire area. She walked toward them and you could see how pleased she was having it all done already.

"This is amazing, you've cleared it all," her voice showed how happy she was.

"Just as you asked of us, my lady, they're a great help too," Ranforray smiled at the Gramudds, letting them know how much they were appreciated.

"The day has gotten away from us; everyone has done so much here to help let us return." She placed her staff into the ground the green light appeared. They were all walking through it when she again stopped Ranforray. "Hold on, I need to put these in the ground."

"What are those, my lady?" He could see they had a golden glow to them.

"They're part of an old friend and they'll help." She went to each end of where the house used to be, planting each piece into the ground.

"Decoration?" he had no idea what she was doing.

"Ranforray," she looked up at him and smiled, liking his wise comment, "not decoration but protection, so this will never happen to him again." She rose up after planting the last one with a big smile. "It's all ready, come on, let's head back." She put her arm around him as they walked into the light.

Then just as they walked through the light and it was gone, that's when the true magic of Dawla and Lanila began. Suddenly, from where the house used to stand, the spots she had just planted parts of the tree began to glow brightly. It had the same look as the golden light from the willow as it began to pulsate. It began to consume the entire area where nothing could be seen. Then suddenly, it let out a powerful pulse of energy and then it was gone. The magic and powers of Dawla had given him a home. Unlike his old home, it had only one level and looked to be larger, the branches she had planted at both ends were now two very large willows. They looked similar to the one on the hill, and they were here to protect him along with this beautiful new home he now had. The power and abilities of Dawla, seeing what she was capable of doing, was enlightening to see as this was what Rell needed. It was showing that indeed, she would be a great ally and friend to both Rell and HaVon.

Chapter Sixteen

With all these new changings happening around Lanila, Rell having no idea of the surprise that awaited him back at his home. The suns were finally beginning to rise into the sky; to think that the two adventurers would still be resting was further from the truth. Instead, both of them were sitting by the lake at HaVon's favorite spot. From the look on both of their faces, it appeared they were ready, no matter what they faced, including any surprises along the way.

"You know, HaVon, so much has changed already. To think, we're about to find out more of what's to come," said Rell as he looked up at him.

"I can remember all the times asking Ravin when I would be able to see the Elders," HaVon grinned a bit. "How much has changed even with you, I couldn't think of anybody better to do it with than you, Rell," he said, smiling down at him.

"Thanks, it means a lot to me. One of the reasons I'm not too worried about what's ahead." He smiled. "I have a dragon!" Then, he started laughing, "A real-life dragon!" The boy in him was coming out as he stood up. Hearing that, you could tell HaVon was just as excited.

"That's right, you do. Together, we can do this, Rell." As he stretched, he did something he hadn't done before; he let out a roar that shook the ground.

"Wow!" Rell exclaimed, taking his hand away from his ears. "Sounds like someone else is ready!"

Then without another word, Rell reached over and touched the mark on his shoulder. It was still amazing how the suit worked its way through the mark, covering his body. With an extremely large smile on his face, he turned and reached out for HaVon, followed by that blinding golden light. They stood there, joined together. HaVon's blue eyes were piercing and the way all his scales were highlighted in gold, unlike before, his legs this time were completely covered. He spread his wings and took to the air with a great force.

They were headed in an entirely new direction of Lanila. Having no idea what they would find ahead of them, but they were excited and ready nonetheless.

Back at the Grelands, Dawla, Ranforray, and the Gramudds had already prepared themselves to settle in from the day. Some of the them had gathered around a fire and you could feel how happy everyone seemed; they were dancing and laughing among themselves. Some of them stood around what looked to be their homes; very sturdy buildings and also seemed to made from the ground and were very roomy.

Dawla approached the waterfall and walked through it; she didn't even get wet. It opened up to an entirely new area that looked to be underground yet it was very bright and visible. There, it was a glamourous home; everything was so alive even without the suns' rays. This home was made of some green jade or crystal, it was spread throughout the area, which would explain how it was so easy to see. It must work as a way to light the area as well; it was truly magical.

Back where the Harbsides lived, Saball and Shalcox were still talking as he reached out and handed him something.

"What do you want me to do with this?" Shalcox asked as he held it up, looking at it. It had a lot of the same properties of the crystals from the land of the reflections.

"Keep it close, you'll know when Shaydon is in need of you." He then rose from the table. "Make sure they're all ready as well." He gave a look of disgust to the ones around, shaking his head with that evil smirk.

"They'll be ready," said Shalcox as he rose from the table and told the ones there to escort him out. "Anything for my old friend to help stop this new beginning from happening. Now follow him out."

"As you wish." Hearing in their voice, it seemed they weren't happy with either of them.

So they led him down the stairs back to where he had first entered. Nudging his way past them, he looked back with that dead smile and laughed, taking off. They watched him disappear into the rain and raised the bridge back up. As soon as it was closed, the one on the left began to look around.

He noticed no one was close so he whispered, "You heard them, right? They spoke of the new beginning." He was positive no one else was around. "We need to tell Berllard what we've heard, this might be the help we need to get out from the clutches and torture of Shalcox."

"Shhh, my friend," the other said as he looked at him, "we must be careful. These walls have ears, Shalcox must not know that we heard them, for the rest of us. Let's go." It confirmed that indeed, they seemed to be listening to Shalcox against their will.

This Berllard they spoke of, he was one of the oldest Harbsides still around; he had told stories to them of what Shalcox and Saball had been talking about. It was then that they realized, it might have not been just a story but the truth. They walked down the halls into a different area of the castle, then entered a room where there were many of them gathered together. In the center of them all was Berllard. He had aged many more cycles than the rest around him. He seemed very strong and alert as he saw them enter, and he enjoyed telling stories to them all. It was his way to help them with the life that they were forced to live, always wanting the best for the Harbsides. He knew that Shaydon gave Shalcox control of this area, with these allies they knew of their powers and were forced to listen. Berllard knew that was the only way to keep all his people safe.

"Berllard, how are you today?" they walked up to him.

"The days are getting better and better," he answered, very alert for being older, "but I feel something out there is different." He looked up.

"Saball returned," they said, looking at him.

"Do you know what was he here for?" Berllard took a drink from a mug next to him.

"He gave Shalcox some crystal, saying they would call upon him in time," they told him, hoping he might know why. "We also over heard them mention something about the new beginning."

"You heard them say this?" he asked as his eyes lit up.

"We did," they look at one another. "Is this the same one you speak of that can help us?"

"Listen carefully please, everyone," they all gathered close, "we must not speak of this again. If he knew that we have found out about this, you know what would happen." They all nodded, knowing he had always looked out for them.

"Berllard, what if it's true?" one of them asked.

"Shhh, it's true, but you must trust me," he said, looking at them. They could see the truth in his eyes.

"We always have," they all seemed to answer at one time; it looked as if they too had waited for this.

"For all our safety, we do as Shalcox says, until I can find out more and a way this new beginning can help us." You could see him thinking. "Do we all understand?"

"We do," they all answered.

"We do what?" They were so distracted they had no idea that Shalcox had made his way into the room, seeing how they all were gathered together.

"To hear a story, sir," Bellard lowered his head, quick to respond. You could tell how much he cared for them.

"Bellard, they do enjoy your stories," said Shalcox as he picked his teeth. "After you're done, I need everyone at their posts, understand? I also need some sent to me." He smiled looking at the glove as he turned and headed out.

"That I will, sir." He waited for him to leave, then said, "That was too close. Not another word for now, everyone, please stay strong. Hopefully, not for much longer." You could see how hearing that picked up everyone's spirit.

So he went on to talk with them about how careful they needed to be, as some of the Harbsides left to do as Shalcox had asked of them. They knew Berllard was right about being careful not to talk about it, his glove had the dark powers of Shaydon and it was clear that's how he controlled them. How would they be able to get to this new beginning for help, that itself would prove to be interesting to see how it all would play out. Would they prove to be hidden allies that could help our young adventurers in the quest to change things for the better around Lanila?

There was so much happening at once, the new days ahead would show so much more as well. It has finally started and in time, it would show our young adventurers exactly how important they truly were to all of Lanila. What the Elders had said, how the word of the joining of two would spread throughout Lanila, an example of this just presented itself at the Harbsides. This had just begun and to see how excited they were, would it bring more allies out or worse reveal more that are against them.

As Saball headed back to the land of reflections, Dawla and her team were resting for what was ahead. Our young adventurers were getting closer to the land of the forever trees, but Shaydon was still with Jadard and the valley warriors. They had moved and found their way into one of the caves in the valley. There was a throne-like chair and by the size it seemed to be Jadard's.

They were all gathered around what seemed to be a layout of what looked like Lanila.

"You have done well looking at all the area you have covered for recruits, but what of these areas here?" he could see some places they hadn't covered yet.

"Well, some places we seem to have problems, my lord," he paused looking next to him at who seemed to be his man-at-arms, "especially right here. Every time I send someone, they can't remember anything and wake up in an entirely new area."

"What do you mean?" this got his attention.

"Everyone that can remember anything just mention a blinding light and when they wake up, they're somewhere else." You could see it still confused him.

"Blinding light?" He growled under his breath. "What color was it?"

"My lord, I believe they all mentioned a green light," he replied, hoping that made sense to him.

"I remember what I can't stand about you, Dawla!" his voice was angry after hearing that; he hit the table with his hand.

"Are you telling me this was Dawla, my lord?" Hearing her name got Jadard's attention. "We thought for so long she was gone, you're saying this could be her doing this to my men?" You could hear almost a hesitation in his voice.

"There has to be a reason she's doing this here, if it's even her," he said as he looked at him. "Don't worry about it, just get yourself ready for when I return, that's where we will head."

"Yes, my lord, as you ask," he bowed his head. "What of this crystal you gave me?"

"Just keep it close. Right now, I need to find out about that place your men have problems at, something about this is different." He extended his arm. "I'll return soon, Jadard, just be ready."

He was extremely curious of this area that had been pointed out. As they escorted him out, the look on his face showed he was thinking hard, wondering if indeed this was Dawla's powers they had encountered, why would she be getting involved in that area? Hearing her name come out of his mouth just brought more anger out, it was evident in his steps as each one got louder.

"Jadard, it's good to see how you've been helping my cause," he said, looking at the warriors. "Be ready in time, we'll remind them why this happened in the first place." Then they all began to stomp and grunt.

He turned to leave the valley and it was clear he had the support here for what he had done and was planning to do. He did seem to be very curious of this particular area of Lanila; if she was involved, it made him wonder if the boy and his path had anything to do with it. Since she had resurfaced, it had been only where and when the boy needed help.

"There are still many parts of Lanila we need to get to, it's been too long and I want to know why this spot." He just stood there. "If this was Dawla, it has to be because of the boy," he growled in frustration.

You could see after learning about this new information, it had become his priority for the moment. It sounded like her powers and if it was, he needed to find out why she was there. He became engulfed in the black mass, changing back into his true form and took to the air. He wanted to meet up with Saball, as both of them have been busy, notifying what seemed to be allies to help them stop this new beginning.

The importance of these others that Rell and HaVon were searching for might have become more urgent than first thought. They had made it to their location now and had separated. They just stood there staring.

"I see why we had to land, I can't see through them," Rell was amazed, "they're so much bigger than I could have imagined."

"You can't even see the tops of them," you could hear in HaVon's voice the amazement he felt. "We need to be careful, Rell."

They stood in an area where everything was such a deep green and had so many bright colors everywhere. They looked at one another and slowly began to approach these massive trees. You could see them enjoying all the beauty they saw around. They both began to smile, not feeling any danger, but a welcoming feeling came over them.

"You know, I was worried at first, not knowing what to expect but now were here, I'm not," Rell looked up at him. "I wonder how many more marvels there truly are in Lanila. Look at this place, it's amazing." He was about to reach out and touch the tree's trunk.

"I feel more relaxed as well. You know, I'm sure there are so many more out there." He just gazed at their size. "Hey, be careful, Rell," he said when Rell was about to touch the tree.

"I will, it's just so massive and beautiful." The smile on his face was just as big.

Then as he placed his hand to the trunk of the tree, and his attention was quickly diverted to the white stone on his arm. It began to glow. His eyes grew larger, watching what was happening. He got HaVon's attention when suddenly, a pulse of white light overcame both of them and the tree.

"Rell, are you OK?" HaVon had no idea what he had just witnessed, but wanted to be sure he hadn't been harmed.

"I'm fine." Rell noticed the stone had stopped glowing. "What was that all about?" he asked, looking up at him; you could see he was confused.

"I don't know, Rell, but I have this feeling we'll soon find out," he replied, knowing how things had gone already, it was only a matter of time.

He wasn't further from the truth; as they stood there looking at one another trying to figure out what just happened, suddenly, they noticed the white light was back. It began to engulf the tree. When it did, it revealed an opening. It was even large enough for HaVon to enter. They both just stood there looking at one another. Then they both agreed to walk into it and as they did, it closed behind them. Being inside with it closed, it wasn't dark but bright with the white light they had seen. Then things changed, it suddenly became a blinding light, to the point where they could see nothing. They called out for one another.

"What's happening, HaVon, I can't see anything," Rell cried as he waited for an answer. "Are you there?"

"Yes, I'm still here, Rell. I don't know, but it doesn't seem harmful, just don't move." HaVon couldn't see either, not even with his sight.

"Trust me, I'm not, just don't understand why it's so bright." Not being able to see, Rell sure wasn't moving.

Then just as he asked about the light, it was gone. They tried to get their eyes to adjust. Then at almost the same time when they opened their eyes, they could see standing all around them, just staring, were smaller people. They were half the size of Rell and some were even smaller, but they all looked to be in excellent shape. They all just stood there and some of them looked to be smiling. Seeing this, Rell placed his hand to his heart.

"Hello, my name is Rell and this HaVon," he pointed at HaVon, smiling the entire time. "We're here to meet with King Edbow." He noticed they all began to whisper among themselves and seemed to be pointing as well. "Do you think they understand?" Rell asked as he looked at HaVon.

"I don't know, but something has them whispering," HaVon replied, looking at him with a big smile.

"Where do you think we are?" Rell started looking around. "You know, I think we're on the top of them."

"Top of what?" asked HaVon he looked down at him.

"I know this is going to sound crazy but the top of the trees," Rell replied, looking up at him.

"With everything we've seen already, Rell, it really doesn't but I think you're right," he said, looking around.

The closer they began to look at what they were standing on, they realized he was right – that was why there wasn't a tree in sight, they were below them. But spread throughout were what looked like tree houses, some were very large and were just as magical as the massive trees. Being the top that they seemed to be on was so flat, but what surprised them was that it was able to hold the weight of even HaVon. They stood there, still amazed by what they were seeing, and still not a word had been spoken from who they assumed were the Ludes. They just continued to stare, each of them getting the other's attention and pointing as well, when suddenly from the crowd a deep voice could be heard. "Seeing you is a relief, how we've waited so long for this!"

One of them walked through the crowd; he was the same height but more muscular than the rest and carrying a club, which looked to be made of the same white crystal as on Rell's mark.

"I'm King Edbow and we welcome you both," he said as he extended out his arm.

"King Edbow, it's an honor to meet you. My name is Rell and this is HaVon," he extended his own arm.

"Well, you are an impressive dragon and your size is breathtaking." King Edbow walked up to him, looking up. "She mentioned it and let me tell you, I understand seeing you now."

"You said she?" Rell looked at HaVon.

"I hear the curiosity in your voice," Edbow turned and looked at him. "She mentioned to me you would ask and wanted me to let you know she's a friend."

"A friend," HaVon lowered head down to talk, "so you know who we are?"

"That I do." The king turned to HaVon. "May I ask, do you?" A big smile overcame his face.

"We're learning more every day, that's what has brought us to you. We're searching for one of the others and were told you be able to help." You could see how much HaVon hoped King Edbow would have the answers they searched for.

"Indeed, I might be able to help. One of the others, you say…" he smiled at all the Ludes. "Come, let's get to know each other." The crowd split and they follow him to an area where they could sit down.

"We've been trying to figure out where all the trees went," Rell asked as he sat down next to the king.

"They're still here. You ask because you can't see them, but do you have to see them for them to be present?" Edbow chuckled with another smile. The manner in which he spoke seemed confusing. "The reason they're not visible is because we walk on what you seek."

"You were right, Rell," said HaVon as he lowered his head.

"Yes, she said your knowledge was growing stronger every day," the king looked at Rell. "Now what questions do you both have? Maybe, the answers I have are what you are searching for." He chuckles again as the rest of the Ludes joined them, sitting down.

"What was that blinding light we encountered and how did we get here?" Rell was curious.

"That was the power of teleportation," King Edbow smiled. "We had to get you here."

They both looked at each other and knew this was going to be an experience to remember.

As they sat and learned more of the Ludes and King Edbow's story, Saball had returned to the land of reflections and was searching for Shaydon. When suddenly from the distance, he saw him coming. As he approached, he hit the ground with force.

"My lord, I saw Shalcox and he said they would be ready whenever we need them," he kneeled, pleased he had had no problems.

"You gave him the crystal?" Shaydon asked as he walked past him.

"I did," he rose and followed him.

"Well, when I saw Jadard, I found out about an area of Lanila they seemed to be having a problem getting to." He stopped. "I told them I would return but instead, I'm going to send you, let them know you will go and find out why then you will inform me of what you find." He paused again. "They mentioned a green flash of light, that's why you must go."

"That sounds like the same thing that happened to me," he knew not to mention her name. "I'll find out, my lord."

"I need to know if this is her and why would she be protecting this area." Shaydon walked toward the cave. "Have them show you where they had these problems."

"Do you think this has to do with the boy?" Saball asked, remembering she had only been seen where he was. "This might be the answer we've been searching for, since we have lost his direction and can't seem to find out where he went."

"That's what I'm hoping, Saball." He stops at the bottom of the valley wall below the cave. "Keep me informed about what you find, there has to be a connection."

"I will return to Jadard and let them know I'll take care of it. We'll soon find out what it is, my lord," he said as he knelt before him before turning to head back to the valley warriors.

"I'm going to find out what it is you're protecting," said Shaydon, talking to himself as he entered the cave.

Instead of returning to help Jadard like he had first said, he sent Saball to search for the answers why. Meanwhile in the Grelands, Dawla and Ranforray had begun their new day, walking and talking to one another.

"How many of the Gramudds will we need today for his home, my lady?" he asked as he wanted to be prepared.

"Oh, Ranforray, always on top of things for me," she smiled at him, "but no need. Let them enjoy this great day; we won't need any of them."

"My lady?" You could see the confusion on his face. "I thought we were rebuilding it today?"

"Come with me, my friend, we shall return soon." She spoke to some of the Gramudds that were around, then raised her staff, and they disappeared into the green light.

With Saball headed to the valley warriors to search for answers, Dawla had taken Ranforray back to the home to show him what the powers and magic of Lanila had done. Meanwhile, back at the forever trees, Rell and HaVon had been learning so much about the Ludes, but still waited for the answers to what they were searching for – one of the others.

"So like I've told you, this is a great thing seeing the two of you standing before us," King Edbow was enjoying the time he was spending with them.

"The same can be said for us as well," Rell being sure he knew they enjoyed it as well. "I like your crystal," he added, noticing he wore the same type that was on his suit around his neck.

"May I say the same for yours," the king winked, "but are they so different?" Once again, his answers were more like questions.

"No, not so different at all, but as you would say the same," Rell smiled. "I believe it has brought us together for a reason; for you to know it's begun and to hopefully be united with one of these others."

"Oh, Rell, she had said how impressive your thoughts and feelings were." King Edbow held on to the crystal necklace. "We know now we're the same, looking for what we have lost."

"What's that?" HaVon spoke up.

"Hope, my friend, and it's standing in front of us," he smiled. "So, you keep asking of the triplets?" He looked at the Ludes as they started talking among themselves, still holding on to the necklace.

"Triplets?" You could hear the confusion in Rell's voice.

"I'm sorry, Rell, I mean one of the others." Edbow then rose to his feet.

"So the triplets you're speaking of are what we're searching for?" He now had the attention of them both.

"But, Rell, I ask you what makes you so sure what you seek is just one?" Once again, the biggest smile came over his face. You could see how much he enjoyed twisting his words, making you wonder what you asked.

"So the one is three?" he was even more confused.

"Are they here now?" curious, HaVon began to look around.

Then all King Edbow did was smile, still holding on to his necklace and Rell could see it had begun to glow. At that same moment, the mark on Rell's suit did the same and he brought it to HaVon's attention, then for the first time, all the Ludes while sitting down looked to the sky. Then they all leaned forward, placing their hands to the ground. The young adventurers looked at one another, having no idea what was going on. King Edbow then winked at them, as they noticed the blue skies above them began to get blanketed with white clouds. It took a moment, as they watched this happening; suddenly, they watched as the clouds moved around. They seemed to have come to life; as the white clouds began to move until all they could see were three above them.

"Girls, it's time. They've come," King Edbow spoke up and they both wondered who he was talking to.

Their attention was soon changed, noticing something was happening to the three clouds above them. The look on their faces was that of astonishment at the magic that they were seeing right before their eyes; the three clouds were surrounded with same bright white light. They watched each cloud begin to form into a dragon, but smaller.

"That's what we're searching for?" Rell looked over at King Edbow, who was smiling. "It's one of the others, HaVon!"

"But it's three. I'm confused, they don't seem too big," HaVon was at a loss a bit as he looked at them.

He was speaking of their size and from a distance, they did seem smaller. As they got closer to them, they both could see they had a sparkle to their white scales. They also noticed each of them had a blue chest that went down their under belly; they were truly beautiful to see. The Ludes all stood, you could see how excited everyone was to see them all together. As they landed in front of them, Rell and HaVon were amazed what they were seeing.

"Hey, Dad!" they all spoke at the same time, then looked at HaVon. "Well, aren't you a big one," once again, speaking at the same time.

"Dad?" Rell turned to King Edbow.

"Is it Dad or just a person they know loves and cares for them?" he said as he smiled. "We are all family here in the forever trees and look out for one another."

"That we do, Dad," once again they all answered at the same time.

They stood before the both of them, noticing they were smaller, about a third of the size of HaVon and they also seemed to be juveniles as well. Looking at their scales closely, you could see that each scale was highlighted in shade of blue. They all had eyes of white with a hint of light blue in their irises; they were beautiful but eerie at the same time. They both noticed their wings were so much larger than their bodies; at least three times bigger.

"These are my girls." King Edbow patted each one of them on the head, you could see how much they did care for him.

"Hello, girls," Rell spoke up as HaVon smiled. "My name is Rell and this is HaVon."

"Hello, little ones," HaVon lowered his head to talk to them. "You are a sight to see and a relief at the same time. It's been so long since dragons have been around, I look forward to our future together."

You could see in Rell's face how happy he was to hear him greet them in the way he did.

"You three are truly beautiful," Rell said as he approached them with his hand out.

"It's OK, girls," King Edbow smiled at them and they approached him with eagerness.

"I could never have imagined this," he said as he looked back at HaVon, "seeing and touching even more dragons." You could hear the kid in him coming out, he was so excited.

"It's a new beginning!" HaVon responded.

"It truly is, my friend." A big smile came over his face. "You're so amazing and beautiful." He touched them all. "What are your names?"

"We're the girls," they respond at the same time.

"Don't be alarmed, Rell," King Edbow could see his reaction and explained, "for their entire life, all we have called them are 'our girls,' plus, since they looked so much alike, it seemed easier."

"I understand that." He could see they were enjoying the attention he was giving them.

"It won't be so hard remembering their names," HaVon chuckled under his breath, followed by a smile.

"Well then, girls, I know the Elders will be pleased we found you," Rell said and smiled.

"The Elders?" speaking at one time, you could see this was how it would be like talking with them.

"Yes, girls, they are the protectors of Lanila that go back many cycles as long as I can remember," King Edbow answered them, "along with our lady."

"Our lady?" This got both Rell and HaVon's attention. "You're speaking of Lady Dawla, aren't you?"

"Oh, Rell, is that who I speak of or who you ask of?" Once again King Edbow's answers were more like questions as he smiled, placing his hand on his shoulder.

"It seems his answers are the questions," HaVon looked down at Rell.

"It does, HaVon, but I understand as well, that our questions are our answers," he said, smiling at King Edbow.

"Wise, she said," King Edbow shook his head with a smile. "I'm so happy; we've waited so long for what I see and hear from you both."

"Thank you, we are just as excited," they both answered at the same time.

They continued to talk, letting them know what they had been told and learned, during which time, Dawla and Ranforray had appeared from the green light at Rell's. Ranforray couldn't believe what he was seeing. When they had left, there was nothing here and now, there was a beautiful stone home. It looked larger than what was there, with two massive willows at both ends.

"He's going to be amazed by this!" said Ranforray as he walked toward it. "Those willows are amazing and all the green jade I see!" He smiled at her.

"I truly hope so, but unlike before, this will have the protection he needs," she referred to the willows on both ends. You could see how happy she was.

"How did this happen?" He looked at all the detail on everything.

"It was just little magic of Lanila," she answered, smiling at him.

"Little magic?" he asked as he laughed a bit. "It seems bigger than the last one."

"It is, but I gave him just one level." A tear appeared on her face. "He lost so much with that top floor, he'll always have the memories, so I hope he'll start and remember all new ones."

"Magic, huh?" He was smiling as he listened to what she said. "I believe he will, my lady, when he sees this. I'm sure as well it will be a little hard for him too," he said as he looked at her.

"I thought that as well and I had an idea. When he does come back, I'll send you to meet with him, let him know that besides HaVon, there are others that care and want to help." You could see she had thought hard about this and, by her smile, knew this would help.

"As you wish, my lady," he bowed his head with a smile as he knew she had thought about it.

You could see how they were sure it was time for them to meet some of those that cared. He followed her as she began to point things out to him so he could show Rell when they met. It was clear she was letting him know of all the benefits this house would give him. You could see he seemed really excited that he was going to meet them finally. She could see it as well as she smiled and continued to lead him throughout the area. He listened to every word she spoke, being sure not to miss anything; he knew how important this was.

"Thank you, I'm excited to meet them." You could tell he'd been looking forward to this. "My lady, may I ask why not you?"

"In time," Dawla said as she smiled. "Right now, he just needs to know there are more pulling for this new beginning." She then places her staff to the ground and the green light appeared. "Come on, Ranforray, let us return." They disappeared into the light.

As they returned to the Grelands, at the forever trees, the adventurers had moved to an entirely new area; it was large and enclosed but well-lit and very bright.

"This is amazing!" Rell took a moment and appreciated what he was seeing.

"It really is," HaVon agreed; he had more than enough room.

"This is the very center of the forever trees." He could tell they were amazed.

"So right now, we are inside of a tree?" Rell looked at HaVon.

"We are," the girls answered, while climbing all over HaVon as he smiled. It was great to see the bond they were forming.

"So you said earlier about the Elders that they would be happy to hear you found us, and you also mentioned they would want to meet them?" King Edbow already knew the answer.

"They will, it's all part of this new beginning, but I think you already knew that," Rell smiled at him, "but I also feel that it might be safer for now if we return and let them know." He had made a great point; with all that was going on, this seemed like the right thing to do, not wanting anything to happen to them.

"I agree, Rell, but what if they want to see them?" HaVon looked down at him.

"We're bonded now." The girls all jumped down, looking at Rell.

"Bonded?" Rell was confused.

"With the crystal on your suit," King Edbow approached him. "Whenever you need the girls, just touch it and they'll feel you calling."

"We'll know you need us," the girls added.

"So I just touch it and then what happens?" Rell was even more confused.

"You see, Rell, not only are the forever trees beautiful in sight and our home but they give us all the ability of teleportation, like I told you." He raised his hand out and the girls came to him. "No matter where you are, they will always be there for you, whenever you call upon them."

"Anytime you call us, we will be there," the girls responded.

Knowing now how they could move around and hear, it just amazed both of them.

As they continued to talk, Dawla and Ranforray were walking through the Grelands, talking.

"I thank you, my lady, for the chance to meet them, but how will we know when he returns?" he asked as he looked at her.

"It's important that they know there are more out there that want this and have been waiting," she smiled. "I'm going to go and see some old friends; they can help to point him in the direction of returning to his home."

"Do you need me to go with you, my lady?" They had stopped.

"No, you go ahead and help the Gramudds here, I'll return soon." She put her hand to his shoulder.

"As you wish. Be careful, my lady," he said as he bowed before her.

"It's finally happening!" Smiling big, she placed her staff to the ground and disappeared into the green light.

Chapter Seventeen

It was like she had said, the time was coming that everyone had waited so long for. It seemed that she was very excited going to see old friends.

By this time, Saball had made his way to the valley warriors. Jadard appeared to be very active in the distance with his warriors, they looked like they were preparing when suddenly, a grunting went out and he saw it was Saball approaching.

"Where is Shaydon?" he asked as he extended his arm out.

"He sent me to look into the area you spoke of." Saball stood taller and more muscular. "He wanted you to show me a map." You could tell he wasn't one that wasted time and was very direct.

"Saball, this way, let me show you." Jadard may have been waiting for Shaydon, but also knew if he was there, things had changed and no one crossed Saball.

"Your warriors look strong and ready, this will please Shaydon to hear." Unlike at the Harbsides, he liked what he saw here.

"We do as we're asked, they'll be ready." He was pleased to hear that as they entered the cave and approached the map. "Here is the place he wanted to check on."

"That's where the land and water meet?" It seemed he was familiar with this area. "He told me all your warriors can remember is a green light?"

"They do and that's when he mentioned Dawla," Jadard said as he looked at Saball. "How many of my warriors do you need?"

"I'll take care of this," Saball said as he smiled. "He just wants you to be ready." He turned to head out.

"I'll be sure we all are," Jadard replied as he followed him out.

"I'll let him know of your progress," Saball said and extended his arm out.

"Until he calls upon us and our paths cross again." You could see Jadard and his warriors would be ready.

Now that he knew the direction of this unknown green light they had encountered, plus having seen the valley warriors preparing, there was little for him to do except go check that area. But there was a possibility while doing so, he could encounter Dawla, so he needed to be careful. He took off in a new direction of Lanila with a good force; meanwhile, back at the forever trees it seemed as if Rell and HaVon were preparing to leave as well. They were all now back at the base of the tree where it all began.

"Thank you, King Edbow and girls, it was an honor to finally meet you. We look forward to the journeys with you ahead," Rell spoke as HaVon agreed.

"The same for the both of you. Finally seeing you brings joy to us all," said the king as he looked at the Ludes and the girls.

"We're just as excited too," the girls spoke, "remember, wherever and whenever you need us, we promise to be there for you." You could feel the excitement in the air.

"We'll return soon, I promise King Edbow. Come on, HaVon, we need to head back," said Rell as he looked at him with a smile.

"We'll miss you," said the girls and rushed to give HaVon a hug.

"I'll miss you too. Be good, little ones, we'll see you soon." You could see he was enjoying the hug as he smiled.

"You two, be careful while you're out there, so many things are changing now." King Edbow knew it wouldn't be easy.

"We will and ask the same of you and all the Ludes," HaVon answered. "Also, you too, girls, please be careful, they might know of you now."

"See you soon." Rell reached over and touched HaVon and everyone was blinded by the golden light.

"Wow! It's been worth the wait," they all responded at the same time, finally seeing in front of them what they had been waiting for. They took to the air as everyone watched them fly off.

"That's what we've been waiting for, everyone," said King Edbow as the biggest smile came over his face.

"Amazing, look at them!" the girls spoke watching them fly away, you could see they were amazed by what they had just seen.

It was clear that this was new beginning that everyone had been waiting for and it was upon them, you could see and feel the excitement already and to think, all of it was just starting.

They flew off in the direction of the Elders, who were gathered around the pool of gold. They looked to be talking when they were suddenly distracted by a green light from behind.

"My old friends, Cliffon and the Elders, it's so good to see you." It was Dawla, and it was the Elders she had left to meet. "I have missed this place so much, it still looks amazing," she said as she looked around, smiling.

"Oh Dawla, how pleased we are to see you," said Cliffon as he approached her. "You've been watching over him, haven't you?" he smiled.

"You know as well as I do how important this is to Lanila," she answered with a smile.

"We do and when he mentioned what happened with Saball," they all gathered around the golden pond, "we knew it was you."

"I couldn't let anything happen to him, not until they are ready to protect themselves." She looked at them all. "That's why I'm here, I need you to tell him to return home."

"We saw what you and the Gramudds have done for him," they all looked at one another, "it will make a difference and help him even more."

"I hope he really enjoys it." You could see how happy she was. "They should be back soon; I know they've left the forever trees and have found the girls."

"They did find one of the others?" You could see how pleased they were. "They still have so much ahead of them, but we'll let him know, Dawla, when he returns."

"They do, it's about time we let those that are still waiting know. Thank you, Cliffon, it's finally happening – the new beginning of Lanila is upon us," she said, smiling bigger than ever.

"It truly is, please be careful," all the Elders responded at the same time.

"See you soon, old friends. If you need me before then, I promise I'll be here." She then disappeared into the green light.

If it wasn't any clearer now hearing the stories of this new beginning and seeing the excitement in everyone, this is what Lanila had missed and needed for so long. As she returned back to the Grelands, Saball was making his way to where the land met the water. He couldn't stop thinking about her, wondering if it was why she would be watching over this area. The closer he got to his destination, he noticed how the lighting seemed to be changing as well Somehow, the suns were causing reflections off the area that caused everything to have different shades of green. Seeing this himself, he began to wonder if this was what they had seen and maybe it wasn't Dawla after all. As he continued on his way, Dawla had returned.

"It's good to see you, my lady," said Ranforray and bowed. "Were your friends able to help?"

"It was good to see them and yes, they were," she smiled larger than he had ever seen.

"By your smile, I'm glad to hear that it went so well," he said as he began to walk with her.

"I'm so happy." She stopped and looked at him. "No more hiding in the shadows, waiting; it's finally here and they all need to know it's time to fight and get back what we've all lost." You could hear the excitement "After you see Rell, return to me so we can start a plan on letting everyone else know the time is here."

"I will, my lady." He knew this was just as important.

With the young adventurers getting ever so much closer to the peak of the Elders, in the land of reflections even Shaydon had been keeping busy. He was standing in front of what looked to be some sort of crystal-type creatures. He must have created them from the crystal formation on top to help with their plan to stop the young adventurers. Being large-sized, you would think their mobility would be slow, but it was just the opposite – they seemed very flexible and had some similarity to Saball; just wider with four arms.

"My Crytions, it's important that you're not seen until you're needed." His voice was without a tone as he looked down at them and immediately, they became transparent. "I knew you understood, you will be a surprise to them all!" His evil laugh filled the valley walls.

This seemed to be something he planned out and would be a real test to the adventurers when their paths would cross. Time had passed and the moon was getting higher into the sky. As the Elders were talking, they looked up in the distance.

"Here they come," Cliffon smiled; you could feel it in the air how excited they were.

"We're finally back!" Rell could see the peaks and the Elders.

"They're going to be so happy and pleased we found one of these others." You could hear the relief in HaVon's voice as well, seeing they were finally back.

"What's on your mind? Are you OK, HaVon?" Rell felt as if something was bothering him.

"I am, it's just amazing to know there are more of us out there." He now understood.

"I had that same feeling too until I met you." Hearing that lifted HaVon's spirits even more. "This is only the beginning for us, my friend, you never know how many more we'll find hiding and waiting," Rell continued.

"What do mean waiting?" HaVon was slightly confused.

"Seems like they all have been hiding, waiting for us to find them and bring them out of the darkness." They approached the ledge and they separated. "This place still amazes me," said Rell as they walked side by side.

"The power of the Elders always amazed me as well." HaVon had been raised on the stories his whole life.

They walked down the path and saw all off them gathered around the pool. You could see how pleased the Elders were to see they had made it back safe. They knew this was only the beginning of the journeys ahead.

"We're so pleased to see you." Cliffon approached them. "How was your journey to the forever trees? Did you find any answers to the whereabouts of the others?" They already knew but kept it to themselves.

"We did, when we met King Edbow and the Ludes," Rell smiled. "That place was amazing, and how happy they were to see us!"

"We told you once the word of the joining spread, it would lift spirits. You'll see in time how many more have been waiting." Cliffon could see and feel the energy between them.

"Their spirits sure were," HaVon smiled, "especially the girls. Seeing them was amazing!"

"The girls?" this got Cliffon's attention.

"Yes, they're one of the others we were searching for." Rell looked up at HaVon. "Well not exactly one," he shrugged with a grin, "but now we're connected."

"So you did find the Ludes, but why the hesitation about being one of the others?" Cliffon didn't quite understand.

"Well, what I meant was…" he paused thinking how he could explain it, "I'm thinking it would be easier just to show you." Rell smiled at HaVon and he nodded.

As the Elders stood there looking at one another, trying to understand what he was saying, they saw them both smiling. Rell reached down to the white crystal on his suit, touching it like King Edbow had told him. Meanwhile, back at the land of the forever trees, King Edbow was talking with the girls about the changes that would soon come.

"He's calling us, Father." The girls could feel him as soon as he touched it.

"Then go, my girls, help them bring Lanila back." He embraced each one of them seeing how proud he was. "Tell them I said hello."

Just as soon as Rell removed his hand from the crystal, the Elders noticed clouds forming above them; they looked at one another, curious. They didn't know what was happening as they were seeing this for the first time. The clouds started to take shape then there was a blinding white light. The two adventurers looked at one another and grinned.

"It worked!" Rell was amazed.

"We told you we'd be here for you whenever you called." The girls came out of the light, landing next to them.

"Girls, so good to see you!" HaVon was happy to see them.

"HaVon!" They were just as happy.

"Well, aren't you three a beautiful sight!" Cliffon now understood what Rell was trying to say. "We're all so happy to see you." Standing in front of them was the beginning to what they had been waiting for.

"Wow, where are we, this place is so pretty!" The girls asked as they began to look around. "Father says hello too."

"Hey girls, good to see you." Rell reached out touching them. "These are the Elders we spoke of," he said as he pointed them out.

"Hello, Elders, we've heard about you from them and our father," the girls said as they approached him. "Are you made of gold?" they asked, curious as they looked him over.

"We are, little ones," the Elder replied, smiling at the others and enjoying their curiosity.

"What's this?" the girls then asked as they approach the golden pool.

"This is the key to the beginning," Cliffon answered, looking down at them.

"The key?" Rell was a little confused.

"Rell and HaVon, things are not always as they seem," he smiled.

"Elders, the key to what?" the girls asked as they looked up at him.

"What do you mean, Cliffon?" HaVon walked up to his side.

"Like you said to us earlier, it will be easier just to show you." All the Elders were smiling.

Cliffon ensured the girls they had nothing to worry about, that this was just a part of joining they needed to go through. He then told them what they had to do, explaining that each one of them needed to place one of their legs into the pool of gold. Looking at each other, you could see they were timid at first, until they turned to see the smile on both Rell and HaVon's face. Seeing how they were, this had to be a part of what they had talked about. Everyone watched all three of them place one leg into the pool. They watched how the golden pool began to glow, as it began to climb just up their leg and stopped, then it was gone.

"You may now remove your legs, girls." A big smile came over all the Elders' faces.

"What did it just do to them, why did it stop? Are you OK?" Rell was confused with what he just saw.

"We're fine, Rell," they answered, looking at one another, not sure what just happened.

"They are now bonded with the mark as you two were," Cliffon pointed to each of their shoulders.

"Well, look at that!" Rell walked up to them to see what he was pointing at. "It looks like mine," he said, looking at his shoulder.

"They're the same!" HaVon lowered his head to get a closer look.

"It's the mark of Lanila's new beginning," all the Elders spoke at once.

"Mark of Lanila!" said the girls looking at it. "What does it do?"

"It will reveal a completely new side of you, showing you powers that you didn't even know were there," he said and chuckled.

"In what way?" both Rell and HaVon looked at him.

"Let them just show you and you'll understand," he looked down at the girls. "I need you to stand over there, then at the same time, girls, I need you to touch the mark on your shoulder."

"Like we did in a way, girls, I promise you'll be fine," said Rell, letting them know not to worry, but you could hear the excitement in his voice, wondering what would happen.

"Is this good?" They walked over to the spot, still admiring the mark on their shoulders.

"It is, girls, it's now time." The Elders were smiling.

With everyone watching and waiting to see what he was talking about, the girls all looked at one another and did like he said. Suddenly, as they touched their marks, everyone was overwhelmed by a blinding white light with hints of light blue in it as well. Everyone just stood there, waiting to be able to see what happened. Rell and HaVon turned to each other, smiling, as they saw what was happening, then standing before them when the light was gone were the girls. But what the mark did was merge them together into one dragon. The excitement everyone had as they smiled at the breathtaking sight that stood before them. They were now almost the same size as HaVon and their white scales had a sparkle to them, like diamonds. Their chest was now a deeper blue with the same sparkle to it and their eyes were a very light blue.

"How are we almost seeing eye to eye now, HaVon?" the girls spoke. "Wait, what happened to us?" they were confused.

"It's OK, girls. Wow, look at you!" Rell walked up looking at them. "It takes a bit of time to get used to." He turned to HaVon, smiling. "Look at that, they bonded like we did."

"They sure did!" You could see how happy Cliffon was with what he saw. "You're just as amazing," he said and walked up to them and looked them over.

"Rell, why are you down there, what happen to you?" they asked, looking down, then it all began to make sense. "So, it's like when you two join, we now have that same ability?" the girls looked at the Elders.

"I would say you do." Even HaVon was amazed.

"It's the mark, like yours, Rell; when they touch it, they become one. Then, girls, when you want to be three, just touch it again," he explained, looking at the them with a smile.

"Wait until Father sees what we can do now," the girls' youth was coming out and you could hear how excited they were.

"He'll be just as amazed!" HaVon agreed then turned to the Elders. "So, these others you've spoke of, like the girls there are more of us out there?" You could see how excited he was as Rell smiled.

"Yes, HaVon, it does." They knew how happy he would be to hear that.

"So we're not the only ones?" the girls turned to each other, smiling.

"This is only the start to what Lanila has been needing and is in store for," Cliffon said and looked at the Elders.

"Then we should return to the boulders." Rell looked up at HaVon. "If we found out about the girls there, maybe we can get the other boulders to open to find out more of these others that are waiting for us."

"That sounds like a plan," he agreed, "but what about the girls?" He turned to Cliffon.

"They'll return back to the forever trees for now, but we need to talk to them first." He walked up to them both. "You both now have seen and understand how important this is."

"We do, Cliffon," they both responded.

"We'll be there for you both anytime you need us," the girls looked at them, smiling big.

"We know, with just a touch. Thank you for believing in us, girls." Rell pointed to the crystal with a smile.

"Be safe, our young adventurers." Cliffon was happy to see they were returning to Rell's home on their own.

"Hey!" the girls touched their shoulder and became separated. "Wow!" they exclaimed, looking at one another and smiling. "We'll miss you." They bum rushed both Rell and HaVon with affection. Seeing this, the Elders all smiled.

"See you again soon, we promise," they both answered, smiling, you could see how happy everyone was. Then they turned and headed to the ledge, merging together.

"Now that's what amazing!" said the girls as they watched them leave.

"It truly is, girls," Cliffon walked up next to them, "but so are you. Come with us, let's talk."

There was still so much our young adventures would discover, as they headed back to Rell's. The suns had gotten lower into the sky while the girls learned more from the Elders of how important they were to all that was happening. With a surprise waiting for Rell when he returned home, meanwhile Saball was getting closer to where the land met the water. He was sure the green shadows he had seen were not from Dawla and were what the valley warriors encountered, but it just wasn't making sense to him the more he thought about it, so he continued.

"I've seen no sign of her here, I don't understand," he grunted, looking around, when suddenly, he heard something coming through the brush and hid. "I wonder who this is so far out here?" he said to himself as he watched.

As he hid there out of sight, he saw what looked to be six men on horses and were getting closer. The one in the middle was wearing a robe and looked to be bald, the other five looked to be protecting him. They had some sort of blue armor on.

"Where did they come from?" He talked to himself staying quiet. "Where are they going?"

You could see he started wondering if this had anything to do with what happened to the valley warriors, so he decided to follow them, staying far enough back not to be spotted. He knew this was something; Shaydon would want to know about it, so he watched these people trying to figure out where they were going.

While back at the peaks, the girls had finished talking with the Elders.

"We'll see you again soon, girls. Thank your father for us, please," Cliffon smiled.

"Thank you, Elders, for all you've told us," they all spoke at once. You could see whatever the Elders said they seemed very excited. "We'll be sure to tell Father." They smiled, looking at one another. As the white light appeared, they disappeared into it on their way back home.

"This is so exciting; so many cycles have passed," Cliffon said as he looked at the Elders and approached the pool, speaking into it. "Dawla, they're headed back now."

At the exact same time he said that, back in the Grelands, all of the Gramudds, including Ranforray and Dawla, were having what looked to be a large banquet. She suddenly looked to the air and smiled.

"Thank you, Elders." She then turned to Ranforray and said, "Soon, my friend."

He smiled at her, knowing it was almost time.

With the girls returning home and Saball trying to find out who the people were he was following, he needed to find out where they were going. The young adventurers too were on their way back to Rell's.

"I can't believe what happened with the girls, this mark is pretty powerful," said Rell as he was still trying to grasp hold of the changes.

"To think the Elders said this is only the beginning too. So you really think the boulders hold the answers like before?" HaVon was wondering too.

"I hope so, because it's got me excited even more now to find more of these others," the kid in him was coming out.

"I know what you mean, I feel it too." HaVon was just as curious.

With each stroke of his wings, getting ever so close to Rell's, Saball was following the people he had seen to the exact spot he had been heading to.

"Hmm, now I'm curious," he grunted to himself and watched.

Having no idea that they were being followed, they approached the edge where the water began. Spread throughout the water were what looked like smaller mountains but just the tops were visible. This really got Saball's attention when he saw the one wearing the robe got off his horse. He watched him approach the edge of the water and wondered what he was doing just standing there.

"What are you doing, little man?" Saball was trying to focus in on him.

Suddenly, the man pulled back the hood from his head and he reached inside his robe. Saball kept watching and saw him holding a large green jade sword. He wondered if this was the connection he was searching for, but even he couldn't have imagined what would happen next. The man held the sword up then kneeled, driving it into the ground.

"What did he do that for?" Then Saball noticed the ground began to slightly tremble.

Suddenly, the peak closest to them in the water began to rise. The man pulled the sword from the ground and returned to his horse. Saball just watched what was going on; the peak kept rising from the water and when it stopped, it was the size of a mountain. He just stared as the ones on the horses seemed very calm, then he noticed a path also rose that connected the land to this large mountain. Saball couldn't believe what he was seeing; he knew now why he hadn't seen them before now. Then he watched them walk down the path as this mountain began to open up, he focused in on it, seeing a lot more of them inside and even more had armor on. Then he realized.

"The Farlands, I knew that armor reminded me of something," he whispered, speaking to himself. They couldn't see him, being at such a far distance and he had made himself visible. "I thought we took care of them at the great battle. So this is where you have been hiding." He began to laugh.

He realized just then that they had been hearing about them for many cycles, being the survivors of the great battle that first drove Lanila into what it was today. They were never found until now. He watched them walk into the mountain and it closed up behind them. Then the mountain and path disappeared into the water to where all you could see was the peak.

"Why have they stayed hidden for so many cycles?" He stood there staring. "Seeing them here, Dawla might have something to do with this after all and I need to let Shaydon know." A smile came over his face as he turned and headed back to the land of reflections.

You could see how important this was to him, finally finding the Farlands who they thought were gone; he took off with great speed.

By now, the young adventurers had finally approached the hill with the willow on it.

"I've missed my old friend. Just as I remember, still beautiful," Rell spoke out as they flew over it.

"I know, that's good to see." HaVon could feel how excited he was to be back.

"It really is, HaVon," said Rell then looked ahead. "Do you see that, what happened?"

"I'm not really sure, Rell." The closer they approached, HaVon could feel how happy Rell seemed; there was an excitement as they approached the ground and separated.

"HaVon, what happened to all the debris? Do you think this is mine now?" He just stood there, amazed. "What in Lanila would do this?" he asked, looking up at him.

"I don't know, Rell, but now you have a home again," HaVon answered, looking down to see him, smiling.

"I really do," said Rell, realizing how right he was. "Look at those!" he said, pointing out the large willows on each side. "You know they both remind me a lot of—" he stopped, looking at HaVon, then back toward the willow they had just flown over.

"Reminds you of what?" HaVon looked at him.

"My willow on the hill!" You could see him thinking. "Do you think?"

"Do I think what?" you could see this was confusing HaVon, not finishing his sentence.

"It's probably nothing, I'm just so excited right now to see this," he smiled, shrugging, "but you know, I remember my mom telling me the story of Dawla. She presented that willow to my father for me," he said, pointing back to the one on the hill. "Seeing this with all that's happening to us, I thought there might be a connection."

"There might be," even HaVon wouldn't be surprised.

"It's just an idea, I'm just thankful for what I'm seeing right now." You could see a smile; he was enjoying it all.

"Rell, look at the door," said HaVon, pointing out the mark that was the same as on his shoulder, "it has the mark of Lanila."

"Look at the detail on it," said Rell, reaching out and rubbing his hand along it.

Enjoying all they were looking at and having no idea how it happened or who might have done it, they were totally unaware that very shortly they were about to have a visitor.

In the Grelands, when he touched the door, it must have sent a signal to Dawla, so she turned to Ranforray and smiled.

"They've returned," she said.

He stood up from the table.

"Yes, my lady," he bowed. "I will let them know what you have told me." You could tell he seemed a little excited.

"Thank you," she said, placing her staff to the ground and he disappeared into the green light.

With our young adventures looking around, taking in all they were seeing, Rell pointed out how much larger this one seemed. They pointed out different details each of them saw and suddenly, they noticed a green light coming from behind them.

"Rell!" said HaVon after seeing it and getting into a defensive stance to protect him.

"What do you think it is?" Rell asked as they both watched. "Hold on, I remember that green light." Rell watched from behind him.

"What do you mean you remember it, I haven't seen it before," said HaVon, still being protective. When they saw Ranforray walk from it, he let out a thunderous roar that shook the ground.

"It's OK, no need to growl. I'm a friend," said Ranforray, raising his hands and smiling as he walked toward them slowly.

"It's OK, HaVon," said Rell, walking out from behind him. "I know you from somewhere." You could see him trying to remember. "I've got it. When Saball tried to attack us, that's the same green light that helped us. Remember, I told you about the lady I saw?" he looked up at HaVon.

"My name is Ranforray, I serve my lady and Lanila," Ranforray said, placing his hand to his chest and kneeling before them. "You're right, Rell, but I was frozen and you both were motionless," he explained as he stood up.

"Rell, that's the lady you kept talking about?" said HaVon, thinking he did keep repeating seeing a lady that helped, as he chuckled. "That's not quite a lady," he said, smiling while looking down at him.

"No, HaVon," said Rell, shaking his head looking at him with a grin, "that's the creature that was frozen, he's with her."

"She said your mind and powers were like nothing Lanila has seen before," said Ranforray as he laughed, "she wasn't kidding." He walked past them, smiling. "She has sent me here to show you around your new home." He turned, looking at them. You could see they were still catching up to what he had said. "I must say, what an honor and pleasure it is to meet you both, how long Lanila has waited to see you!" They could see how excited he seemed, like everyone they've already encountered.

"Thank you." Rell looked up at HaVon. "You keep mentioning her, is it Dawla you're speaking of?" he asked with eagerness, waiting for an answer.

"You are very wise, Rell, for being so young. She said right now it is important that you find the others, to help bring Lanila a new light which it has never seen." He walked up to Rell, placing his hand on his shoulder. "She will always be watching over you though," he smiles. "Come, there is so much to show you." They headed toward the front door.

"I'll be right back, wait for me," he said as he looked up at HaVon.

"HaVon, around back, my lady has something for you as well, she wanted you two to be close." Ranforray smiled, encouraging him to go see.

"Go and see what it is." Rell shrugged. "I'll follow him, then join you. It has me curious too." He smiled.

"I as well!" Now HaVon was eager to see what Dawla had had prepared for him.

Chapter Eighteen

With HaVon heading around the back of the house to see what he was talking about; she had done something just as special for him as well. Around the front, Rell followed Ranforray into the house. When he entered, his eyes became wide open. All he could do was stand there; he couldn't believe what he was seeing – the size of the ceiling and how much room there was now inside the house. The floors looked like a marble of some kind, and he also noticed the stone work looked like green jade spread throughout the place. The entire back of the house instead of having windows was one solid peace of crystal, it was clear as glass; he was amazed how easy it was to see through. Rubbing his hand over it, he couldn't believe how smooth it was, but it also seemed very strong and solid.

"What's this exactly, I've never seen anything like it before." You could see how amazed he was.

"She thought it was important for you to be able to see through it." He could tell Rell was enjoying this. "She also wanted you to never forget," he said, pointing toward the fireplace. Rell noticed it had something on the face of it.

"What's that?" he walked over to where Ranforray had pointed, and a tear fell from his eye when he got close enough to see it. "Mom!" It was a portrait of her sketched into what look like marble, it showed her true beauty so detailed.

"My lady felt it was important for her to be part of your new home," explained Ranforray, seeing how happy it made him.

"I miss her so much." He turned smiling as he wiped his eyes. "Please be sure to tell her thank you, it's beautiful and exactly how I remember Mom."

"I will. Come, there's so much more to see." He led Rell from that room into an entirely different one. "She felt that there was no reason to have two floors anymore," he spoke and stood out of his way. "She wanted you to have more room."

"Look at this, all the detail work, there are dragons all over!" Rell exclaimed, looking closely at the columns and the fireplace as well, but unlike the other room, the back wall was solid with pieces of the clear crystal spread all around, it was just enough to see through and worked as a way to light the room. "That's my bed? I didn't know they could be that big," Rell wondered and started jumping on it excitedly, it was so much larger than his old bed.

Rell was lost in all that he was looking at; he felt so lucky. Meanwhile, HaVon had made his way around back and was just standing there. Looking around, it seemed so much larger than he remembered, but there was nothing that stood out to him. He began to look around for any sign of what Ranforray was talking about, when suddenly, something got his attention as he walked up to it. He saw sculpted into it was a dragon head from the same marble that was in the house, then all of the sudden, it began to glow in gold and began highlighting the dragon's head. He decided to place his foot to it and when he did, the ground opened up in front of him. It was large enough for him to enter and he saw it began to glow in a familiar blue that he recognized.

When he saw this, a warm feeling came over his entire body. He began to walk down it and the further he went, the more it opened up. Then he realized how it looked so similar to his cave, it had the same blue spring which explained the light he was seeing but was so much larger. Also, he saw different colors of grass which he had never seen before, even the bushes and trees had so much life. Seeing this, he knew now this was what Ranforray had told him to look for, he couldn't believe and felt so thankful for what she had done for him as well.

"Look at this place, she wanted us to be close to one another!" You could see how happy he was.

Looking around, he saw a place that looked to be where he would rest. It was so grassy and tall, he walked up to it and sat down; you could see by his reaction the comfort he felt. Still stunned by all of it, he just sat there enjoying this moment.

Rell and Ranforray had made their way out of the house and stood on the porch in front.

"This is something you could only dream of!" They walked side by side and as Rell looked at him, he was twice as tall. "Let her know as well how much I love those." He pointed at the willows.

"Like the willow on the hill, they were put there to help protect your home," he said, as they looked up at their size. "Sure hope HaVon is as happy with what she did."

"That's right, where is he?" With so much he was taking in, he had forgotten about the surprise for HaVon.

"Come with me, I'll show you." Ranforray led him around the tree and toward the back.

"There is not a word to describe how I feel about all that I'm seeing." He continued looking at the house and all the stone work. "So where is he?" he asked, not seeing HaVon anywhere in sight.

"He's there, Rell," Ranforray pointed as he smiled, walking past him toward the marking that HaVon had touched. He placed his own hand to it.

"What did you just do?" Rell asked as he watched the ground open up. "You're telling me he's down there?"

"My lady knew it was important for you to be close to one another. Come, let me show you." He walked down the path and Rell followed. The further they got down the path, they could hear splashing. Ranforray smiled. "I would say by that sound he likes what she's done."

"Likes what?" At about that time, the space opened up and there was HaVon, swimming in the spring. "It looks like his cave, but it's so much bigger and look at those plants!" Rell was awestruck.

"Hey, Rell!" HaVon saw them after coming up from the water. "Look what she did for me, you see this place?" They both could hear the excitement in his voice.

"I see you're enjoying it," said Rell as he smiled. "This place is amazing and beautiful; it reminds me of your cave." Rell was happy to see him so relaxed and having fun.

"Well, my lady will be very pleased to hear that you're happy, HaVon." He placed his hand on Rell's shoulder, smiling. "Now that I've had a chance to show you everything, you know now that the two of you are not alone in Lanila and they would enjoy this as well." he winked at him. "It's getting late and I need to return."

"Thank you for everything," Rell extended his arm out.

"Thank you both," replied Ranforray as he extended his own. "You need a place to feel safe, you are the hope that all of Lanila has been waiting for." He then bowed to HaVon, smiling. "I'll return soon. I'm ready, my lady," as he speaks into the air the green light appeared. "Remember what I've said, you're never alone and have new friends." He winked at them both again and smiled before disappearing into the light.

"He was nice," said Rell as he turned looking at HaVon. "Hey, he winked again?" Rubbing his hand through the tall grass, he asked, "How's the water?" He then touched his mark and as his suit disappeared, he ran toward the spring and jumped into it, making a splash.

"This place is huge and he was great to show me all he did," he said and dived under the water, enjoying the moment.

For the moment, there wasn't a worry at all, as the two experienced something amazing and were enjoying it. What Dawla had done for them was something really special, giving them a place of safety and no worries, which appeared to be working. They continued to have fun.

Ranforray meanwhile appeared back at the Grelands and began talking with Dawla about his visit.

"I'm so pleased and happy to hear they liked it." She had been listening to all he said. "Now that they know there are more of us standing with them, we need do think about going where the land meets the water; they've been waiting as well."

"That would be a pleasure, my lady, just let me know when." Ranforray placed his hand to his chest. "I agree, the time has come to let them know."

"I believe it's time for all of Lanila, but the Farlands are just as important as the Ludes and King Edbow to this beginning." A look came over her face. "You must be sure to be careful!"

"I always am, my lady, but you have my word," he smiled. "Time to rest for what's ahead, I feel it will be all new and exciting." He bowed and then turned, heading to where he slept.

So hearing what she said confirmed that indeed it might have been Dawla that the valley warriors had encountered, as she said she had been watching over the Farlands. She had no idea that earlier while Saball was scouting, he had found them and was on his way to Shaydon to inform him. As the Grelands began to get quiet and rest for the new day ahead, back at the forever trees the girls and Ludes including King Edbow seemed to be celebrating. You could feel the excitement in the air, seeing how they danced and laughed.

"I'm so proud and happy for you girls," King Edbow said as he hugged them. "Seeing the mark of the Lanila and the powers it gives you to come together, how much joy it brings to us all seeing the changes that are happening."

"Thank you, Father." All three smiled and were just as happy and excited.

"That was the most amazing thing to see you three merge, I could have never imagined." He thought for minute. "You will always be my girls, but what if…" he paused again.

"Father, you have done so much keeping us safe for this very moment, what's your idea?" They were excited to hear his idea.

"Well, I thought when you're one, everyone could call you Destiny." He hoped they would like it. "I believe it's your destiny to be a part of this new beginning." All three of them looked at one another smiling.

"You have done so much for us, Father; we'll call ourselves Destiny." Everyone was excited thinking what a great name it was for them. "Can't wait till we tell Rell and HaVon."

All of the Ludes began to cheer and clap, hearing what they would call themselves when merged, what a great name! They continued to celebrate and enjoy the night. Meanwhile, Saball has made his way back to the land of reflections, calling out for Shaydon with excitement.

"What did you find, Saball?" He came out from the cave. "Did you find a connection with Dawla and what the valley warriors had encountered?"

"My lord!" he kneeled. "I didn't see any sign of her but, it doesn't mean she's not involved," he said, standing to his feet as Shaydon approached him.

"What are you talking about?" Shaydon asked, standing in front of him.

"Well, while I was scouting the area, I did find something we had stopped looking for, thinking they were all gone – the Farlands, and I know where they've been hiding." He knew how pleased Shaydon would be to hear this.

"I knew they had survived and you found them?" He then lowered his head, thinking. "They didn't see you, right?"

"No, my lord," Saball answered as he shook his head.

"With you finding the Farlands there, I know she is involved, but I don't understand why." He started walking and Saball followed. "I can't believe they have survived this many cycles, but it makes me wonder if they have connection to all this." You could see him thinking.

"What do you want us do about them?" Saball asked.

You could tell how happy Shaydon was to hear he had stumbled upon them, but there had to be more to it and he needed to know.

With the suns beginning to set and the blue moon starting its climb, Rell and HaVon were talking in the tall grass in his new cave.

"I can't believe what she's done for us, we both have new homes to rest that are close to one another," You could hear the relief as he looked at him, "to know there are more out there pulling for us."

"It's amazing and exciting at the same time," HaVon looked at him, smiling.

"Look at this place, how big it is, we're not going to let anyone down." Rell smiled, feeling confident. "I've been thinking about what he said and how he winked before he left." He had HaVon's attention. "You know, he did say we have friends now and the girls crossed my mind, they really would enjoy seeing this as well and this could be the place where we can get together, where it's safe to talk and I don't know but it seems we might need a place to better all of our abilities for what's ahead."

"A place to get away with no worries, you might be right about being prepared as well." HaVon smiled as Rell touched his shoulder and the suit began to work its way over his body. "You're going to call them, aren't you?" You could hear a little excitement in his voice.

"I am," said Rell, touching the crystal. "They're a part of us now that we're fighting for Lanila, they would love to be a part of this as well." This would be a great gesture.

"Look, here they come." HaVon looked at him with one big smile. After being blinded by the white light, there they stood.

"HaVon and Rell!" the girls ran up to them, even though it hadn't been that long since they'd seen one another, you could tell they missed them both.

"Hey, girls!" they were just as happy to see them.

"Father says hello," they said and began to look around.

"Look at this place where are we?" they seemed lost in all they were seeing.

"This is my new home now and we wanted you to know you're always welcome here, it's a place where we all can be safe and prepare for whatever is ahead," said HaVon as he looked at them and smiled.

"Thank you for that. What do you mean a place to prepare?" they asked, looking at all the space that was around; it had so many different colors. "Oh we almost forgot to tell you, Father came up with a name for us when we are one," they said, speaking at the same time.

"What is it?" Rell curiously waited along with HaVon.

"Destiny! Is it OK if we look around?" You could see how distracted they were.

"Like we told you, this is now your place as well to enjoy and have fun." HaVon could see that's what they wanted to do.

"Thank you." Just as soon as they said that, they were off, the both of them just stood there smiling. They knew this was a great idea.

"Destiny, you know that really does fit them," said Rell as he looked up at HaVon.

"It does, Rell," HaVon said, smiling. "Boy, they have a lot of energy and with so much ahead us, but, it's good to see them having fun," he chuckled.

"Can we jump in here?" they asked, pointing at the spring.

"Hold on, girls," HaVon stood up, looking at Rell. "Be right back!" With a grin, he began to run toward the spring. As he jumped high and into the water, it caused a wave that overcame the girls, soaking them wet.

Everyone was laughing, having such a great time, Rell saw what he had done and the girls looked at one another, smiling as they jumped in, splashing him. Rell just sat there watching with a solid smile on his face. He could have never imagined not just one dragon but he was looking at four. They were having so much fun and he shook his head, laughing; they were right about being prepared, seeing what they already had encountered. He wanted to be sure they were just as strong and knew it would take time.

"You all look to be having so much fun," he stood up. "The new day is not far away, so I'm going to go ahead and head back to the house, HaVon," said Rell, needing his rest, and they were having too much fun to interrupt.

"All right, Rell. Are you OK?" HaVon asked as the girls continued to splash him.

"I'm fine and, girls, great to see you." He waved and headed up the path.

"Good to see you too. Where's he going?" the girls asked as they watched him walk up the path.

"His home is above us. He's just tired from the day, unlike us, he needs his rest." He turned to them and they continued to have fun. You see, dragons could go days without sleep, unlike Rell.

These two were learning so much about each other, and to learn that there were possibly more out there waiting and finding out that there were those around that want to help them as well. HaVon and the girls were enjoying this very moment, having no idea what the new day would bring. There would be challenges along with it, but the young adventurers did realize they needed to be prepared for anything they would have to face. As Rell came out from the ground and it closing behind him, you could see the pep in his step along with a smile he couldn't lose. Looking up, he had no idea the blue moon had risen so high into the sky, while in the land of reflections, Shaydon had come up with a plan. He explained it to Saball and what he must do to find out if there was a connection with the boy.

"You want me to do that again?" After hearing his idea, Saball just looked at him.

"I don't care if you don't like it," said Shaydon. "This is the only way to find if there is a connection and if Dawla is protecting the Farlands as well."

"If that's what you ask of me, my lord." You could tell he didn't seem too pleased with his idea. "I can't stand when I have to be one of them," he said, growling under his breath.

"You'll do this and find out if they're involved." Shaydon's tone of voice left no room for defiance. "I want to see their hopes for this fail."

"How are we so sure they'll invite me in?" Saball asked, looking at him. "You don't think they'll be more cautious?"

"The Farlands live by a code and if you have survived, they will help, that's why this will be so easy, that's their weakness, Saball." He knew of their code and their way of life. "We're going to find out what's going on and stop it."

He had thought all the Farlands had been destroyed, but since Saball had seen them, he knew now they had spread out. It seemed they had spread apart to survive and now they were coming back together, he wanted to know, why realizing things did seem different. He was thinking the disguise had worked before when they took it all down, plus this was just to find out what was going on inside of this place they were hidden at. The plan was for Saball to change his appearance, infiltrate their hideout to find out what brought them there and if it had to do with the boy or Dawla.

"Saball, find out what they're up to and keep me informed. If you see her or the boy, leave immediately," instructed Shaydon. He was sure this would work.

"I will, my lord." Saball bowed, placing his hand to his chest. "Hopefully, it won't take that long to find out. I can't wait till this is over, being one of them makes my skin crawl," he growled.

"Saball, be patient, we'll find out. Now go while the moon is still up," said Shaydon, turning back toward the cave. Saball headed to where the land met the water.

They were going to do as before but the difference was, this time they had to find out the connection, Saball took off with the blue moon highlighting the land.

Rell had made his way back into the house. Looking around with a big smile on his face, he was so thankful, and still trying to grasp how or why Dawla would do something so special for them. He had such a long day as the yawns became more regular; smiling, he walked over to the fireplace and looked up at his mother's portrait.

"Mom, I miss and love you so much," he said, blowing a kiss and touching the portrait. "So much has happened today. I'll see you in the morning," he said, rubbing his eyes as he entered the bedroom. "Today was like nothing I could've imagined. It makes me wonder what surprises the new day will bring. I do know we'll need to be ready; I have this feeling it's only going to get harder," he said as he fell back into the bed, yawning.

The day's end was upon him and he was right about being ready. Lying there, he thought about this Saball. He smiled at times, even talking to himself as he did; it seemed he wasn't worried. His eyes were getting harder to keep open, he was fighting to stay awake but it didn't work and he fell asleep. The same could not be said for HaVon and the girls; they continued to have fun with not a worry in the world. This day, they had found out so much; what they call home now and the new allies they had for this quest of freeing Lanila. With one resting and the others enjoying themselves, Saball meanwhile had almost reached where he needed to be.

"I can't stand being around these small, mindless people," he said, talking to himself. "I just want to find out what I need and get this over with." He picked up speed.

Seeing what they were up to, knowing he had done it before, it was scary to think about, and even Dawla had no idea. She was planning to send Ranforray soon to let the Farlands know it had started, but when she would finally send him, would he be able to see through Saball's disguise?

"Let's get this over with," he growled, touching the ring.

He was overcome with same black mass when Shaydon changed his appearance, he couldn't be seen but when it disappeared, there he stood. Saball had the look of them but was smaller than average size, wearing ragged clothes and looking as if he had been struggling for some time. It did give him the appearance of someone in need of help; he smirked and couldn't have picked a better time to change his look. When he came from the brush, he startled the same bald man he had seen earlier, reacting in a panic when he saw him. Acting as if he was scared, hoping they hadn't seen what he had just done, Saball cried out, "No, no, please, don't harm me." He fell to the ground, covering himself.

"Don't be alarmed, my friend, I'm not going to harm you," he said, removing his hood and looking down at him. "You scared me as well." He looked around for sign of anyone else.

"Please don't hurt me," he still acted scared and it seemed to be working.

"Brother Ben, what is it?" He wasn't alone. From the brush came a man wearing armor and carrying a sword. "Are you OK?"

"Yes, lower your weapon," he said as he kneeled down to Saball. "My friend, where did you come from?"

"I-I don't remember," he made his voice high-pitched, "I've been searching for days, looking for anyone."

"What is your name, my friend?" You could see how helpful this Brother Ben was trying to be.

"My name is Basall," said Saball, very quick coming up with that. He sat up, feeling it was working. "Who are you?" he looked up at him.

"My name is Brother Ben and this is Billum, he helps keep us safe," he smiled, helping him up.

This Billum he spoke of was taller than them both and very muscular, his armor was blue and he wore it like nothing he had seen before. It was very detailed from head to foot. He stood behind Brother Ben, just looking around you could see he wasn't comfortable with what was happening,

"Billum, put your sword away and help me," Brother Ben said as he helped Saball up. "You look like you could use a good meal, my friend."

Saball was doing a great job making it seem hard to walk.

"Brother Ben, are you sure?" Billum was cautious as he grabbed his arm, he wasn't as convinced with his story.

"Billum, the Farlands always help all that need it."

Saball lowered his head as if he was in pain, but he was grinning at what he was hearing.

"We do, Brother Ben," he nodded and helped him walk.

"So, Basall, are there more of you?" he asked as he and Billum looked at one another.

"No, all is lost," he cried as he faked being in pain.

"What of that necklace?" Billum saw it around his neck.

"It's all I have left of my love." He could tell that this Billum might be a problem, but he stuck with it, wiping his fake tears from his face.

"You'll be safe now; we have food and also some change of clothes." You could see how caring Brother Ben was. "I'm glad we found you, Basall."

"You have no idea how happy you've made me." He even made as if it was hard for him to talk. "I'm just so weak."

"We're almost there, hang on." They cleared the bushes. The blue moon was shining over the area when they approached the water's edge.

"I don't understand, where are you taking me?" Saball was pulling this off, so he asked this even though he knew better.

"Don't worry," he smiled. "Billum, hold on to him please." He walked to the edge and placed the jade sword into the ground.

"What's he doing?" he looked up at Billum and he just stared back at him, not saying anything.

Then, as he had seen earlier but not at night, the mountain and the path rose, but this time, it was glowing as it lit the area for them to see.

"He's not very talkative, is he?" he asked as Brother Ben grabbed his other arm to help him.

"Billum is cautious," Brother Ben said, letting him know that's how he was, but you could see Saball wasn't so sure.

"This is your home?" he struggled to look up.

"This is the new home of the Farlands, come with me." They started their way across the path. "We have been surviving since the great battle, waiting for the sign," Brother Ben said as he looked at Saball.

"We all remember the great battle," he coughed, "but you said waiting for a sign?" he asked, hoping he would say more.

"Brother Ben!" Billum cut him off and just looked at him, feeling he was telling him too much.

"You're right, Billum. For now, let us just worry about getting you better, friend." You could see how open he was, but the same could not be said for Billum; he was more cautious having been through so much already.

"Thank you for your help, Brother Ben." Saball was pulling this off.

"You're welcome, Basall." As they got to the opening, more came out to help assist them. When they did get inside, Saball looked back to see it closing. He smiled – it had worked.

Well, with what Shaydon wanted to do seemed to have worked as he was now inside with the Farlands, but seeing the way Billum acted toward him, he knew to be careful, knowing he would be watching over his every move. But it didn't matter now that he was inside, he just needed to find out more of what they knew and who was involved.

Chapter Nineteen

The changes in Lanila were happening and could be seen by everyone. A new day had already begun at Rell's and they had been busy. He was working outside his beautiful home and was not alone.

"I can't thank you enough for helping with this," he said as Dawla had also put in a garden for him, "Seeing her portrait, I thought to myself how much she loved hers."

"I'm just so glad to help you with anything." It was Ranforray who was helping him. "My lady was so happy to hear what you've done, also to see the girls enjoying it as well," he said as he looked up.

"We are too, especially HaVon. It's good to see him like that," Rell replied as he smiled.

They were right about that, as the girls and HaVon were flying in the air; they looked to be almost playing tag between them. It was good to see this after staying with him through the night, seeing all four of them together, enjoying one another's company. For HaVon, it brought memories of what Ravin used to do with him, and how much fun they were having together. But this was his way of helping them prepare for whatever they might face, he and Rell just wanted them to be ready.

"You know they're coming along so well," Rell said as he continued to put plants in the ground.

"We all thank you for getting ready and preparing, it shows your growth as well in such a short time." Ranforray lay the plants out ahead of him.

"Thank Dawla for me, these plants are like nothing I've seen before," he said as he smiled.

"Knowing what you wanted to do, she thought these would be a nice touch." Ranforray had brought these from the Grelands. "Any more signs?" he asked as he looked to the boulders.

"I haven't seen any," he stopped and looked at them. "I don't know why, that's what I've been wondering." You could almost hear a bit of frustration in his voice as he looked at his shoulder.

"She thought it might be bothering you," Ranforray said as he looked at him. "My lady wanted me to tell you not to worry, look at how much is already changing around Lanila." He pointed up to the sky.

"It really has!" said Rell as he looked up, smiling. "I know there is still so much ahead for us," he said, putting in the last plant, "this is why instead of worrying, we've decided to be ready like the Elders and Dawla have advised." He then stood to his feet, cleaning off the dirt from his clothes.

So indeed, what HaVon was doing with the girls was preparing, putting them through the same kind of training he did with Ravin. The girls followed each other while flying around, and Ranforray helped Rell around his home, the Grelands were busy in their own preparation. Then from the waterfall came out Dawla and she was not alone.

"I thank you so much for coming, Motia," she said, looking up at him as they walked.

"Like you, we too have been waiting and as soon as word spread to us, I had to come." He stopped. "The Caps of Lanila stand with you and want to help any way we can."

The Caps were going to be yet another ally for the young adventurers in their quest. Motia was tall, twice the size of her, and very muscular. His skin had almost a blueish tint and he had white hair with blue streaks. He wore a chest protector and leggings that were very detailed with dragons on them. Around his waist was a dark blue crystal band, also detailed with dragon heads, on each side of his waist were long daggers of gold color.

"They will need it, I feel as if Shaydon and Saball have been too quiet for some time now," she continued to walk and he followed, "I'm afraid we'll soon find out why."

"Knowing what you have told me and with what they have already tried, it wouldn't surprise me at all." You could see he shared the same feelings as she did. "I haven't seen Ranforray, is he OK?"

"He's back with Rell at his home, I want to help them any way I can," she said as she smiled. "Plus, I think he really enjoys being around them."

"By the way you speak of them, I understand why. So we shall do as you ask, Dawla, and I'll keep my eyes open," he said, looking at her. "When you need us, we will be here for you and our new beginning," he said, placing his hand to his chest.

"Thank you, Motia, I'm going to send Ranforray to the Farlands when he returns," she told him as she extended her hand. "Like you, they will be pleased to hear and need to know."

"Be careful please," he said, looking at her. "Tell Ranforray the same for me and if we see any sign of either of them, I will let you know." He turns and whistled extremely loudly.

The ground trembled slightly, and suddenly, from the distance what appeared to be a large horse but three times the size approached. It looked to have a very light-blue under skin and had long fur which had never been seen on a horse. It was white in color and the tips were blue, it had large eyes of yellow. As it stopped by his side, Motia climbed on.

"I've forgotten how beautiful she is," said Dawla as she approached, putting her hand to its head as it purrs.

"She's always been my girl, we help each other," he said as he patted her on the side and she purred louder. "We shall keep our eyes open. Stay safe, Lady of Lanila." He smiled and they took off.

She watched as they disappeared toward a part of Lanila we've not seen yet, by her smile it was apparent how happy she was to see him. It seemed to be indeed the young adventurers' allies were growing every new day.

Back at Rell's. they were all gathered in HaVon's new cave and were talking among themselves.

"Girls, you are doing so good with what HaVon is teaching you." Rell walked up to each of them, rubbing his hand along their heads. "Your father would be so proud."

"Speaking of Father, we should head back and see him. After staying all night, we don't want him to worry," the girls said as they looked at them both, "if that's OK, we know how important this is."

"Girls, please do." HaVon looked at them. "You never have to ask that, it is but as well to never forget what has brought us to this moment," he said as he smiled. "Last night was fun."

"You should, girls, and thank him for letting you spend so much time with us," said Rell as he walked up next to him. "Stay the night and we'll start again when the new day gets here."

"I should also think about returning as well. My lady might have something for me to do," said Ranforray as he stood up. "Thank you to everyone, being a part of this is something I'll never forget."

"We thank you as well." The girls approached the young adventurers with affection and a smile. "We'll see you on the new day."

"Be careful, girls," they both responded at the same time.

"Both of you as well," they said and disappear into the white light.

"I will tell my lady what you said, Rell. Thank you again for this." Ranforray bowed before them and spoke into the air. As the green light appeared, he walked into it, waving.

"You know I remember not too long ago I thought I would be alone," said Rell as he looked up at HaVon. "I'm so thankful for you and this."

"I remember too," HaVon replied as he looked at him. "I'm glad you're here with me. Those days are behind us now," he smiled, "we're only beginning; to think, how many more we'll meet along the way."

"I talked to Ranforray about that," Rell said, looking at his shoulder. "I told him it kind of bothered me."

"You're talking about not seeing another sign yet?" HaVon lowered his head. "I know it will come to you; I believe there has to be a reason."

"I believe you're right about that." Rell smiled. "Plus, what we're doing is needed for all of us. I know we'll be prepared for whatever is ahead."

"We'll be ready, Rell, I believe that," HaVon said as he rose up and headed toward the spring.

"Yes, we will," smiling, he followed him.

You could tell how much he wanted to see another sign to find the others, at the same time also knowing how important it was to stay and train for what was ahead. As they enjoyed their time in the spring, at the land of reflections, Jadard and some of his warriors seemed to be talking with Shaydon. A solid wall of crystal now surrounded the entire area around them.

"Have you heard anything new on the boy or Dawla?" Jadard asked him.

"No, we haven't," Shaydon paused, "but I'm sure it won't be much longer before we do." He grinned.

"So have you heard from Saball, is he still with the Farlands?" It seemed as if he knew of their plan.

"Yes, he is, and they still have no idea the last time I heard from him," he snickered and seemed very pleased. "Now that this wall is complete, I think it's time we spread out and find anyone else that believes in this new beginning and destroy them." His laugh echoed through the valley.

"As you wish. We stand with you, my lord, but where do we start?" Jadard paused. "You know, we've heard from a scout while they were out, they came across the Talasis of the wetlands."

"Those people are weak with few numbers, what did he see?" You could tell he wasn't too concerned.

"My lord, he told me their numbers have grown. When he saw them, they looked to be celebrating." He then turned to his man-at-arms and he nodded.

"Celebrating what?" Shaydon growled.

"He told me they were dancing around a statue we've never seen before." Jadard felt this would be a good place to start. "Let me take some of the valley warriors and end their celebration."

"Go, Jadard, let's remind Lanila what we're capable of," said Shaydon as he grinned. "Find out what they're celebrating and take the leaders, then destroy the rest, including this statue you speak of."

"As you ask, my lord," putting his hand to his chest, Jadard kneeled.

"Take them with you," he turned as two of the Crytions became visible.

"Where did they come from?" Jadard noticed their size. "They resemble Saball slightly."

"They do have some similarities, but their own abilities, and I need to know where they need to improve." He smiled. "It's time they learn of our changes and my Crytions." He let out a laugh.

"Looking at them, I can see why," said Jadard, amazed at what he was seeing. "We will destroy everything and capture the leaders, to find out what they know." Seeing these creatures, he was even more confident.

They were speaking of the Talasis that lived in an area of the wetlands; they were very small and peaceful individuals. They lived in the area that was tall with grass that grew from the wet grounds, which they used to protect and hide in. It might be considered a marshy environment and over the cycles they had found a way to grow in numbers. They too had heard of the hope that was coming but might not have a chance to see it with Jadard and his valley warriors coming.

They may have not seen any sign of the boy or Dawla, but it was clear they had plans of their own and were not worried. They were about to remind Lanila why they all had been scared.

Back at the spring, the young adventurers had climbed out and were talking as the day had grown long.

"You know, HaVon, we should go on the new day and see the Elders," Rell suggested as they lay in the tall grass, with Rell leaning his back against him.

"If that's what you want to do, you know how much I enjoy being there." You could see the bond was growing stronger between them. "We could take the girls and after we see them, we could go by where I used to live." HaVon smiled.

"Hey, that's a great idea," he said, looking up at him. "You're not wanting to return there for good, are you?"

"I would never leave your side." He could read the look in Rell's eyes.

"I know," replied Rell as he smiled, "but also the memories you have there is the only reason I ask."

"I do, Rell, but she is always with me," he said as he touched his heart. "I truly appreciate and know what you mean, but our memories are just beginning and I wouldn't miss any of that." He lowered his head down to him. "You're my future." He smiled.

"You're mine as well." Rell reached out, placing his hand on HaVon's head. "It's getting late, my friend, the new day will be upon us soon." He yawned.

"It will be." He looked to see he had fallen asleep against him. "Rest well for the new day," he said as he smiled. "I will never let anything or anyone ever harm you." He curled up around him and they both fell asleep.

You could see how much HaVon cared for him. As they rested for the new day, seeing this as they lay in the tall grass would touch anyone's heart. The new day would show them all new challenges; what we wonder is if it might come from the Farlands. They had invited an evil in they had not yet discovered, and with Dawla planning to send Ranforray on the new day, what would that bring to the plan?

Chapter Twenty

You could see Lanila was trying to find itself again with all that was happening. But over at the Farlands, Saball's plan was to find out what they knew and their involvement in what was ahead; he had told Shaydon it had worked but he wanted to know how they had survived for so long.

Saball was surprised to find that their dwelling had so much room on the inside. The top being open gave it enough sunlight and there were trees and streams; it had as much life in here as Lanila did on the outside. It was very active with a lot of people, and there were cabins and structures spread throughout the area. It had gardens and towers and was very efficient looking around. Looking at everyone, Saball noticed how happy and relaxed they seemed. It seemed as if everyone had a purpose that they were actively performing, except one and that was Saball. He still acted injured and slow to move. They had lain him down in a cabin when they brought him in.

"Basall?" Brother Ben knocked on the door before entering. "How are we, any better on this new day?" He smiled.

"Brother Ben," said Saball as he sat up. "I want to think I am," he said in his high-pitched voice.

"Good to hear." Brother Ben placed a bowl of what looked to be food next to him. "Here's something for your energy, we're heading out to look for more of us."

"More of who?" he asked as he grabbed the bowl.

"Of those who have survived and are waiting," Brother Ben answered as he turned to head out.

"Brother Ben, waiting for what?" You could see Saball was searching for answers.

"For what we all have been waiting for," he smiled. "Hope. See you later, my friend," and he left.

"Hope!" Saball was disgusted hearing that. He got up from the bed, noticing a large group of them were leaving with Billum in front.

He seemed to be playing his part well as the new day was here and he was still acting injured, this was their plan to be able to get inside. Seeing them leave, he knew he had to explore the area and find out what they knew as he brought himself out of the cabin. He saw truly how large of an area this was, for the sides were not visible to the eye. He looked around, making sure no one saw him and proceeded down a path. Saball looked for anything that would help. Meanwhile, Ranforray had returned to the Grelands.

"It makes me so happy to hear he enjoyed the plants we sent," she smiled, "also hearing what they've been doing to prepare," she said as he filled her in on his visit.

"Rell really seemed excited to make the garden," Ranforray continued, not wanting to leave out any details.

"While you were gone, Motia came to see me," said Dawla as she began to walk and he followed.

"I'm sorry I missed him, my lady. How are they all doing?" he looked at her.

"They're all good, he did ask where you were." He could see her thinking. "After seeing him, I think it's time we tell the Farlands." She started walking again. "You know how much it would mean to them and it would give you a chance to make sure it's safe," she turned and winked at him.

"I was wondering when you might send me, I'll make sure to check," he grinned. "I'll let them know, my lady."

"Ranforray, please be careful and return safely," she said as she placed her hand on his shoulder, "we need to be sure everything is OK."

"My lady, I promise I'll return as soon as I can," he answered, placing his hand to his chest.

He was headed in the direction of the Farlands to inform them, also it seemed she wanted him to check on something as well. When he would arrive there, would he be able to see Saball and what he was up to? She smiled, happy with everything, but that would soon change. As an entirely new conflict would occur and it had to do with what she asked; it would have her terribly troubled when she finds out.

Meanwhile, Jadard and the valley warriors that were with him, along with the two Crytions, were headed toward the wetlands and were getting close.

They wanted to capture the leader and destroy the rest, as Shaydon wanted to send Lanila and those around a message, which they would differently do and destroy this statue as well, but also they would find out that there were more preparing than he realized.

"Jadard, do you think we'll have any problem with them?" his man-at-arms asked, walking next to him.

"By them, no," he said as he smiled at him, "but keep your eyes open. Things are changing." He may not have been worried by the Talasis, but he was smart enough to know never be unprepared.

"I will," he replied, as he like the most of them carried double-sided axes and spears. "Jadard, what about them?"

"Shaydon called them the Crytions and wanted Lanila to know of them," he answered as he looked back at them. "I'm sure they'll be fine."

"What do they do, sir?" the man-at-arms looked at him.

"Guess we'll soon find out," Jadard replied as they continued getting ever so close. "But if they were created by Shaydon, I can only imagine," he said, knowing of his power.

With them getting closer, Saball also had found an area that made him curious; it was a path into the wall itself. He was about to investigate, he knew something was there when he heard something coming, so he redirected what he was doing, hoping whoever it was hadn't seen him. So he began to stretch and act as if he was in pain from walking and sat down, needing to be careful as he knew he wasn't alone.

"Is someone there?" his high-pitched voice called out.

"Did I scare you?" from the brush came Daniel; he was about ten cycles and was the son of Billum.

"Daniel, right?" You could see the look of frustration in Saball's eyes at having been interrupted. "I didn't realize you followed me."

"That's right, I saw you leave and Father said you might need help," he said as he approached him. "Plus, I was bored. You look to be feeling better."

"I'm a trying to get better, I thought a walk would be good for me." He knew he needed to be careful with what he said.

"Father does say that helps," he said as he picked up a stick and started swinging it, "but you should still be careful, no one would know if you needed help if something happened." Like any young boy, Daniel was talking non-stop.

"You're a very smart young boy," Saball commented. He realized he needed to be careful, the last thing he needed was for his father to find out. "So that down there seems so pretty, I just wanted to see it all," he pointed. "Daniel, where does that go?"

"It's very nice here," he swung the stick around. "We should wait for Father; only if he goes can we go." He looked around. "Let me go and see if he's back."

"You know, it's OK, my leg is starting to hurt. Can you help me back?" Saball asked, wanting him to help and hoped he would forget what he asked.

"Yes, that's what we Farlands do, we help." You could see he had been raised with this belief.

"Yes, you do." As Daniel helped him walk, he knew where he needed to look but it would have to wait.

They headed back in the direction of the cabin where he came from as the day had grown longer, and he hoped the boy would forget. Only time would tell that for by the end of this day, so much would have changed. The new day ahead would have an impact on all of Lanila and truly test this new beginning.

While this was going on, Jadard had made it to the wetlands. They were spying on the Talasis as they hid in the tall grass. waiting for orders to attack, looking for the leader. They could see the Talasis were still celebrating, totally unaware of the danger awaiting them. Jadard's warriors were sure the leader was in there so Jadard decided he would grab the entire group; each of them began to spread out and surround them. He watched the warriors get into the place waiting for a sign to attack, but little did they realize to get to the caps of Lanila, you had to travel through the wetlands.

You see, Motia had done a few other things before deciding to return home. At this time, he was closing in on the wetlands, having no idea what he would encounter. The suns were climbing closer to the ground and with the moon rising as well, then from the distance he heard what seemed to be screaming and yelling.

"What was that, Meke?" he stopped to listen and heard it again. "Come on, let's go." He patted her on the side.

What he was hearing was Jadard and the rest attacking the Talasis. The closer he got, the more uncertain he was about what it was so he stopped and got off of Meke.

"Stay here, girl," he looked at her. "You'll know if I need you." He stroked her around the neck and she purred softly.

He proceeded ahead, being careful. The sounds became louder the closer he got, then finally, he could see what it was and he couldn't believe it. He had no idea who it was attacking these peaceful people. He was overcome with anger and rage, seeing the Talasis being treated and harmed this way. Looking at all the destruction they had caused, he couldn't take it anymore. He lunged from the brush and landed by them.

"I'm thinking you might want to let them go," he said, holding both of his daggers in his hand, he was just as big with more muscles.

"Take care of this," Jadard looked at his warriors. "I'm taking them, destroy the rest."

"I ask you not to move." Motia lunged into the air, hitting his daggers in the ground. When he did, it threw a shock of energy that knocked them off their feet, showing the power he had.

"Do something!" Jadard looked at the Crytions. "Men, let's go!" A few of his men grabbed the Talasis they had decided to take as they sneaked off.

Motia was so busy fighting the valley warriors that had stayed, he was unaware that Jadard was escaping with some of them. He was proving to be a challenge for the warriors, exchanging blows between them, Motia was winning too when he was hit from the side, suddenly knocking him to the ground.

"Don't move." The warriors gathered around him, wiping the blood from their faces. "Wipe that smile from your face," they said. You could hear the anger in their voices.

"I warned you," Motia said as he rose to his feet, smirking, and looked at what knocked him down. "What in Lanila are you?" He then whistled really loudly.

Then suddenly, their attention was diverted as they heard a loud purr, when they turned to see what it was; there was a dragon that resembled Meke, did she have the ability to transform, it had the same blue tint with white fur.

"Where did that come from?" The valley warriors looked astonished and forgot about Motia.

"I told you!" Motia began to take each one of them out. "Meke, get them!" Motia yelled as he pointed at the Crytions.

As she hit the ground so hard, it threw them off-balance and they crashed to the ground. After he knocked the rest of them off their feet, he headed toward the Talasis still alive. He passed Meke and winked as she roars for the first time, then instead of breathing fire her breath looked like a stream of ice as she hit each one of them and they were frozen by it.

"Meke, that should be good!" He smiled at what she had done. "It's OK, I'm here to help," he said as he knelt down, releasing them from the rope.

"Thank you, stranger," said one of the rescued Talasis.

"You'll be fine," Motia spoke to the few left.

"What about the rest?" One of the young ones asked.

"Rest?" Motia looked at them.

"They took our wise while you were fighting," the older one spoke out.

"Why would they attack you, you're such peaceful people?" He was trying to figure it out. "Do you know where they came from or who they were?"

"No, we haven't seen them before, but they asked us about our statue." You could see the look on their faces seeing it destroyed. "They wanted to know how we knew of the two powers."

"The two powers?" Motia then realized who could have been behind this.

"The hope we all have been waiting for," he looked at him, "a new beginning." The man lowered his head. "But see what happens when you believe?"

"Listen to me, even though someone challenges your beliefs," seeing how they felt, he knew they needed to hear this, "know that it's happening. Look at what they're trying to do, stop you from believing."

"But what do we do now?" they all looked at him.

"You all with come with me." Motia then looked at Meke. "Prepare the circle." They both started drawing around all of them, until they were standing in a circle with designs around the edges. "They won't stop us!"

As he and Meke got into the circle, he smiled at them and held out his daggers. Raising them into the sky, he forced them into a design at the top of the circle. When he did that, they were overcome with a blinding snow. Motia assured them they would be fine as they disappeared out of sight. The warriors that were frozen were now free of the ice as it suddenly broke, they gathered themselves but the same could not be said for the Crytions; they were destroyed.

"Where did he go?" One of the valley warriors looked around. "Where's that dragon as well?" They all began to search.

"Wherever he went, the rest of the Talasis are also gone." said another one of the warriors who couldn't find them either. "Looks like they didn't make it." He looked at what was left of the Crytions.

"We need to get back and tell Jadard what happened, about this stranger and the dragon we saw." They gathered themselves and headed back.

By this time, Jadard had no idea what had happened. As he reached his valley, he informed his men to take the ones they brought back to a secured area. With his men watching over them, another was sent to inform Shaydon of their success. He too was curious to find out what they knew of the change he had been hearing about. There were things happening all over Lanila and this was only the beginning. He waited to hear from Shaydon and the warriors he had left behind.

The young adventurers were still resting for the new day ahead and Ranforray returned to the Grelands only to be sent back out to the Farlands. At the land of the forever trees, the girls and Ludes seemed to be very active, even King Edbow seemed to be giving the area around extra security. It seemed they are getting it ready to protect them from the dangers that might come.

"So you think this is all necessary, Father?" The girls landed next to him carrying some sort of crystal shards. "With us, Rell, and HaVon, we would never let anything happen to you."

"I know that, girls." He smiled, placing the shards they brought into the trees themselves. "So much is changing, girls, and this will help us in case my girls or our new friends can't be here." He used his club to fix them into the trees. They became as solid as the crystals he placed in them. "When do you return?"

"We're supposed to continue preparing for the new day," they all spoke at one time, "we've learned so much from them, Father."

"I'm so happy to hear that, girls." He looked at what they had done with the trees. "You know, this is enough for now. Why don't we head back up and you can show all of us?" He knew how happy this would make them.

"OK, Father." He was right, you could hear the excitement in their voices as they took off to the top.

"I'm so proud of them," King Edbow said to himself as he headed toward the base of the tree and disappeared into it.

All of the Ludes got together to see what they had learned and to celebrate. While this was happening, Saball and the Farlands were also gathered for eating and talking. The ones that had left earlier had returned, finding no one but bringing food. Brother Ben began talking to Saball about his day.

"I heard you went out today, Basall?" he asked as he handed him a crink.

"I needed to," Saball replied, uncertain what he knew. "Yes, Daniel scared me while I was out and had taken a break."

"He laughed about how he scared you!" smiled Brother Ben while sitting down next to him. "Even Billum found an interest in what he had said."

"You know, young ones always having fun," Saball replied, hoping he had not told them too much of when he saw him. "I can't get over how amazing this place is," he said, taking a drink.

"So, Basall," Billum approached them, "my son said you went out today."

"Yes, and I feel it," Saball answered as he rubbed his legs and arms, "needed the air." He took another drink.

"Yeah, needed some air, good to hear." You could see the look in his eyes. "Brother Ben, I need a word with you."

"Now Billum, it takes time." He placed his hand on Saball's shoulder. "Basall is doing better and that's good. I'll be right there, Billum," he said as Billum walked off.

As Brother Ben got up and headed over to Billum, you could see the look on Saball's face as he wondered what the boy might have said. He had always felt uncertain about Billum and knew he needed to find out what was in that cave. Suddenly, he noticed everyone's attention had been diverted to the entrance. It seemed someone had caused it to open and by the reaction, it seemed everyone was excited, but Saball couldn't see what it was and when he did, it was a creature. He looked twice at it and you could see him thinking, he couldn't place it but the creature looked familiar to him.

"Ranforray!" Daniel ran to him, excited.

Then it hit him – that was the creature that had jumped in front of the boy when he tried to get him. He sat down quickly, looking around. The last time he had seen him, Dawla was also there and knew if she showed up, they would feel his presence, so he decided to head to his cabin as quietly as possible. When he rose to his feet, it was just in time to see Ranforray transform into his normal appearance. Seeing the excitement everyone had for him, he knew he needed to act before the new day was upon them.

Chapter Twenty-One

The Farlands welcomed Ranforray with open arms. Everyone went up to greet him and by his reaction, he seemed just as happy to see them. You could feel the relief almost in the air; like before, he wasn't there just to visit and check on whatever Dawla felt was important there.

"We've missed you, Ranforray," Brother Ben and Daniel were the first to greet him.

"The same from me, my friends, I've missed you as well." He greeted them both with a hug. "My lady sends her wishes to everyone."

"She won't be joining you?" The rest greeting him smiled; they were all excited.

"I'm sorry, not this time, but she wants you to know she's always watching over you." He then approached Billum. "Still strong as ever, I see," Ranforray commented, smiling.

"Seeing you, Ranforray, is a good thing." For the first time, we see him smiling as he embraced Ranforray in a big hug; doing so, he picked him up off the ground.

"Like I said, stronger than ever," said Ranforray as he gasped for a breath. "Easy, big friend, I come with great news!" Taking a deep breath after being put down, he smiled.

"Come, we have just started to enjoy our meal. Join us and we can talk." They walked back toward the fire, everyone feeling the excitement he brought.

They brought themselves together back around the fire, they placed his chair in the middle and Daniel brought him a plate. While they seemed to be catching up, we travel to a place we have yet to see. This was what Motia called home the Caps of Lanila, this was a place of dreams with all the different shades of blue and white. Looking at how high this place was would explain the name, there looked to be a white powder covering everything. The outside area getting here was cooler, but once inside it wasn't the temperature of the air was very comfortable.

The center was surrounded by walls that had a light blue color spread throughout, making it look like a city inside with a fortress of massive size. On each corner on top of what looked to be crystal guard towers were massive creatures, but they were statues and very detailed with faces and covered in fur. This was a very clean and active area with people that resembled Motia, then there were others that didn't, making this seem like a place you would feel safe. Spread around the area were pools of dark blue water that emitted steam, which would explain it not being as cold as you might think. Close to this fortress was a large circle that resembled the one he had drawn to escape. It was overcome with the same blinding snow and there he stood with Meke and the Talasis.

"Motia!" cried a female. She came running up to greet him.

"My dear Addie!" he said as he embraced her as well.

"What happened to you?" she asked, looking at the marks on his face. "Meke, are you OK?" she turned to see her.

"My love, we're fine," said Motia, smiling. "Aren't we, Meke?" She approached purring and it brought a smile to Addie's face. "Men, help our friends feel welcome. Please follow them and they will help you with any injuries and a place to rest."

The guards escorted the rescued, showing the compassion this place had, as they made their way inside.

"The reason I love you so much; always helping. Where did they come from?" Her smile showed this was nothing new to her.

"I came across them in the wetlands and they were being attacked. With all that Dawla told me, I had to help them." He sat down and she began to clean him up.

The inside was just as beautiful as everyone was helping while some cleaned up Meke.

Addie was a beautiful being, having the same tint to her skin. Her hair was the opposite though; blue with streaks of white. She was also tall, with eyes of the most gorgeous blue.

"How is our lady of Lanila doing?" she asked as she cleaned up the cuts.

"She is doing good, my love." He stopped and looked at her. "It's happening, they've joined. She told me and I told her we'll be there by their side." They hugged and smiled; like everyone else, there was an excitement.

"That's what we've wanted to hear. What do we need to do to help them?" she asked as she looked at him.

"Help all of those that need it like we've been doing," he stood up holding her hand. "We need to be there for her and the two powers, but first, we need to help the Talasis and make sure that every one of them are healed."

"We shall, my love," she replied, squeezing his hand and smiling.

The compassion and the way they cared for those in need, with Addie by his side, was remarkable. Like him, she was fit and also had a passion for others. They began caring for the injured and clothed them as they both started to help.

"You said they were being attacked in the wetlands?" Addie asked she walked over to Meke, showing her love as Meke softly purred.

"By warriors I haven't seen before, my love," he replied as he too walked over to Meke. "I warned them to stop and they didn't, so they found out the hard way what happens if they ignore my request." He winked at her.

"Having not seen them before, where could they have come from?" she wondered as she brushed Meke.

"Well, Dawla did mention that things were changing, she's was afraid that there would be danger by those that oppose it." He stopped and looked at her. "I'm not sure but I'm afraid this has to do with Shaydon or Saball."

"Motia!" she looked in his eyes. "You have to be careful if they're involved, we made a mistake before misjudging his power and haven't had to worry in so many cycles about them." They walked out together where they could look over the area.

"I know, but until I can talk with Dawla, I cannot say for sure." He turned and placed his hand to her face. "You know me." He smiled.

"That's why I say that, my love." She smiled and hugged him. "It's exciting though, we've all been waiting for this, but it scares me as well. They're both so unpredictable."

"Hey, we're not alone," he said as he embraced her tightly. "No matter what they try, you know we'll be ready." He smiled at her.

They cared deeply for one another and wanted to help. Their trust in Dawla showed how they would be great allies for the young adventurers, the entire place and the way everyone was active and helpful showed their hearts, how they all were always ready to help anyone in need; this was the way they had always lived, showing the true light of Lanila's old ways.

Ranforray meanwhile had been filling the Farlands in on everything that was happening; you could tell everyone was listening attentively and seemed even more excited now.

"Hearing you say this is great." Billum looked at the rest who were smiling. "Before long, no more hiding for any of us." He raised his hand and they all cheered.

"See, Basall, I told you," Brother Ben looked toward Basall but he was nowhere in sight. "Has anyone seen Basall?" he asked.

"That's a name I haven't heard before. Who's Basall?" Ranforray looks at him.

"We found him not too long ago," Brother Ben said as he stood up. "I'll be right back."

"So, Billum," Ranforray looked at him, "where did you find this Basall?"

"Not far from here, when we were out scouting and came across him," he replied as he looked at Daniel. "Why don't you go with Brother Ben and help him?"

"Yes, Father." He stood and ran to catch up.

"By your expression, Billum, you don't seem so pleased by him." Ranforray could see the uncertainty in his eyes. "Why is that?"

"After everything we've gone through, I'm not as easily convinced like Brother Ben." He added some more wood to the fire. "It's just that feeling I can't shake."

"Hearing that, I'm curious to meet him now," Ranforray said as they continued to talk.

As they enjoyed the fire and waited for Brother Ben to return, Daniel had finally caught up to him as they approached the cabin.

"Basall!" He knocked on the door before entering. "I wanted you to meet someone special to us. Are you OK, my friend?"

"I'm sorry," said Saball, knowing that's what he didn't want to do. "I felt so weak all of a sudden and needed to lie down." He was pulling off not feeling good again.

"If you feel better, please let me know, I really wanted you to meet him," said Brother Ben looking at him. "Just rest then, Basall, OK? On the new day you will see what I've been saying about believing." He smiled and left.

"I've got to get out of here before it's too late." He watched them walk away. "I need to find out why that path leads to a cave." His time here was coming to an end, but he felt as if they were protecting something and needed to see.

He wanted to give it a little more time before leaving so he waited. Brother Ben and Daniel by then had made it down the path and were enjoying the fire.

"Were you able to find him?" Ranforray asked as he saw them returning.

"He wasn't feeling well so I left him to rest," he said as he sat down next him.

"He seemed just fine earlier." Billum looked at him.

"It's fine, Billum," Ranforray looked at him, "if he's not well, we have time." But now, he was curious to meet him seeing the way Billum acted.

"So you'll be staying with us?" You could see how happy they seemed after hearing that.

"Yes, but then I'll need to head to the Grelands before too long." There was so much to do.

With everyone smiling, he went into detail why he was there; you could see they all listened as he told them of the new allies and people that were now in his life. They held on to every word and no one made a sound. Seeing the look on everyone's faces, it was clear this was what they had been waiting for. The moon was climbing even higher into the sky as he continued, and Saball had sneaked out and crept through the brush, staying hidden and wanting to get back where Daniel had seen him.

"I feel that they're hiding something and I have to see." He had to be careful as he moved along. "With this Ranforray here, I need to be even more cautious, he could ruin everything."

As he got closer to what he had seen earlier before Daniel saw him, and no one was even aware of his intentions, he looked through the brush to see the path and could see a light coming from it. He entered slowly. He wasn't sure what it was as the light got brighter the further he went. When it opened up, he stopped in his tracks and just stared at what he saw.

"Well, what have we here, is this what you've been hiding?" He approached closer and saw a dragon egg. "Where did they find you?" It was a shade of red as he looked closely at it. "Oh Shaydon needs to know this."

He grabbed a hold of the necklace and closed his eyes; he seemed to be in a trance and communicating with Shaydon with what he had found. By his smile, you could see how pleased he seemed with what he had found, then all of the sudden, above him a black mass began to form. As it got larger, he transformed back into his original form, but little did he know Daniel was behind him. The child screamed for help but no one could hear him and Saball smiled.

"Tell everyone we're coming back for you all and this, I'm taking from you." His laugh echoed through the walls as he disappeared into the mass.

When he did, it let out a shock wave of power, knocking Daniel to the ground. He hit his head on a rock and lay there motionless. If this egg was what Dawla had them looking after, it was now in the hands of Saball. The Farlands had no knowledge of it being gone or of Daniel's disappearance.

Saball appeared in the land of reflections. "My lord!" he said as he knelt before Shaydon, holding the egg out. "This may have been the reason Dawla was involved with them."

"Did you see her?" Shaydon asked, worried he might have been spotted.

"No, my lord, but that creature I mentioned that interfered with getting the boy was there." He rose to hand him the egg.

"Where did they find you?" He looked it over, smiling. "This might be the answer to what we've been needing." Shaydon was pleased with what he had found. "We must keep this hidden until we find out more about it."

Just as he said that and they looked it over, suddenly from behind, a valley warrior came through the wall.

"Jadard has done as you asked, my lord, he along with the prisoners wait for you back at the valley," he said as he placed his hand to his chest.

"Tell him he will see me soon." Shaydon's voice was spine-tingling. The valley warrior turned and left to inform Jadard. "I want you to take this to Shalcox, tell him to hold it until I come."

"If that's what you ask, I will do it, my lord." Saball took the egg from him and started to head back to the Harbsides.

"Saball, be warned and careful you're not seen. It will be only a matter of time before they know it's gone. Take a couple of Crytions with you," he said as two appeared just then. "They'll be able to help if you have any problems, plus they can stay there to help keep it protected."

With Saball heading out being escorted by the Crytions and Shaydon was going to see Jadard, back at the Farlands everyone was resting. Billum entered his home and found Daniel was nowhere to be seen.

"Daniel!" he called out and whistled for him. When he didn't get a response, he left and hurried to Brother Ben's. You could see he was worried. "Brother Ben!" he called out.

"Please come in, Billum." Ranforray was there too.

"Have you seen Daniel?" He was unsettled; this wasn't like his son not to be in bed.

"We'll help you find him." Ranforray could see how upset he was. "I'm sure he's fine; like you, he's strong," he said, trying his best to ease his mind.

They all walked out of the cabin and began calling out for him. This got the attention of the rest of the Farlands as they heard them and they came to help. They had everyone searching for him and as they did, Billum was becoming more worried. This was not like his son; usually he ran when called. Suddenly, someone called out they had found him. Billum ran as fast as he could and when he saw his son, he went to pick him up.

"Oh no, Daniel!" Tears appeared in his eyes. "Son?" He was still unresponsive.

"Billum, let me see." Ranforray placed his hand to his head. "He'll be fine, get him back to the cabin."

"Thank you, Ranforray." For the first time, this strong man weakened, like any parent would be in this situation as he carried his son out.

"Oh no, this isn't good." Brother Ben walked past him to see the egg was gone.

"Don't tell me," Ranforray walked up next to him. "Where is it?"

"I don't know, Ranforray, we saw nothing." He became panicked, looking around for any sign of it. "Maybe Daniel knows."

"Tell everyone to stay alert," even Ranforray became worried, "I'm going to go see Billum and check on him."

"I will," Brother Ben stopped him. "I'm sorry she trusted us and it's gone." He lowered his head.

"Brother Ben, it's fine, right now we need to help Billum and Daniel," Ranforray said, lifting his head up. "Let everyone know to keep searching and I'll be back."

Right now, his priority was the boy's health. He hoped when he woke up, he might be able to shed some light on what happened. He was worried about the egg as he came to Billum's cabin, knocking on the door and entering as he saw Daniel in bed with Billum cleaning his face.

"Ranforray, who would do this to a boy?" he asked, looking at him. "My poor boy!" he cried, rubbing his hand on his forehead.

"I promise you, we'll find who did this to him. Whoever it was, they took the egg as well," said Ranforray, kneeling next to him.

"How did we not know this? We saw nothing to warn us." You could see both the aggravation and worry in his eyes.

"Listen, it's OK, Billum," said Ranforray, trying to assure him things were fine. "Right now, he's my priority." He placed his hand on Daniel's arm.

"You're right, Ranforray. Thank you for being here." They both sat there waiting for him to wake up.

With all of the Farlands on their guard, they looked for any sign of where the egg may be, and also kept their eye open for whatever might have done this. But unfortunately, they were too late and the egg was not here anymore. When Daniel would eventually open his eyes, they would soon find out who was behind it.

The suns were breaking over the horizon at Rell's, where the two of them were still asleep in HaVon's cave. He still leaned up against him. As he began to move, HaVon did as well and when their eyes began to open, they saw the girls were there, staring at them.

"How long have you been there?" Rell sat up, rubbing his eyes.

"Hey, girls, good to see you." HaVon stretched as well.

"We didn't want to wake you," they said, speaking at the same time. "Father has always taught us never to wake one from resting." They smiled. "And Father says hello."

"It's OK, girls." Rell smiled. "Nice to see how ready you are for the new day and what's ahead."

"We are," they were smiling big, "we have a surprise to show you."

"Wow, a surprise?" HaVon was curious.

"Well, when we were showing Father and the Ludes what you have taught us and we can do now," the girls looked at one another, "let us just show you."

"Please do, now I'm just as excited to see what it is." Rell walked up next to HaVon, and they both were smiling.

They both were watching eagerly to see what it was they were talking about, as the girls touched their shoulder and merged together.

"Boy, that's still awesome to see!" Rell looked up to HaVon who agreed.

As they watched them, it even surprised them more to see this. They smiled and let out a roar as they both watched. When they did, instead of breathing fire, what resembled a lightning blast came from their mouth and it destroyed the boulder they were aiming at.

"What in Lanila was that?" Rell amazed as both of their mouths fell open seeing what they did.

"How did you find out you could do that?" HaVon looked at what was left of the boulder.

"It was Father, he suggested we see what we could do when merged." They smiled so big, and were so happy to see their reaction. "You want to see what else?"

"Well, yes, of course, we do. After that, we're excited to see what else," they both answered, smiling.

With the both of them watching, you could see they were excited. Destiny began flapping her wings to where she was hovering in front of them. Telling them to hang on as they looked at one another, Destiny suddenly brought her wings together with such a force, it sent a shock wave so strong and powerful that it knocked them both off of their feet. Seeing what they did, they separated and rushed to help them.

"We're sorry, are you OK?" They looked over them both and all they could see was a big smile as they started laughing.

"That was awesome!" Rell sat up and hair was blown back.

"How amazing was that!" HaVon looked at them smiling. "We're fine."

"This is how we're going to change Lanila," Rell said as he stood up, brushing his hair down. "Your father is amazing, wait till the Elders hear of this."

"The Elders?" the girls were honored and surprised to hear that.

"Rell, you're right, they said in time we'll learn of our powers, we'll grow stronger together, teaching one another." HaVon looked at them with a smile. "This is just the beginning." They were excited.

"It is, I'm going to go and clean up." Rell said, touching the girls on the heads as he passed, "then we go see the Elders. You're awesome!" There was a pep in his step as he walked away, smiling.

While he proceeded up the path to get ready in his house, the girls had their opportunity and ran, jumping into the spring. HaVon just smiled; he knew they enjoyed it and followed their lead. Rell reached the back of the house, excited, as he looked at his shoulder. Talking to himself, he came to the front and entered the house. When he did, he heard a familiar voice and knew who it was.

"I'm so proud to see you all are getting so much stronger. You shouldn't worry so much, son, it will show in time like before." His mother had appeared in a golden glow.

"Mom!" he whispered as his eyes moistened. "I miss your talks, they always helped me in times like this."

"I do as well." She came closer. "I'm so very proud of you and seeing this place, then the garden as well." She placed her hand to his face and a warm feeling came over him.

"It's hard without you at times," he smiled, enjoying the touch.

"Remember you're never too far from me," she said, placing her hand to his heart. "Plus, seeing the way HaVon looks out for you, then the girls, they are special as well."

"He really is great, Mom." Then it hit him. "The girls? I haven't seen you since at the lake by HaVon's old cave."

"Son, I'm always watching over you," smiling, she proceeded over to this large table and he followed. "Let's catch up," she sat down.

"OK, Mom!" the kid in him came out; he had missed this so much.

So as Rell filled his mom in on all that had happened and he had gone through, she already knew but could see how happy it made him. She sat there smiling and listening to all he had to say.

Meanwhile, back at the caps of Lanila, Motia was talking with Addie about all he had learned from Dawla. It seemed that the Talasis he saved were doing much better, as they came up to him showing the gratitude they had for what he did and they told him of the ones that were taken.

"I'm so happy to see you all up and feeling better, but who were those that attacked you? Do you know where they came from?" Sitting there, he still had to look down to talk with them.

"I know the leader referred to someone they called Shaydon," one of them answered, then another said, "He said they were there to remind us who controls Lanila and to stop believing things were going to change."

"That's why they did this and burned that statue. This has to stop." He turned to Addie. "Dawla needs to know, I promised her if I saw anything…"

"We've all waited for so long." All of the Talasis spoke out at one time.

"My love," Addie looked at him, "I understand."

"Don't stop believing, all of you," Motia said as he looked at the Talasis and smiled, "I want you all to stay here and feel as if this is your home."

"Thank you for this," they all bowed their heads.

"Please come back to me, my love," Addie embraced him.

"I will, my dear." He winked and turned to his men. "Keep your guard and keep the caps safe till my return." He raised his arm.

"We shall," they all answered at one time and stomped on the ground.

He embraced Addie one last time and then he whistled. Meke came in the form of the large furry horse. Having heard what had been said about who it was, Motia knew Dawla needed to know. He promised and wanted this change to happen as well. He climbed up on Meke and then turned to his love, smiling, raising his arm to the air. With the sound of heavy stomping, he took off.

Back at Rell's, his mom's spirit had left and he was already cleaned up. By the way he smiled and moved, it showed talking with his mom had helped.

"Thanks again, Mom," he placed a kiss on the portrait, "you've always had the right thing to say." He then turned to leave and opened the door.

"Hey, Rell!" HaVon was just outside with the girls.

"Hope you haven't been waiting long," Rell said, closing the door behind him. "I was thinking about what you showed us, girls, it makes me wonder what we're capable of." He smiled at HaVon walking off the porch. "Ready to go see the Elders?"

"We can't wait!" the girls seemed excited to go with them.

"I'm glad to feel you're more relaxed," HaVon looked at him, "it helped seeing her, didn't it?" He smiled.

"It did, HaVon," Rell replied, looking at him, "she just reminded me to relax, and know that it will come in time." He touched his shoulder as the golden suit worked its way over his body.

"Told you she always seemed wise with her words and guidance," he smiled.

"You know what happens to us when we touch our mark is amazing, but to see how that suit works over his body is unlike anything we've ever seen," the girls enjoyed what they saw.

"HaVon, she really is and thank you girls," he reached out to touch him and they merged together.

"They're so breathtaking when together," the girls spoke out. "Father was right, they're special to Lanila."

"We're not the only ones that are special to Lanila," they heard Rell say; he wanted to be sure they knew how much they meant to them.

"We know but seeing you both like this, you're what they have been waiting for," they ran up to hug them.

"Your father has done well raising all of you." HaVon looked at them. "Are you ready? Come on, let's head to the Elders," he said, and spreading his wings took to the air.

He climbed higher and looked back to see the girls merge together and follow. This was a sight that had not been seen in so long and how amazing it was. Two beautiful and breathtaking dragons flying in the air, the suns shining brightly off of them both as they flew side by side on their way to the Elders. The confidence on both of their faces as they fly,

Meanwhile, back at the Farlands, everyone was gathered around as Daniel finally began to move.

"My son!" Billum said, seeing his eyes open. "You had me so worried," he spoke as he helped him to sit up.

"Father, I saw Basall change into a large creature," the look in his eyes showed he was scared. "He looked like a dragon almost, Father, but stood on two legs and he took Makia," he said, taking a deep breath. "I'm scared, Father, he said they're coming back for us."

"Listen, everyone, I need you to stay here where you're safe," Ranforray stood up. "When I leave, do not raise from the water until I return."

"Ranforray, we'll do as you ask but where are you going?" Billum asked as he looked at him.

"I'm going to get help." You could hear in his voice how serious this was.

The look in his eyes showed it had happened what they feared, and he had to let Dawla know. Ranforray transformed himself into the creature and took off with great speed. The Farlands could see how serious this was and lowered themselves into the water, waiting for his return; they had no idea what to expect from what Daniel described but they would be ready.

The young adventurers, along with the girls, were heading to the Elders, having no idea what had happened and the impact it would cause. Motia, after rescuing the Talasis, was headed to the Grelands as well; he knew Dawla would want to know about the attack and hoped she would know where he could find the rest. Saball, with the egg that they took and a couple of Crytions, headed to see Shalcox; could this be the opportunity that the Harbsides had been looking for. Berllard wanted so much more for his people; they had suffered for so long, and Lanila was going through more than anyone could have imagined. What's ahead would prove to be a challenge for the two young adventurers; it would truly test them and their new allies. To everyone in Lanila that thought the dragons were gone forever, well, they were wrong, and it was just getting started…